Psychic Sleuth

Alan's eyes were shut, his hands resting lightly on the cover of the missing boy's geography book.

Out of the blackness came sounds: a chuckle, dry and coarse as sandpaper; a low, obsessive moaning; the rustling of wind through tall trees. And he shivered through his sweat, because the sounds were aimed at *him*. But how could that be? *I'm looking for a kid,* his rational mind complained, in confusion, but no one was listening.

His mouth was dry; blood pounded in his head, turning the blackness red. *What about the kid?*

Don't worry about the kid; worry about yourself.

And then a face appeared, and he forgot about the kid, forgot about himself. A face as beautiful as Boston, as fragile as a dream. Its almond eyes begged him to come, begged him to stay away; they wanted him, they warned him. Alan's confusion was total now, but other emotions were more important. Fear. Desire. *I don't want to hear that moaning. I want to touch that face.*

But it too disappeared, the mirror clouded over . . .

Kelliher was staring at him. "Alan? You okay, Alan?"

Marlborough Street

Richard Bowker

BANTAM BOOKS
TORONTO · NEW YORK · LONDON · SYDNEY · AUCKLAND

This edition contains the complete text
of the original hardcover edition.
NOT ONE WORD HAS BEEN OMITTED.

MARLBOROUGH STREET

A Bantam Book / published by arrangement with
Doubleday & Co, Inc.

PRINTING HISTORY
Doubleday edition published February 1987

Grateful acknowledgement is made for permission to reprint the following:
Excerpts from "California Dreamin'," words and music by John Phillips and
Michelle Phillips. Copyright © 1965, 1970 by MCA Music Publishing, a division of
MCA Inc., New York, New York. All rights reserved. Used by permission.

Bantam Spectra edition / March 1988

Bantam Books are published by Bantam Books, a division of Bantam Doubleday
Dell Publishing Group, Inc. Its trademark, consisting of the words
"Bantam Books" and the portrayal of a rooster, is Registered in U.S.
Patent and Trademark Office and in other countries. Marca Registrada.
Bantam Books, 666 Fifth Avenue, New York, New York 10103.

PRINTED IN THE UNITED STATES OF AMERICA

O   0 9 8 7 6 5 4 3 2 1

To Craig, Victoria, and Jeff

Marlborough Street

Chapter 1

The Public Garden at twilight: the Swan Boats bedded down for the night, the Beacon Hill matrons home clipping coupons, the bums gone to the Pine Street Inn. A gaunt, white-haired jogger, face twisted with pain, pounded past a couple of teenage thugs sharing a joint. A young woman walked her Doberman and silently dared the thugs to try something. Alan Simpson hummed a leitmotif from *Lohengrin* and tossed the last of his peanuts to some eager pigeons, who crowded around him as if he were giving the Sermon on the Mount.

Alan wore a rumpled gray suit coat and corduroy pants. His brown hair needed a trim, and he had nicked himself shaving in a couple of places along the sloping line of his jaw. He looked like a perpetual graduate student, a preppy after a hard night.

When the peanuts were gone the pigeons wandered away, and so did Alan. The Red Sox were on TV tonight, and he had to get home. He tossed the empty bag onto an overflowing litter barrel, crossed over to Marlborough

1

Street, and walked past the fragrant magnolias and old-fashioned streetlamps to the town house that contained his apartment.

Dusty meowed irritably as he entered. It was late, and she was hungry. "Yeah, yeah," Alan muttered. "Pigeons have to eat too."

The phone began to ring as Alan was opening a can of Tuna 'n Liver Feast. He hesitated for a moment, then let it ring. He fed Dusty and stuck a frozen dinner in the toaster oven for himself. Then he popped open a can of Budweiser, picked up the phone, and dialed a number.

A hurried voice answered. "Kelliher."

"What's up, Jim?"

"Where've you been?"

"Feeding the pigeons."

"God help us, he's going soft. Can you come right over?"

"I haven't eaten. People have to eat too."

"Come to O'Rourke's. I'll have a cheeseburger plate waiting."

"Who pays?"

"The goddamn taxpayers of the city of Boston. This is important, Alan."

Alan took a sip of his Bud and decided Kelliher was probably right. "Okay. I'll come."

"Ten minutes. Take a cab."

Alan walked. He wasn't fond of cabs. O'Rourke's was on the other side of the Back Bay, past the tony stores and the expensive condos, the Neo-Gothic grandeur of Trinity Church and the blank immensity of the Hancock Building—around the corner from police headquarters, at the edge of the seedy side of town. It was a small bar and grill with uncomfortable stools and vinyl booths that were cracked and taped; it stank of cooking oil and stale beer; it was always crowded.

Kelliher was in a cramped booth at the back, next to the men's room. He was a big man with thinning brown hair and the pushed-back nose of an ex-lineman. His polyester tie was loosened at the collar. A cup of coffee sat untouched in front of him. The cheeseburger plate was waiting, as promised.

"You walked," Kelliher said as Alan slid into the booth.

"Were the taxpayers going to spring for the cab?" Alan loaded his cheeseburger with ketchup and began to eat.

"I don't think you've ever taken a cab in your life. I don't supose you'd start just because it's a matter of life and death."

"You just told me it was important," Alan said between bites. "The Red Sox are on TV tonight, by the way."

"Screw those bums. Listen."

"I'm listening."

Kelliher leaned forward, competing with the raucous off-duty cops at the bar. "His Honor the Mayor has a kid, name of Todd. Eleven years old. Goes to this fancy private place, the Cadbury School, over in your neck of the woods. I guess His Honor doesn't think too much of our public school system; can't say I blame him. Anyway, Todd didn't come home from school today."

"Probably playing pinball in Harvard Square."

Kelliher shrugged. "The mayor called us around four o'clock. We went over the route the kid usually takes home—along Newbury, over to Beacon, up the Hill. One of the men found this at the corner of Newbury and Clarendon." Kelliher reached down beside him and picked up a faded-green hardcover book.

"Have you dusted it for prints?" Alan asked.

"We're not total incompetents," Kelliher said.

Alan read the title. "*Our Fascinating World*. Isn't it, though? Geography?"

Kelliher nodded and set the book down on the table.

"Anybody call the mayor up demanding twenty million dollars in Krugerrands?"

"Not a word."

"The media know about it?"

"His Honor wants to keep it quiet, at least until we're sure the kid isn't playing pinball. Wouldn't look good to have these little domestic problems on the six o'clock news."

"Meanwhile—"

"Yeah, meanwhile the kid could be rotting in some alley. So I thought—give my young friend Alan a call. What do you think?"

Alan looked at the book. "I can but try."

A burly fellow wearing a Celtics T-shirt came out of the men's room, jiggling his fly. "You want to do it back in my office?" Kelliher asked.

"Doesn't matter. I should finish my cheeseburger, though."

Kelliher rolled his eyes and leaned back. "And he never gains an ounce," he muttered.

"That's 'cause I walk instead of taking cabs." Alan gulped down the cheeseburger and wiped his hands carefully with a napkin. Kelliher slid the book over to him.

Alan laid his hands lightly on the cover. Children in cute ethnic costumes smiled up at him from between his fingers. Most of their faces had mustaches carefully drawn on them. Alan smiled back. The crowd at the bar was laughing at something that was going on in "Family Feud." Alan was vaguely aware of Richard Dawson's unctuous voice, the clinking of glasses, a conversation about variable mortgage rates. Kelliher's hands closed around his coffee cup.

Alan waited and tried to relax. He wanted, as always, to force it our of his synapses or the ether or wherever it resided, but he knew that to force it was to lose it. It was a gift, and one does not demand gifts. So instead he hummed Mozart to himself, letting the music carry him along, hoping the gift would get bored or jealous and finally appear, dismissing the melody, dismissing everything but its own strange reality. His mother had once said, "It's like having the whole universe inside your head, waiting to surprise you." Alan had never quite decided whether such a state of affairs was delightful or terrifying.

He began to sweat.

The children's faces grew larger, their mustaches became ominous. He was struggling briefly, then his grip on the book seemed to loosen, and the children's faces fell away, spinning into blackness.

His eyes were shut. Was it over? No. Out of the blackness came sounds: a chuckle, dry and coarse as sandpaper; a low, obsessive moaning; the rustling of wind through tall trees. And he shivered through his sweat, because the sounds were different from the struggle, the sounds were aimed at *him*. But how could that be? *I'm looking for a kid,* his rational mind complained, in confusion, but no one was listening.

His mouth was dry; blood pounded in his head, turning the blackness red. *What about the kid?*

Don't worry about the kid; worry about yourself.

And then a face appeared, and he forgot about the kid, forgot about himself. A face as beautiful as Boston, as fragile as a dream. Its almond eyes begged him to come, begged him to stay away; they wanted him, they warned him. Alan's confusion was total now, but other emotions were more important. Fear. Desire. *I don't want to hear that moaning. I want to touch that face.*

But it too disappeared, the mirror clouded over, and in its place were the children's faces once again, smiling up at him, happy to be drawings on a book cover. The audience cheered wildly on TV. Kelliher was staring at him. "Alan? You okay, Alan?"

"I . . . don't think I liked that cheeseburger," he replied slowly.

"You get anything?"

He shook his head tentatively. "It was all muddled."

"Well, was he kidnapped?"

"Oh. Oh, yeah. Pretty sure about that."

"Is he still alive?"

"I think so. It was kind of a . . . blur."

"What do you mean?"

Alan paused, then shook his head again. "Sorry, Jim. I just don't have the words." He knew Kelliher wasn't satisfied, but if he didn't understand it himself, how was he going to make Kelliher understand? "I think I should go home. Thanks for dinner. Give my love to Connie."

"You looked pretty scared there for a second," Kelliher remarked. "I've never seen that before."

"The kid was scared. I guess I felt his fear. That isn't going to help you find him, though. Listen, the Red Sox game is starting pretty soon and—"

"Oh, all right. Get lost. When're you coming over?"

"I'll call. Sorry again." He pushed the book back to Kelliher and walked out of the place, feeling Kelliher's eyes on him until he stepped outside into the growing darkness.

The walk home did little to clear his head of the muddle. He wasn't even sure he wanted it to go away. Nothing like this had ever happened to him before, and it seemed to be worth some thought. The trouble was, thinking about one of his visions was like trying to grab hold of mercury. It just slithered away, back into the ether, leaving him no wiser than before. What was the use?

Back in his apartment he opened a beer and turned on the TV. Dusty sauntered in from the bedroom, stretched, and jumped up onto his lap. The vision faded. Why should he even bother with it, when reality offered such contentment?

The question remained unanswered for about an inning, long enough for the Red Sox to fall behind and that face to bubble up in his memory. It was real too. Almost a child's face, yet more worldly-wise than he could ever hope to be. A calloused strength beneath the vulnerability; horror beneath the beauty. And why hadn't he described it to Kelliher? He suddenly felt much less content.

"What have I accomplished today, Dusty?"

The cat purred. She had been fed. What more did the man need to accomplish?

"From a cosmic perspective, I mean. Can a cat look at things from a cosmic perspective?"

Dusty shut her eyes, eliminating all perspectives entirely.

Alan sighed and sipped his beer. "You're a big help." Finally he got up, spilling Dusty unceremoniously on the couch, and turned the TV set off. "If I'm not back in two hours, organize a search party," he said. Dusty eyed him grumpily, then trotted into the bedroom. Alan headed back out into the night.

He walked hurriedly over to Newbury Street, past the darkened boutiques and art galleries to the corner of Clarendon. He saw a policeman talking to a fellow with the double-knit look of a detective. This was the place. He stood on the curb and hummed a Mozart aria.

A couple of minutes later the aria was over, and Alan's mind was still stubbornly in the realm of the rational. He stopped and considered. Try another corner. He crossed the street and leaned against a no-parking sign.

> *Non più andrai, farfallone amoroso*
> *Notte e giorno d'intorno girando*
> *Delle belle turbando il riposo—*

Get in the car.
What the fu—

He felt his arm being wrenched, the book falling, a dive into darkness. Then movement. All right. He followed the movement.

It was like chasing a nightmare—except that he was moving through *this* reality as well, dodging real cars with real drivers shaking their fists at him, bumping into pedestrians and mumbling apologies *now*. And meanwhile, in his synapses or in the ether, afternoon sun glinted off a yellow Volkswagen that sped down Clarendon Street with a woman and a boy inside.

He had never done this before; till now his gift had been resolutely immobile. He wasn't sure how, but he managed to maintain a precarious balance between the two realities, walking through the nighttime world in pursuit of the afternoon car, his mind somewhere between or beyond both of them.

. . . Except for the part of it that was impatiently inquiring: *Why are you doing this? Why not call up Kelliher, tell him: Yellow VW, beautiful brown-haired girl heading south on Clarendon?*

And, as the questions remained unanswered: *You're heading into the South End now, Simpson. It's dangerous in the South End.*

He stopped on the overpass above the turnpike and listened to the cars hissing by below. The VW faded momentarily, but he knew (don't ask him how) he could get it back. Police headquarters was just a block east. He knew that he was about to get into more trouble than he wanted to have in his life, and it could all be avoided by crossing the street and heading for Kelliher's office. *Tell me what to do*, he asked the night, and the face appeared once again in his mind.

Clear enough. He let the gift do its work, and the VW appeared immediately, a hundred yards away, ready to lead him on the chase. He took a deep breath and followed.

. . . Past the sleazy bars on Tremont Street, the drunks lurching toward him looking for a handout, past the walleyed, toothless bag lady, the little black man with the porkpie hat, the pimpmobiles, the closed and grated shops; beyond, into the shadowy streets lined with row houses, half of them gentrified, half still filled with rats and roomers. And then it was gone, flickering away like the end of a movie reel, and he was alone on a dark unfamiliar street. He started searching through the nighttime world for a yellow Volkswagen.

It was parked on the next street over. California license plate. He tried the doors. Locked. He looked at the row houses. Which one?

He had a headache now. His feeble brain was not used to this sort of exertion. *Just a little bit more*, he pleaded to the deity who was in charge of such matters. He grabbed the VW's door handle again and waited.

The images came. Dragging the dead weight. Hot tears. Up the steps. Thirty-eight. Fear, and darkness, and waiting.

More?

"Ju— Ju— Ju—," he muttered, like a Tremont Street drunk with the DT's. He shook his head, found the street number, and climbed the steep steps to the front door.

It was a rooming house. The entryway was littered with handbills and broken glass. The inner door was open, its lock twisted out of shape. The first floor reeked of pork chops. A Spanish radio station blared from somewhere up above. A baby cried. Alan hesitated, then went up the stairs.

How about the room number? he asked the deity. *Por favor.*

Ju— Ju— . . .

He walked down the short hallway to his left. What would Jim Kelliher do now? Well, in the first place he wouldn't be here by himself. In the second place he might conceivably have a weapon of some sort. All Alan had was his gift, which was not the most reliable of companions.

He stopped in front of a door. He touched the knob and knew that it was the right one. What now?

He closed his eyes and knocked rapidly. "Open up, Julia," he commanded.

It was not his voice.

There was silence. Alan waited, motionless, frightened by the unfamiliar sounds that had issued from him, frightened by everything. Then there were footsteps, and the door opened.

Chapter 2

Her eyes were wide with terror. She tried to shut the door on him, but his foot was blocking it. He pushed past her and glimpsed the boy lying—asleep? unconscious? dead?—on a small bed. Then she was attacking him, clawing and kicking desperately. He managed to grab her arms and pin her against the faded-yellow wall. She struggled for a moment and then went limp. "Who are you?" she gasped.

Alan didn't answer, as the image in his mind merged with the frightened face inches away from his own. She was young, perhaps no more than twenty, and model-pretty, with high cheekbones and fine brown hair tied back with a scarf. But her careful makeup couldn't completely hide the traces of tears, and her almond eyes reflected what he already knew: that she was in terrible trouble, and he had to help her. She was wearing tight designer jeans and a powder-blue Lacoste jersey. Kidnapping clothes. Her arms were smooth and warm in his grip. Her perfume was rich, arousing. *We've got to stop meeting like this*.

"Are you a cop?"

He shook his head. What was he supposed to do now?

"How did you find me? How do you know my name?"

He considered. "I'll try to explain later. We have to go now."

"Where? What do you mean? *Who are you?*"

"You can't stay here, Julia. You know that. Come with me. I'll protect you."

She shook her head wildly and fought against his grip. "I can't. Seth will— I can't. No."

"I called the police. They'll be here in five minutes. You'll be arrested. Come with me. Is the boy okay?"

She looked over at the mayor's son. Tears leaked out of her eyes. She seemed to go through one last interior struggle and then yielded. "He's drugged," she whispered, "but he'll be all right."

"We'll leave him, then. Take your stuff."

Alan let go of her arms and watched her obey silently, picking up her Coach bag, traveling case, car keys, sunglasses, a paperback. Then he led her out of the room. In the hallway the Spanish music had been replaced by the Red Sox game. Top of the fifth, Sox trailing. He hadn't missed anything.

"We'll take your VW," Alan said when they reached the street.

Julia looked at him but said nothing. Not much point asking him how he knew about the car, if he wouldn't explain about anything else. They walked over to where it was parked. "Are you going to drive?" she asked.

"Don't know how. I'll direct you."

Inside the car, Alan smelled sweat and fear, but his aching brain couldn't produce anything more. He gazed at Julia's profile as she drove: tight-lipped, expressionless, beautiful. Was this all it was about, rescuing a pretty girl gone wrong? If she had been ugly, would he have become an accessory after the fact, or whatever the hell he was now?

Maybe not. But he knew there was more to it than that, even if he had no idea what it was. "Park anywhere," he said when they reached Marlborough Street, and eventually she found a space. He held her arm as they walked back to his apartment, feeling like a solicitous escort bringing his date home. When he opened the door, Dusty was meowing for attention in the darkness. He picked her up and let Julia go. "Have a seat," he said pleasantly. "I've got to make a call."

She went with him into the kitchen and sat down at the small table littered with breakfast crumbs. Alan put the cat down and dialed a number.

"Kelliher."

"Thirty-eight Dwight Street, second floor rear. The kid is there by himself. He's unconscious, but I'm pretty sure he's all right. 'Bye."

"Wait a minute, Alan, what's going on, why didn't you tell me this before?"

"Just figured it out. If I knew how these things worked I'd be the smartest man in the universe. Be grateful for small favors."

"Wait a minute. What about the kidnappers?"

"Beats me. I can't do everything for you." Alan hung up. "Please excuse the mess," he said to Julia. "Bachelor squalor, you know. Hungry? Want something to drink?"

She stared at him. "You said you'd already told the police," she whispered accusingly.

Alan nodded. "I lied. Sue me. Want a beer?" He got a couple of Buds out of the refrigerator and started making salami sandwiches.

"Couldn't you please tell me who you are and how you know—what you know?"

"Sure. Let's go into the living room first." He finished making the sandwiches and brought them out along with the beers. Julia followed and sat down in an overstuffed armchair well scarred with claw marks. Alan turned the Red Sox game on softly, then sat down on the sofa and popped open a beer. "My name is Alan Simpson, and I'm psychic," he said, keeping his eye on the game. "I have a friend in the police department who calls me in once in a while when he thinks I might help him on a case. That's what happened tonight. This beer is yours if you want it."

"But why did you bring me here? Why didn't your friend arrest me?"

Alan watched the Red Sox batter hit into a double

play. It was the bottom of the eighth. "Don't know," he said finally. "I guess I saw something. I felt an urge to protect you—from everyone."

"What does that mean?"

Alan pondered. "Don't know."

Julia shut her eyes. She looked very tired, very . . . vulnerable. But the kid had looked vulnerable too, and Alan had left the kid behind. He picked up a sandwich and bit into it reflectively. This wasn't going to cure his damn headache. And he wasn't going to cure it thinking about the question that remained unasked: What happens now?

Julia didn't seem to want to ask it just yet. Perhaps she was afraid of the answer. She opened her beer and watched the game for a few minutes. Then she got up and wandered through the room, reading the titles of the books stacked haphazardly on the plywood shelves, examining his stereo system, his opera posters, the stack of *New Yorkers* in the corner, the wilted plants on the grimy windowsill.

She was making Alan uncomfortable. Not many people came into his apartment. It was squalid, but it was his own squalor. "If you go into the bathroom you can see Dusty's litter box and my deodorant," he remarked.

"Are you a professional psychic?" she asked him.

He shook his head.

"What do you do for a living?"

"I'm a private secretary to an eccentric Beacon Hill millionaire."

"Are you putting me on?"

"I wish I were."

"But you're incredible. Why can't you—"

"Perform in nightclubs, consult with heads of state, win a fortune at the races, right? First of all, I'm not incredible. Mediocre is more like it. And second—what if I don't enjoy doing that sort of thing?"

"You don't?"

Alan paused. "Not always."

Julia stared at him again, then continued her inspection of the room. She was trying to get inside his mind, just as he had already been inside hers. That was what bothered him, of course. Well, tough for him: fair was fair. Besides, what in the world did he have to hide?

She sat back down, eventually, and they both watched the game in uneasy silence. Whatever her thoughts were now, they were hidden from him, except for the obvious tension in her features. *Everything's going to be all right*, he wanted to murmur to her, but the future was no clearer than her thoughts, and he was not at all sure that anything would be all right.

The front-door buzzer did nothing to ease the tension. Julia jumped up, shaking her head. "No, please, no."

Alan thought for a moment, then went over and spoke into the intercom. "Yeah?"

"Kelliher."

Alan hesitated, then pushed the door-release button. When he turned back, Julia was crouched in a corner of the room, still shaking her head. "I thought you were going to protect me," she whispered.

"Relax. You'll be safe if you stop acting like a mental patient. Have a sandwich."

There were footsteps in the hall and a knock. Julia hurried back to her armchair. Alan waited until she looked reasonably normal, then opened the door.

Kelliher stepped inside. Dusty rushed over and curled around his legs. "Alan, we've got to talk about this business."

"Gee, I'd love to chat with you, Jim, but I've got a date."

"What?" Kelliher looked past him into the living room and saw Julia, who managed a smile. "Oh, excuse me, didn't mean to—"

"That's okay," Alan said.

Kelliher stared at Julia for a moment, then took Alan's arm and leaned close to him. "What is this, Alan?" he asked in an undertone. "You didn't mention anything to me about a date. And since when do you bring a girl into this hellhole? And since when—"

"Gee, Jim, I'd really like to discuss my love life with you, but the game is in extra innings, and my date and I are both getting very excited."

The detective gazed at him in perplexity, then shook his head. "Call me tomorrow. I want to talk to you."

"Right. Tomorrow."

Kelliher nodded briefly to Julia and left.

She slumped in her chair and finished off the Budweiser. "That's your friend?"

"Yeah. Want another beer while I'm up?"

She shook her head. "Does he suspect me?"

Alan returned to the living room and sat down. "Don't see why he should, at the moment."

"But eventually."

Alan shrugged. "He's a good policeman—and you *are* guilty, after all."

"Then why did you let him see me?" she asked, her voice trembling. "Why am I here?"

"I don't know, Julia," he said quietly. "I wish I could . . ." his voice trailed off as the Red Sox pitcher gave up a towering home run into the left-field screen.

Julia stood up. "I should leave then. This is crazy."

He looked at her, looked at the face in his vision. "Don't go."

"Why should I stay here and get arrested?"

"Maybe you won't be. And maybe there are worse things than getting arrested."

An expression of utter panic appeared on her face for a moment, and then she shook her head as if willing it away. "This is crazy," she repeated, and she headed for the door.

It was Alan's turn to panic. He didn't want that face to disappear from his life. He rushed after her. "If you go I'll turn you in," he said. "Yellow Volkswagen; California license GT54627. You wouldn't make it to the turnpike."

She turned and faced him at the door, and her expression was hard now. "I get it," she said evenly. "A little blackmail. Kind of kinky, huh—fucking the kidnapper? And then you'll just turn me in when you've had enough."

Alan felt himself blushing. Damn it, it wasn't true. But there was enough truth there to prick his conscience. He desperately wanted her not to think of him like that. "I'm a hopeless romantic," he replied. "I just wanted to help a damsel in distress. Go, if you think that's what you should do. I won't call the police. But listen to me: you're in a hell of a lot of trouble, and I just have this feeling that I'm the only person who can possibly get you out of it. I may be mediocre, but sometimes my feelings are *real* accurate. If you want my help I'll try to give it. Otherwise, you're on your own."

She gazed at him for a moment, then past him into the sloppy living room, into the center of his life. And which of her neurons were firing now, what horrifying images were being processed in her cortex? He wished he knew. After a few moments she walked back into the living room and sat down. "What happens now?" she asked softly.

The question at last. Alan smiled and followed her. "Beats me." The Red Sox were making their final out. "Bums," he muttered and turned off the TV. For once the loss didn't seem to matter, though; Julia was staying. "You can have the couch. The toilet runs. Jiggle the handle after you use it. I get up at seven-thirty, go to work at quarter to nine."

"What do I do when you're at work?"

"Keep Dusty company. She gets lonely during the day. Any more questions?"

Julia shook her head.

"I have one for you then: we haven't been properly introduced. What's your last name?"

"You don't know that along with everything else?"

"These things come to me or they don't."

She gazed at him appraisingly. "Then I'll just keep it to myself. Might as well have some secrets from you."

Alan nodded; fair was fair. "Good night, then. Nothing but pleasant dreams allowed in this apartment."

Julia produced half a smile. "I'll do my best."

Chapter 3

"'Chapter Three. A Sense of Purpose. The child of five, of eight, of twelve, has but one thought, and that thought is *me*. His is a solipsistic universe. Parents, siblings, schoolmates—all revolve around the central ego of this Ptolemaic cosmos. Maturation is each individual's Copernican revolution, his movement from solipsism toward altruism, toward an understanding that others are as worthy of regard as oneself.

"'But this movement never occurs easily, without pain or pathos. Many adults end up locked helplessly between the two poles, perceiving dimly that something is wrong with their lives but unable, such is their obsession with their own happiness, to perceive that it is precisely this obsession that is their problem.

"'What is needed is a sense of purpose. But how does one find the purpose? One cannot simply say: work for peace on earth, seek a cure for cancer, improve the lot of the working class. How can these goals, laudable though they may be, compete with the constant need for self-gratification, for the man and woman who cannot see beyond self? One must somehow find the key that will link person with purpose and enrich both. That key is, simply, the key to happiness.'

"What do you think?" Pottston Phipps asked, lowering the sheet of paper and stroking his gray goatee.

"Trite," Alan replied. "And badly written."

Mr. Phipps stared at him in astonishment. "What do you mean, 'badly written'?"

"Ptolemaic cosmos my foot. You're forcing your metaphors, as usual. And you're mixing them too. Keys lock, they don't link."

Mr. Phipps's strokes turned to nervous tugs. His bushy eyebrows wrinkled menacingly, and his gaze darted here and there around the room, as if looking for weapons. "Your objections are trivial, Alan. As usual you refuse to look at the big picture, to see the cumulative power of the prose. It's the fault of your Harvard education, I'm afraid. I begin to realize that our differences are irreconcilable. You may take two weeks' salary in lieu of notice. Have the financial records ready for my inspection before leaving."

"You want me to fix it up?" Alan inquired, pointing at the sheet.

"Yes, yes," Mr. Phipps replied irritably. "Minor modifications only. Spelling and the like. Ptolemaic gave me a lot of trouble. Leave my metaphors alone."

"And those galleys need proofreading."

"Yes, certainly. Take care of that, would you, Alan? I'm feeling quite exhausted. And pick up those books at the Athenaeum on your lunch hour, if you would."

"After my lunch hour."

"Of course, of course. I didn't mean to suggest—" He gestured vaguely and walked out of the room. He would wander upstairs, Alan knew, to his pitch-black, book-strewn bedroom, where he would lie on his elegant four-poster until the fragment of another chapter came to him. That might refresh him enough to endure another contact with the human race.

Alan opened the long draperies covering the French doors, and sunlight flooded his office. Mr. Phipps claimed to be allergic to sunlight. Then he sat down at the Queen Anne desk and set to work on his employer's baroque prose.

At precisely twelve-thirty he stopped working and

took his brown-bagged lunch out of the bottom drawer of the desk. There were several books of poetry beneath it. He selected one by Wallace Stevens and shut the drawer.

He looked at the phone. *Surely I could call her,* he thought. *I could even walk back to the apartment, see how she's doing.* He remembered that he was supposed to get in touch with Kelliher. Let him wait. He picked up the phone and dialed.

It ran a long time. Finally there was an answer—a quick, almost inaudible "Hello?"

"It's Alan. I'm just checking to see if you're okay— regular bowel movements, normal blood pressure, low resting pulse—the usual."

There was a pause, and the hint of a laugh. Or was it just his desire to hear the laugh? "I'm fine."

"Do you have enough to eat? There's peanut butter, and Hungry Man soups, and—"

"Yes, there's plenty. How come you're not fifty pounds overweight?"

"I guess I just have a cooperative metabolism. Are you getting along with Dusty?"

"I fed her some tuna fish and we made friends."

"Oh, good. She's spoiled rotten," he said approvingly. "Well, I—you know—I'll be home about five-thirty."

"Okay. I'll be here."

That was what Alan wanted to hear. He hung up, took his lunch and book, and walked out through the French doors into a small garden surrounded by high brick walls. *Have to get estimates on repointing the bricks.* He sat in a rusty folding chair next to a lopsided sundial, ate salami sandwiches left over from the night before, and read "Peter Quince at the Clavier" several times.

Julia sat by the window and looked past the wilted plants at the quiet, sunny street below. The stillness in the apartment had terrified her at first, but now it seemed almost soothing. She didn't want to leave it; she wanted to clasp it around her, an invisible cloak that would protect her from all harm.

Where should she be now? Somewhere in the Midwest, probably, with the kid still doped up under a blanket in the backseat, listening to the news and praying no state troopers would pull up alongside her . . . but instead she was here, in this stranger's apartment, feeding his cat, more afraid now than if she *had* been on the road, doing what she was supposed to.

She had nothing else to do here but to try to understand why. But that was like trying to understand why she was who she was, and she had never been able to get very far on that question. You begin to think you know, and then instead of heading straight out to the turnpike, you return to the room you've rented, and stare at the grimy walls, and tremble at what you've done, and you're back at the beginning once again.

She got up and went out to the kitchen; Dusty eyed her sleepily from the sofa. She looked in the refrigerator for a Tab; nothing there but Budweiser and flat-looking root beer. Maybe she could go out and buy some, but she didn't want to go anywhere just now. Just being close to the front door made her uneasy. What if the phone were to ring again? She retreated to Alan's bedroom.

It was dark in there, with the shade drawn. Like the living room, it was overrun with books and magazines; on top of them were strewn toilet articles and scraps of clothing. Somewhere toward the center she could make out his bed, a mass of rumpled sheets that looked as if they had been there since he moved in. She sat down on the edge of the bed, not knowing quite why, and hugged her arms around her.

I felt an urge to protect you—from everyone.

And why did he want to do that? Why was she worth protecting? She didn't know and neither, apparently, did he. But there was no denying it now: she was safe here, and that was due to him.

She leaned back among the sheets and stared at the gray ceiling. He was not an immediately attractive man:

he was really kind of a mess; but, like his messy apartment, he had a certain charm. She liked his smile. She liked the way he had blushed when she accused him of wanting to sleep with her. There was a sort of, well, purity about him that went beyond blushing. *This is how I live*, he seemed to say: *take it or leave it*. And if he had seen something in her that made him want to take her into that life, should she assume that he was a fool? Perhaps, but perhaps she should give him the benefit of the doubt.

It was so strange that he was a psychic. Maybe that was part of the attraction. And maybe that was just what she needed to save herself, now that she had made her impulsive break with that other world. He too would be able to look into her soul, but instead of evil there would be . . . what? *What if there is nothing else?*

And suddenly she wanted very much to stay here, to let herself be protected in Alan Simpson's small, quiet universe. She turned over and buried her face in the sheets, and imagined that there was nothing in the world but this dark room, no one else but Alan, drinking beer and watching the Red Sox game. What more was needed? Couldn't she find happiness here if she could find it anywhere?

Something touched her on the shoulder. She screamed, grabbing the sheet to her face and whirling around. Back arched, Dusty glared at her from the floor, then calmed down and jumped back up on the bed. Julia reached out tentatively and stroked her. "It's all right," she murmured. "We're safe here."

After lunch Alan went to the Athenaeum and got the books for Mr. Phipps; on the way back he stopped off at the printer with the galleys. When he returned, he found Mr. Phipps pacing back and forth in the stuffy, unused third floor, past long bookcases crammed with *Vanity Fairs* and turn-of-the-century encyclopedias. Alan dropped the books on a side table. "They didn't have *Pulling Your Own Strings*," he said. "I could buy it, probably, without cleaning out your checking account."

Mr. Phipps fidgeted with his bowtie. "No no no no, try the public library. It's supported by my taxes, after all."

Alan sighed. "Would you like to talk about repointing the back wall?"

Mr. Phipps looked at him vaguely. "I am developing more thoughts on a sense of purpose," he said.

"Perhaps I should come back later then."

"There are other topics, of course. So many topics. So much to do. Perhaps I should think about . . . How to Understand Yourself. That certainly will require its own chapter. How . . . to . . ."

"I guess I'll come back later then."

Mr. Phipps resumed his pacing.

Alan didn't bother to come back later. He worked away quietly downstairs, and only saw Mr. Phipps again as he was leaving at five o'clock. Mr. Phipps was sitting halfway down the narrow front stairs, his well-chewed pencil in the air, legal pad balanced on bony knees.

"Good evening, Mr. Phipps," Alan said.

Mr. Phipps lowered his pencil hesitantly. "Ah, oh," he began and fell silent. "I had a thought," he began again.

"About how to understand yourself?"

There was a pause. "Would you happen to know," Mr. Phipps asked, "was I headed upstairs or down?"

"Down," Alan guessed.

Mr. Phipps brightened. "Down it is, then," he cried, and arose. "You're a good fellow, Alan. Give yourself a raise."

"Yes, sir." Alan shut the heavy oak door carefully behind him.

No pigeons tonight. Alan headed straight back to his apartment, nervous and excited. It felt decidedly odd to have someone besides Dusty to come home to. When he opened the door, Julia's perfume mingled with the apartment smell and the odor of something cooking—

chicken?—and it seemed right and natural. He relaxed—and as he relaxed he sensed the fear like an untreated wound, still there, beneath everything, festering. "It's only me," he said quietly.

Julia came out of his bedroom. She was wearing his "Beethoven Made Overtures to Leonore" T-shirt, and the thought of her sitting in his bedroom, wearing his clothes, made him a little weak. "You all right?" he asked.

She nodded.

"Nice jersey. Is that chicken I smell?"

"It was the only decent food I could find in the place. I'm afraid I'm not much of a—" The phone rang, and Julia flinched.

"It's okay," Alan muttered and picked up the receiver. "What?"

"What in the world is going on?" a throaty female voice asked.

Alan pondered. "Don't know."

"You know enough," the voice said sharply. "You know the evil. But the *danger*. Oh, Alan. Can't you feel it?"

"Sure, but—"

"But what? What are you *doing*, Alan?"

"Don't know," he sighed.

"Oh, Alan. Be careful, child. Be careful."

Alan grimaced and hung up.

"Who was it?" Julia asked anxiously.

"Oh, just my mother. Conversations with her tend to be a bit"—he struggled for the word—"elliptical. She was just warning me of the danger I'm in. I'll bet the chicken tastes great."

"Is she psychic too?"

"She's the all-star. I'm just a minor leaguer, compared to her. Regression to the mean is the technical term, I think."

"And—and what sort of danger did she say you were in?"

"She didn't. She thrives on vagueness and melo-

drama, like most psychics. She doesn't really know, I'm
sure. Actually, I was hoping you might be able to tell
me."

Julia gazed at him silently for a moment, then
walked over and looked out the window at the rays of the
setting sun slanting through the budding trees. Her fingers picked nervously at a dying coleus. "This is so quiet
for a city street," she remarked.

"Henry James once said that Marlborough Street
lacked passion. I suppose that's still true."

"The real world isn't like this, though," Julia said
softly. "The real world is full of anger and pain and
craziness and horror."

"Marlborough Street is real," Alan observed.

"But it's helpless. The rest of the world is stronger.
Your reality can be destroyed by anything—a bomb
tossed from a car, a murder—"

"A kidnapping."

"That would be a start," Julia whispered.

Alan considered. "But that doesn't really solve my
problem. I mean, should I wear a bulletproof vest, or
hire a food taster, or what? Speaking of food, that
chicken—"

"Oh Jesus, it's burning." She rushed past him into
the kitchen. Alan smiled thoughtfully and followed her.

Kelliher called while they were eating, and Alan put
him off with a promise to meet him the next day. "Persis-
tent fellow," Alan muttered as he sat back down at the
tiny kitchen table.

"Did he mention me?"

"Your existence may have come up in the course of
the conversation. Don't give it another thought."

"But what if—" Julia paused, then gave up on the
question. "Have you two known each other long?" she
asked.

"Since I was a junior at Harvard—seven, eight
years, I guess." Alan reached for another piece of bread.
"There was a kidnapping—not unlike your unfortunate

little incident. The victim was the only daughter of a guy who owned a bunch of these women's health spas, so he had the bucks. The parents paid the ransom, but no kid was forthcoming. There was a lot of publicity. I was reading about it in the *Globe*, and I got a flood of impressions—of the room where the girl had been kept, of the guys who held her, their cars, their jobs—everything. I called a hot line that the police had set up, and eventually I got shuffled to Kelliher. Luckily they were desperate, or he wouldn't have given me the time of day. He checked out a few of the things I had to tell him, and everything started to fall into place."

"You found the child?"

"Dead." Alan stared at Julia for a moment, then went on. "The perpetrators were apprehended, however, as the police like to say. Since then I've helped him out whenever he asks, and he's taken a sort of avuncular interest in me."

"He's the only one you help?"

"I've tried spreading the wealth, but my gift, such as it is, is awfully finicky. I went up to Bangor once on a missing persons case, and nothing. Just nothing. I was lucky they paid my bus ticket back. I have often given psychics a bad name."

"Does your mother help the police too?"

Alan laughed. "They should be thankful she doesn't put hexes on them. No, she has no use for public authority. I think there's some gypsy in our genes, although she denies it. She's never really forgiven me for collaborating with the enemy."

"Why are you different?"

Alan went to the refrigerator and got them each another beer. "I saw her gift screwing up her life and resolved not to let the same thing happen to me. She's obsessed with her powers—why she has them, how she can use them. I decided the best thing to do with my powers would be to, well, compartmentalize them, get them out of my life as much as I can. I'll do what I can to help people, but I'm not going to devote myself to reading minds or telling fortunes. Anything else I can clear up for you?"

Julia looked down at her plate, then impulsively reached over and grabbed Alan's hand. "Please, Alan, let's be friends," she said. "I know this is really awkward, and there are things I'm not telling you, and we're both scared, but if we're going to be here together . . . can we be friends?"

Her eyes glistened with tears. Alan was embarrassed. "There's nothing I'd like better," he murmured. "Would you care to watch the baseball game with me?"

Julia smiled. "Of course. There's nothing I'd like better."

When the dishes were done Alan turned the TV on and they sat on the couch together, in silence, like a couple who had been married too long to have anything left to say to each other. Alan discovered that Julia was woefully ignorant of the subtleties of the national pastime, and he tried to enlighten her. She was only vaguely interested, though, and eventually he gave up. Around the third inning she leaned her head against his shoulder, and Alan hesitantly put his arm around her. She seemed to enfold herself into him, radiant with contentment and relief. By the fifth inning she was asleep.

Alan barely moved, afraid she would wake up. Dusty, a little jealous, tried to jump up onto his lap, but he shooed her away.

Asleep, in the flickering TV light, Julia looked even younger and more vulnerable than the image in Alan's mind. Just a kid, he thought. But people are complicated at any age. He considered probing her mind, using his gift to try to understand her. But it was unfair—and it wouldn't work; it never seemed to work when it truly mattered. Let her sleep; eventually he would understand.

"We are special, we are different, we are better," his mother kept telling him as he grew up. No reason not to believe it. But he remembered when he was fourteen, listening to his mother downstairs arguing with the latest man she thought might cure her unhappiness. Alan had been in her mind so often it was almost as familiar to him as his own—but not quite. There were always areas— thoughts and feelings and memories—that were forbidden, off limits. Now, in his adolescent loneliness, weary of the inexplicable tears and anger, he suddenly needed to know *everything*. He pressed his face into his pillow and thrust his mind down into hers, feeling in that split second her power, but also her pain, her confusion, the frustrations of a lifetime of unanswered questions, and he realized several things at once: *We are different, but we are not necessarily better; we see more, but we do not necessarily understand more; even though we both have the gift, we are not the same, and the gift by itself makes no one special.* His mother felt him inside her mind, of course, and as he waited for her to finish one argument so that she could come upstairs and start another, he realized that he had stopped being a child.

When the ball game was over (the Red Sox lost), Alan gently disengaged himself from Julia and lowered her onto the couch. He turned the TV off and stood staring at her for a while, counting her breaths. He took a half-step toward her, then abruptly changed directions. He switched off the lights and went to bed.

She opened her eyes in darkness. The dream had been terrible and the reality, for an instant, was not much better. Then she remembered where she was, remembered the warmth of the shoulder, the hypnotic drone of the announcers. The room clarified around her as her eyes grew accustomed to the dim streetlight filtering in the window. *I am safe*, she thought, *I am being protected*. And she felt a surge of happiness that left her breathless for a moment. *Let me stay*, she prayed, *let me stay*. And along with the happiness she discovered something else, equally unexpected. She thought about it for a while and then arose from the couch.

* * *

Alan awoke to hands moving over his body, fumbling at the buttons of his pajamas. He shuddered with delight and reached out. Her naked body came down on top of him, her lips and tongue met his. *A dream*, he thought, but dreams did not give this pleasure. She seemed more experienced than he (it could hardly have been otherwise), so he let her control the pleasure, moving with her, responding to her silent commands. And when she finally brought him inside her, his mind reached out, and it too was inside her, sharing her rapture and, yes, the fear still biding its time beneath it. Every stroke brought him deeper—deeper into her soul, into the truth of her, toward some irreducible essence, some unalterable reality.

But he never reached it. Their cries commingled and his own lonely, desperate reality shot into her, and they were done.

There was a distant squeal of brakes and honking of horns. The toilet was running; someone had forgotten to jiggle the handle. He could hear Julia's heart beat. They moved apart.

Why hadn't he reached it? *We see more, but we do not necessarily understand more*. Too eager, perhaps, too involved in his own pleasure.

His eyes had adjusted to the darkness, and he gazed at the smooth white curves of her body, the small breasts jutting toward him, asking to be caressed some more. Her fingers played in his hair; she smiled softly.

. . . Or perhaps he did not want to reach it. What if he found it, and it was not what he wanted, not what he needed? What if the evil he had seen was at the heart of her? Did he want to know that?

Not now, not now.

He reached out to her.

"You want more?" she asked.

"I want to devour you."

"Parts of me are pretty unappetizing."

"Let me be the judge of that."

"Can I stay?"

"You are forbidden to go."

She snuggled up beside him. The toilet miraculously stopped running. Marlborough Street was silent. The city, the world, bustled with passion and purpose, but here there was only contentment, and peace.

Chapter 4

"Look, Alan, we talk to the kid, and he says he was grabbed by a young white female, brown hair, wearing designer jeans. He also called her a good-looking bitch, but His Honor asked us to ignore that remark. The guy who runs the rooming house on Dwight Street says he rented the room to a pretty brown-haired girl, about twenty years old. I go to your apartment, Alan, and what do I see there but a cute brown-haired girl wearing jeans. So I ask myself: What is going on here?"

Alan took a swig of his beer. "It's entirely proper of you to be suspicious. In fact she's guilty, and I brought her back to my apartment so I could blackmail her into the sack."

Kelliher shifted uncomfortably in the booth. "I could bring her in and show her to my witnesses, get a positive ID."

"You probably could. I could also give her an alibi, since she was of course with me all day."

"You were working. You'd never take the day off to spend it with a girl."

"I'm in love. I'm a changed man. Try getting Pottston Phipps to remember if I was there on a certain day. He's away in Cloudcuckooland most of the time himself."

Kelliher sighed and stirred a Sweet 'n Low into his coffee. "Well, it's all academic at any rate. The mayor told us to lay off. No publicity. It never happened. But that's not really the point. The point is—"

"The point is you don't want me mixed up in this."

"The point is I know a hell of a lot more about the sleazy people in this world than you do. And you're no match for them, no matter what powers you have."

"But what if she's not sleazy?"

Kelliher drained his coffee cup and slammed it into the saucer. "If you believe that, then you're even more naïve than I think." He slid out of the booth. "Just be careful, Alan."

Alan gestured at the check. "Hey, what about—"

"Drinks are on you this time. The advice is free."

They stared at each other domestically and then embraced. "How did it go with Kelliher?" Julia asked.

"Oh, uh, great. The mayor told him to drop the investigation. You're off the hook."

"But he knows."

"Suspects."

"And he doesn't want you to have anything to do with me," Julia said tonelessly.

"What are you, psychic?"

"I don't need to be psychic to figure that out." She broke away from him and went out into the kitchen. Pork chops in tomato sauce. Ecstasy. "What are you going to do?" she asked as she stirred them.

He followed her. "Me? Nothing. If I don't obey my mother I'm certainly not going to obey Kelliher. Especially after last night." He nuzzled the back of her neck.

She closed her eyes and leaned back against him. "Have I ever asked you why I'm here?" she whispered.

"Wouldn't be surprised."

"Let me try it again."

Alan sighed and got himself a beer. "I saw your face, Julia. In my vision, or whatever it is that I have. And I never wanted so much for one of my visions to come true. I couldn't stand the idea that that face might not be real—or that it might be real, and I might never really see it, touch it."

Julia blushed as she leaned over the stove. "There's nothing—my face isn't—"

"Not just the face, Julia, but—*you*. Visions can be more than skin-deep."

"It doesn't make any sense."

"I know. I didn't say it would. Try not to think about it." He returned to her neck. "Maybe we should skip dinner tonight."

Julia laughed. "This is getting serious."

"I'm afraid so."

They lay in gathering darkness. The *Siegfried Idyll* was playing on the stereo in the living room. The pork chops were eaten but the dishes were unwashed: compromise. Dusty was grooming herself at the foot of the bed.

"Walker."

"What?"

"My last name. Julia Walker."

"Pleased to meet you. Do you come here often?"

"No, but I bet you do."

"My, what a filthy mind. I wish I did."

"You will now."

Julia Walker. *That is who I am sleeping with,* Alan thought. *That is the name that goes with the face.* The thought was exhilarating. Did she have more to say, more secrets to bestow upon him? Ask and ye shall receive. "Tell me about yourself, Julia Walker. What brings you to this neck of the woods?"

He felt her body go tense. Not too fast, now. "Begin at the beginning, Ms. Walker. Chapter One. I Am Born. 'Once upon a time, in a magic kingdom far, far away . . .'"

Julia laughed. "There are no magic kingdoms, Alan."

"Who told you that?"

"I've learned it."

"You need a new teacher." He kissed her forehead. "Once upon a time," he repeated softly.

"It's not very pleasant," she said.

"But at least it has a happy ending."

She moved closer to him and, after a moment, began. "Once upon a time there was an actress. An aspiring actress. And there was this movie producer. Beverly Hills, phone by the swimming pool, the whole bit. The actress did what she had to do to get parts. So she had an audition with the producer one afternoon, and ended up with two lines in some costume spectacle—and me. She didn't believe in abortion; that was her biggest mistake. Anyway. My father wasn't a bad guy, I guess, for his type. He wouldn't have anything more to do with my mother, wouldn't acknowledge me, but his accountants sent us a check the first of every month, with an extra something at Christmas. My mother rented a bungalow in L.A., and we lived off the checks."

"And were happy ever after?"

Julia buried her face in his side for a moment before turning back and staring at the ceiling. "Not in this story," she said softly. "My mother wanted to be a star. I mean, she wanted it so bad she could barely function in everyday life. She was one of these people who grow up in a small town and everyone says, 'You're so beautiful you should be in pictures,' and eventually she believed it. And she *was* beautiful. Christ, maybe she had some talent too. I don't know. Maybe life was terrifically unjust to her. But she never got anywhere.

"It wasn't for not trying, though. You have to give her that. She was always taking lessons in something and appearing in showcases and going to casting calls. If she had a chance to make it with some guy who could maybe get her a part, well, she'd make it with him. Anything for her career."

"And you—"

"I was the excess baggage. She'd cart me along

sometimes to her drama class or something. I was a good little girl and everyone fussed over me. But my mother never let me forget that I was holding her back, without me she might already be a star. Maybe she was right. Maybe she missed out on her big chance some day when I was sick and she had to look after me."

"Sounds like she infected you with her way of thinking."

"I suppose she did. It was my fault, it was the world's fault—anything but her own fault. But you know it really was the world's fault, in a way, for letting a place like Hollywood exist, for letting my mother think her fantasies were more important than her child."

"The world just exists," Alan observed.

"Then maybe it should be changed."

"Who's going to change it?"

Julia said nothing.

"What else went on in your magic kingdom?" Alan asked as the silence lengthened.

"Boyfriends," Julia said with a sigh. "It seemed like I was always acquiring a new uncle, who'd hang around for a couple of months until he and my mother got bored with each other and started fighting. My mother liked for people to admire her looks, but she didn't want a husband any more than she wanted a kid. Some of them were nice; they kept me company. Some of them were— not so nice. I guess I thought it was my fault they were the way they were too. When they beat me up, I knew I'd been bad. I just couldn't figure out *how*."

"Poor Julia Walker," Alan said, holding her close.

"Poor me," she agreed. "The boyfriends more or less dropped out of the picture when the drinking started. I guess at a certain point she sort of sensed that her fantasies were never going to become real, so she stopped trying and got them out of a bottle instead. And then, instead of boyfriends beating me . . . Shit." Julia fell silent again. She turned over on her back and stared up at the ceiling. The music stopped; the idyll was over. Alan wondered if this was such a good idea. But really, he had no choice: he had to know, and he had to hear it from *her*.

"It was awful. It was stupid. Because at the same time she was beating me, I was saving her life—keeping her eating right, calling the ambulance when she'd fall and split her head open, hiding the car keys when she was blind drunk. After a while I just couldn't see the point anymore, and I started running away. But I was stupid about that, too, because I kept letting myself get caught. I guess I just couldn't imagine any other life besides the one I was used to. I'd sit in the bus station, and I'd cry my eyes out until someone would take care of me."

"Wouldn't the social workers get involved—take you away from her?"

"Sure, except that my mother was always on her best behavior for them. If they took me away, they took away her excuse for failing. They knew something was wrong, but it could just as easily have been me as her. So I always ended up back in that bungalow.

"Then, when I was a senior in high school, my father died, and the checks stopped. So my mother went nuts."

"Nuts?"

"She tried to kill herself. Screwed that up, of course. I found her on the floor in the bathroom with am empty bottle of Valium. I looked at her lying there, and I thought: *She's still alive*. Why couldn't I have been somewhere else, and found her after she was dead? Then I called the ambulance. When they'd pumped her out it was clear she'd gone off the deep end. So she was committed."

"What did you do?"

"I managed to graduate; don't ask me how. Meanwhile my father's will was probated, and I found he'd left me a decent chunk of money. I guess I was old enough by then so that I *could* imagine another life for me, because I didn't hang around the bungalow long after that."

"And what about your mother?"

Julia sighed. "She's still committed, as far as I know. Before I left town I'd try to visit her when I got up my courage. She'd seem pretty coherent for a while, and then she'd ask me to help her put her makeup on, because she'd heard that the head of casting at MGM was going to tour the ward later on. I was worried at first that they'd let her out, you know, and everything would start all over again, but they tried her in a couple of those halfways houses, and it didn't seem to work, so I guess she's sort of a lifer."

"Does it bother you—thinking about her there?"

"Just thinking about *her* bothers me. I suppose I feel the same damn old guilt: it's my fault she's there, I'm wrong for not trying to get her out. But she's better off in a mental hospital than in the real world. She does less harm to herself, to me, to everyone."

"So what did you do after you left L.A.?"

"Well, I tried junior college for a while, but I couldn't really get my mind on studying. So I ended up spending most of my time at the beach, surfing, smoking dope. I took some jobs, just for something to do, read a lot of books, had some ballet classes. I felt so free, you know, that for a couple of years the freedom was all that mattered."

"But that changed?"

"Everybody grows up. There's more to life than freedom."

Alan waited for her to continue. What the hell did that last sentence mean, anyway? Dusty jumped off the bed, stretched, and wandered away. Alan thought of the mayor's kid, and *his* freedom. How had Julia made the switch from surfing to kidnapping? How had evil managed to insinuate itself into the innocent beauty of her face, her soul? *Come on*, he thought to her. *When will you have a better chance to unburden your soul?*

I can't. Seth will—I can't.

He reached out and touched her cheek; it was wet. He was afraid his cheek would become wet too, because if she couldn't bring herself to tell him why she was sitting in a South End rooming house with a kidnapped child then all her other confessions would be pointless, their being together was pointless. He longed to save her—but from what?

"Who told you that there's more to life than freedom, Julia?"

The silence continued. "I've learned it," she replied finally.

"Then maybe you need a new—"

"The world is evil," Julia said, her voice suddenly hard. "America is evil. It must be purified—so it doesn't do to others what it's done to me."

"The world just exists."

"Oh, bullshit. You protect yourself from the evil, Alan, with your Red Sox and your opera and your funny little job. You're too well protected. How can you teach me anything, how can I make you understand, how can I—" The tears came in earnest now, and her body was racked with sobs.

Well, that certainly cleared things up. Alan held her, and whispered meaningless reassurances. Meaningless, because her secret remained inside her. If she didn't think she could make him understand then he didn't think he could protect her—no matter how well he protected himself. And without protection— He recalled the sound of wind rustling through unknown trees, and she was part of the wind, and the wind was death. And only he could stop the death.

After a while the sobs went away, and he didn't know if she was awake or asleep. He let go of her, put on his robe, and went into the living room. The *Siegfried Idyll* was still on the turntable. *And what happened to Siegfried?* He should tell her to go away, go face life by herself, leave him and his Red Sox and the rest of his world alone. But that would be rational, and he had left rationality behind when her face had first appeared to him, a gift—and a warning—from the future. Here she is. No warranty, implied or otherwise. Best of luck.

The girl of my dreams, he thought wryly.

He put the record away and got out *Götterdämmerung*. He sat on the couch, skinny white legs stretched out in front of him, and listened to the first scene over the headphones—to the Norns passing the rope of fate among them, to the strains of doom as the rope breaks, and they realize that the old gods, and the world they cherish, are about to be swept away.

Chapter 5

Marlborough Street on a spring morning: a softness in the air. A black cat sunned itself lazily on a stoop; a kerchiefed woman dabbed paint onto her wrought-iron fence; an elderly man in starched shirt and bowtie walked a pair of afghan hounds, brandishing his long-handled scooper as if it were a baton to lead some massive, invisible orchestra; a sleek young executive held his little daughter's hand as he took her to the exclusive Montessori school; workmen on the latest condominium conversion clustered around the canteen truck, sipping their coffee, talking about the latest Red Sox loss; Alan Simpson walked, lunch in hand, remembering, considering.

I can't. Seth will . . . I can't.

You know the evil. But the danger *. . .*

I know a hell of a lot more about the sleazy people . . .

You've protected yourself too well . . .

Alan walked faster, and the scene began to blur. The afghans, seeing the cat, snarl and strain at their leashes. The old man dreams of exposing himself to the kerchiefed woman. The executive hurries from the Montessori school to an appointment with a high-priced call girl on Boylston Street. One of the workmen recalls beating his wife last night, still seeing her terror and submission, still feeling the satisfying crack of fist against bone . . .

Jesus. Alan cut over to Beacon Street, with its commuter traffic and college students. Busy, bland, anonymous: no hallucinations there. There was enough horror in the world without making any up.

But in what sense was he making anything up? Perhaps the worker had not beaten his wife, but the evil was there inside him, waiting for its opportunity. Alan's gift had simply found its own expression for it.

His gift.

If he could understand it he could understand anything; he could understand Julia. Little likelihood of that.

"'Chapter Five. How to Understand Yourself. The first thing to be understood is that introspection can become a disease. Excessive introspection can put one on the danger list. It has been said that the unexamined life is not worth living, but too much examining is fatal, because it leaves no time for living.

"'The cure is to strive for a balance. And in what introspection one does, one must follow the doctor's orders. You should not seek relentlessly to discover what you should be, or even what you can be, but what you are. And you should not expect to find answers that are clear and unalterable; if you find them, they will almost certainly be wrong. The nature of life is to pile complexity upon complexity, and the nature of our search must be to look for hints and suggestions of truths about life that can never be completely revealed. What one must strive for are working hypotheses, sensible versions of the truth that will allow one to live most fruitfully and happily.'"

Mr. Phipps paused.

"I liked the part about too much examining— Dr. Phipps," Alan admitted.

Mr. Phipps beamed. "Indeed. I think I'm onto something there. This will certainly be my finest work."

"Can't help but be," Alan murmured.

"Yes, yes, your little joke, Alan. I'm sure you'll find the unemployment line a great source of amusement too."

Alan smiled. "I'll type it up."

Julia sat in a corner of the living room—as she had when Kelliher had rung the doorbell—arms wrapped tightly around herself, eyes closed.

She should kill herself. Surely she could do a better job of it than her mother.

But she didn't want to kill herself. She didn't want to do anything. Alan had forced her to do something last night—to make a choice—and now they both had to live with the consequences. Damn him, why couldn't he have waited? It came too fast, she had given him one fact and he had wanted them all. Was he surprised that ultimately she refused? Three days ago they had been strangers. Was he ready to tell all his darkest secrets to *her*?

They had barely spoken when he went off to work this morning. It had been all she could do since then to get dressed. And now . . .

Now, suddenly, she felt something: cold and powerful, deep inside her. She didn't have to be psychic to understand that feeling. Seth had reclaimed her—and he was coming to get her. She opened her eyes and stared around her wildly. It was foolish. He was thousands of miles away.

No, nothing was foolish anymore. She stood up. She would have to do something now. But what? She couldn't stay here. She grabbed her car keys and ran out of the apartment, out into the sunlight. She felt naked, exposed: where was her car? She found it eventually, a couple of parking tickets plastered on the windshield. She tossed them onto the front seat and drove off.

Where?

She wandered through the streets of the Back Bay with no idea what to do. More than once she passed the entrance to the turnpike and thought about taking off, running away from both of them—to Canada, perhaps. Were there psychics in Canada? But she didn't, and finally she pulled into a parking garage and sat there alone, anonymous, afraid. And she made up her mind.

She would return to Alan's apartment. Not so that Alan would protect her, but so that Seth would be able to find her. The decision terrified her, but she knew it was what she wanted.

At lunchtime Alan stood in front of the French doors, looking at the garden. He had planted some flowers there one spring, but they had died. Now there were just last year's leaves, soggy and rotting, and a few hardy tufts of grass. He wished he knew how to keep plants alive. He walked over to the phone and called his apartment.

There was no answer. After a dozen rings he held the receiver by the end of its cord and let it drop. He watched it spin as the tension unwound. *Go, stay, go, stay.* When the spinning stopped he picked the receiver up and replaced it in its cradle.

What was the point of trying to find out where she was, if she didn't want him to know? What was the point of knowledge, without understanding? What was the point of love, without trust?

Love. He was twenty-seven years old, had big ears and oily hair, and wore white socks. He liked white socks. He had a peculiar job, a peculiar set of interests, a peculiar gift. But he did not feel peculiar.

So who hallucinated about people beating their wives as he walked to work? Who hid a kidnapper from the police? Who fell in love with one, after a three-day whirlwind courtship?

He wondered if everyone felt normal. Pottston Phipps, for example, who wrote self-help books but was afraid to go outside his own house—did he think himself peculiar, sitting on the stairs and pondering his next mangled metaphor? Did his mother feel normal, giving psychic consultations in her overstuffed apartment and pondering the shambles she had made of her life? Deep down inside, perhaps, they felt that theirs was the proper way to live, that the rest of the world was out of step with *them*. Who's to say they were wrong?

Stay. Nothing to be gained either way. He got out his volume of Keats and ate his lunch while reading "La Belle Dame Sans Merci."

Julia was there when he got home from work. He was surprised and absurdly grateful. They stared at each other awkwardly, and then he took her in his arms. "Let's not stay here tonight," he whispered. "Let's go out and enjoy ourselves."

"Whatever you want, Alan. Where would you like to go?"

He considered. "Well, the Red Sox—"

Julia laughed. "Of course. We'll go to the ball game."

So they ate quickly, then walked down Marlborough Street to Kenmore Square, past the discos, the B.U. students playing Frisbee in the snarled traffic, the pizza parlors, the souvenir vendors, then up Brookline Avenue to Fenway Park.

"Why do you like baseball so much?" Julia asked as they circled around to the bleacher entrance.

"That's like asking why I was raised in Boston. If you're a kid here, you're a Red Sox fan."

"But don't a lot of kids—uh—outgrow it?"

"That's their loss." They moved through the turnstiles into the noisy concourse. Alan bought a scorecard and a beer, and they walked out into the stands. The left-field wall loomed in front of them, impossibly large and forbidding. The outfield grass was so green under the bright lights that it looked unreal—which it most decidely was not. In the Red Sox bullpen two pitchers leaned on the railing, chewing tobacco, silently gazing out into the night. Over the loudspeaker John Kiley played "Lady of Spain" on the organ.

"Baseball is the world made manageable," Alan said as they took their seats. The acrid smell of marijuana floated past them. "It's a stylized version of real life. There's drama, disappointment, triumph, tragedy, but the slate gets wiped clean in October and things start all over again. If the manager makes a bad decision, you boo him, but people don't starve to death as a result."

"Players do get injured, don't they?"

"A pulled hamstring, a broken rib. For a couple hundred thousand a year, I'd let you pull my hamstring. Players get old and have to retire, or they don't quite cut the mustard, but if they have any smarts at all they can sell insurance and make a decent living off having been a big leaguer. No need to feel sorry for the players."

"It's like my mother and the movies, I guess."

"How's that?"

"About the only good times we'd have together were when she'd take me to the movies. We'd get some popcorn and sit in the dark and watch *My Fair Lady* or some James Bond movie, and when it was over her eyes would be shining and she'd be so excited she couldn't move. She wanted to be up there on the screen, part of the fantasy, part of the happy ending. For a couple of hours anyway she forgot about the leak in the roof and the parts she didn't get and everything else."

"Well, of course in baseball you don't know if you're going to get a happy ending," Alan remarked. "In fact, with the Red Sox you can be pretty sure you won't. I guess we'd better stand for the anthem."

They watched the game in silence. Alan concentrated on it for a while, and then his attention began to wander. Julia was wearing an old moth-eaten sweater of his and looked so cute he wanted to hug her. But he couldn't. She was a stranger to him again, and there was nothing he could do about it.

But as the game wore on he realized he had to say

something—just as he had had to repeat his question the night before. He just needed to understand too badly. "I called you at noontime, but you were out," he remarked.

She glanced at him. "Oh, yeah, I figured it was about time to take care of my car. It had two tickets on it. I put it in that garage at the Prudential Center."

"Good idea." And maybe it was the truth. "Were you scared?"

She shook her head. "Should I have been?"

"'The real world is full of anger and pain and craziness and horror,'" he quoted.

The Red Sox were in trouble. Their relief pitcher jogged toward the mound from the bullpen, his jacket draped carefully over his two-million-dollar right arm. A fight broke out a few rows below them, and the crowd rose to see what was going on. Julia looked at Alan, and he knew that the ether was carrying his messages loud and clear. "Give me a break," she murmured.

The crowd roared its approval of a particularly good punch. A couple of burly security guards waded in and grabbed the combatants. The crowd booed. Maybe one message had still not been communicated. "I love you, Julia," Alan said.

"The Yankees suck!" someone shouted. The crowd cheered.

"We're not playing the Yankees!" someone else shouted.

"They still suck!"

Julia started to cry. "You're a jerk," she said.

"I'm a Red Sox fan. It's the same thing."

The batter hit the reliever's first pitch for a triple. The other team went ahead; the crowd settled down.

"There's no such thing as love in the real world," Julia said.

Alan considered. "Maybe you're right. Maybe it's just pretend—like baseball. And Marlborough Street."

"Can we go home now?"

The next batter doubled, and another run scored.

The manager walked slowly to the mound. The crowd booed. "Home," Alan repeated, as if it were a word he was thinking of adding to his vocabulary.

On Friday Alan ate lunch on the Esplanade. At twelve-thirty he crossed over Storrow Drive on the Fiedler Footbridge and found an empty bench with a view of the grim joggers, the preseason sunbathers, the sailboats dotting the Charles. He ate his roast beef sandwiches and waited for the warm spring sun to soften his gloomy thoughts. Eventually he saw someone who was neither jogger nor sunbather.

She looked not unlike a bag lady. She was short and fat. Despite the warm day, she was wearing an old woolen overcoat with a button missing. Blue veins bulged out of her thick legs. The vast amount of makeup she wore could not conceal what age had done to her face. A cigarette dangled from her lower lip. She dropped the cigarette, stamped on it, and sat down next to Alan.

"Want a Cheez-It?" he asked, holding out a Baggyful.

"Skip the small talk. It damn near killed me to walk over here."

"You could have phoned. My number's in the book."

"I'm more menacing in person."

"Why menace me?"

She gave him a disgusted look and turned away.

"I don't know, Ma. Honest."

She turned back, and suddenly gripped his arm. Alan didn't like it when she touched him. "Blood," she whispered, her painted eyes wide with horror.

Too melodramatic, Alan thought. Too many palm readings, too many séances. The medium has replaced the message. *Hey, that's not bad.* "What do you mean? Whose blood?"

She shook her head.

"Where do you see it?"

She took his left hand in both her own and raised it to the level of his eyes.

He hadn't expected that. He gently disengaged his hand. "When?"

"The future flows into the present, and the flow is *strong, strong.*"

That was her way of saying *pretty soon.* "What should I do?"

"Give it up, Alan. You are being warned. You cannot save her, you cannot save the world, you can only save yourself. That is what you must do."

There were tears in his mother's eyes. She was sincere, all right. But what was this about saving the world? Alan sighed. "Well, thanks."

"Never mind thanks. Obey me."

He shrugged. She had never gotten him to obey very well. He was a stubborn child.

She shook her head at his willfulness. "Kiss me then."

Alan leaned forward and made a pass at her cheek, almost gagging on her old-lady perfume. They sat in silence for a moment, then he held out the Cheez-Its to her again. She grabbed a handful this time. "You always were a thoughtful boy, Alan." She heaved herself up off the bench and headed back along the pathway, popping the Cheez-Its into her mouth one by one.

It began to rain on Friday night. Alan found the tension in the apartment almost unbearable, so he took Julia sight-seeing on the weekend. He dragged her to the Museum of Fine Arts and showed her his favorite mummies, introduced her to the turtles at the aquarium, bought her knishes and souvlaki and chocolate chip cookies at the Quincy Market. But she was distracted, uninterested, and finally his energy petered out. On Sunday afternoon he gave up and let her sit by the window. She stared out into the rain and said nothing.

Alan put on *The Magic Flute,* hoping Mozart would

help dispel the gloom. Dusty sat on his lap, purring contentedly.

"It's beautiful," Julia said after a while, but her voice was low and toneless. And, as he flipped the record: "Did you get your love of music from your mother?"

"No, she can't tell the difference between a rebec and an alto shawm. I guess it was my father's contribution to my chromosomes, although I can't remember him being very musical either."

"Is he still alive?"

"Beats me. He left us when I was eight or nine. My parents were happily married until I started growing up and they found out I had my mother's gift. The powers were really strong when I was a kid, particularly when I was with my mother: we'd have these long conversations where we'd barely say a word. Kind of left my father out. I didn't know any better—like you. I thought that was the way things were for everyone. My mother should've known; I think she probably did, and didn't care. She'd always made an effort to fit into normal society, but I guess she stopped trying when she had me for a companion. So one day he just wasn't there anymore. He decided he didn't belong in our lives, my mother said. She didn't disagree."

Julia turned back to the window. So much for that. Alan went to the kitchen for a beer. She shook her head when he offered her one. "Did it make you feel guilty?"

"My father leaving? No. Why should it?"

"You were the reason your parents split up."

Alan took a swallow of his beer. "You mean I should feel guilty for having been born? That's pretty all-encompassing."

"It's the way I feel a lot."

"Well, stop it. You weren't the one who decided not to have an abortion."

Silence. Dusty got up and went over to her bowl of Liver 'n Egg Delight. "Do you wish your father hadn't gone?" Julia asked finally. Was she interested, Alan wondered, or was she just passing the time, picking idly at a scab while she waited for something to happen?

"Sure," he replied. "My mother kind of went to pieces after that. From trying to be normal she went to flaunting her strangeness. She got into palm readings and séances and long dialogues with the spirit world. She's good at that sort of thing, of course, since she's not a fake. But it certainly hasn't made her happy.

"It's occurred to me that if my parents had stayed together I might have reacted against their normality instead of my mother's strangeness, and *I* might have been the one telling fortunes at ten dollars a whack. These powers do tend to give one a fatalistic turn of mind: whatever it is that forms us lurks somewhere out of our reach, out of our control. I could be all wrong about that, but an instance of precognition does make you stop and wonder why you're struggling so hard. If I'm boring you just wave your hand."

Julia turned back from the window and smiled uncomfortably. "Have you ever thought of using your powers to try to find your father?"

"What for—to talk over old times?"

"But there must be things you have to . . . work out with him."

"If there are, they're too deeply hidden for me to know about. Look, I'm not saying you should be like me. Resigned acceptance of the status quo isn't always a virtue. But brooding over injustices isn't very useful either, and neither is guilt over things you can't control. If he were to appear at my door we'd certainly have an interesting conversation. But if that conversation never takes place I'm not going to be heartbroken."

"You make it all sound so simple."

Alan suddenly felt irritable, depressed. "Maybe if you'd tell me your problem I could make my advice more complex."

Julia turned back to the window, as he figured she would. He listened to the opera, knowing that the forces of good would triumph, the Queen of the Night would be vanquished. Just like the movies. He finished his beer and crushed the can. A car hissed by on the street. The Red Sox game had been postponed because of the rain. That's life.

Chapter 6

Julia watched Alan walking off to work along Marlborough Street until he was just a memory. The coldness filled her now, and she knew it wouldn't be long before this strange little oasis in her life would be in the past. At the moment she was calm, although she knew that as the hours went by in the stillness her terror would grow. She didn't question her decision—at least not now—but Alan had not made it easy on her. *Love.* He didn't know anything about love. He didn't know anything about anything. She turned away from the window. Someday he would understand.

On the floor by the sofa she noticed a crushed beer can. She picked it up, walked out into the kitchen, and threw it in the trash—hurriedly, before the tears came.

"'Chapter Six. Disappointments. Life is not exactly what we want it to be. The gap between our desires and reality is the measure of our disappointments. Most disappointments are obvious: we are not beautiful, we are not rich, our friends let us down, our bosses ignore us. Some affect us more than others; some we can affect, others we cannot. If disappointments are not to rule our lives we must be ruthless in separating the wheat from the chaff. We must find the *useful* disappointments, the ones we can struggle against and hope to conquer, the ones that will make us better human beings. Otherwise we will forever be—' Alan, are you paying attention?"

Alan looked up at Mr. Phipps. "More than usual, actually. May I ask your advice about something?"

"Uh, well, yes, I—" Mr. Phipps sat down, fingering his legal pad nervously.

"Is it ever useful to struggle against something, knowing you can't overcome it?"

"Well, I suppose it could build character and all."

"What if you don't care about character, you just want to do it?"

"Well, that's all right, I mean, as long as you are *aware* of what you're doing."

"What if it's *dangerous?*"

Mr. Phipps stood up abruptly and started backing toward the door. "These, uh, personal concerns are really out of place at work, Alan. You must, er, learn to keep them separate."

Alan smiled. "Of course. Stupid of me to bring it up."

"Oh, well, not at all. I mean: who better to ask?"

"Beats me."

Lunchtime. Unable to stay, unable to go, Alan wandered away from his place of employment. Sunlight glinted off the State House dome. Pretty girls, shoeless, romped in the fountains at Government Center. The yogurtmobiles and pretzel stands were besieged with customers. A bearded fellow wearing a leather vest and running shorts was singing "The Fifty-ninth Street Bridge Song" *a cappella*. A family of tourists asked Alan to take their picture. Glumly, he obliged.

He went into the Bell-in-Hand and had a beer, but that only gave him a headache and made him sweat. He loosened his tie and started searching for a drugstore where he could buy some aspirin. After a while he stopped, realizing his eyes weren't working. All he saw was evil. His mind was filled with fear. *I should go home*, he thought, but he knew the evil would only grow stronger as he walked along Marlborough Street, and he didn't think he could stand it. This time he would not be going to the rescue of a fair damsel or an innocent boy. This time he had been warned.

He went back to work and sat in the darkened office: a sanctuary of sorts. The manuscript lay untyped; the bills were unpaid; the galleys unproofed. He sat in the darkness, and recalled the time he had gone with Jim Kelliher into the Blue Hills, looking for a little boy who had been missing for several months. Long, fruitless wandering, following vague psychic clues that seemed to lead nowhere, until he saw a pile of leaves and murmured, "There." Kelliher set to work, grunting and straining, and Alan wanted to help but could not. Then Kelliher turned away quickly, shaking his head. "Don't look, Alan," he said, and Alan didn't want to, but he couldn't stop himself, and he gazed past his friend at the naked, twisted body, and the eyes, *the empty eyes, crawling with*—

He stood up, paced the room for a moment, then walked quickly upstairs. Mr. Phipps lay on his bed staring at the ceiling, his legal pad rising and falling on his chest.

"I'm not feeling well," Alan said. "I need to go home."

Mr. Phipps glanced at him. "Oh dear, and I wanted to review the typescript this evening. You're sure you couldn't hold off until—"

"I quit."

"Oh, now, Alan—"

He strode out of the room and downstairs, ignoring Mr. Phipps's cries. Outside, he raced over to Beacon Street and hailed a cab. *I should have a gun*, he thought as the cab stopped at a light.

But what for?

I should have called.

But there would have been no answer.

The cab pulled up in front of his apartment building. The place looked friendly and inviting in a Bosto-
nian sort of way, like a patrician aunt who invites you to
tea. The street was quiet, almost deserted. No clouds, no
cold breeze, only sunlight and budding flowers. Alan
paid the cabbie and walked into the building.

Up to the second floor. Silence. He inserted the key
in the lock and opened the door. No one. "Julia?" The
name rang out futilely. He stepped inside and shut the
door.

If she was gone, why was the evil still here, why
were tears throbbing behind his eyes? *What was wrong?*

He took a step. The silence. The slant of light
through the windows. The dishes in the sink. The faint
odor of her perfume, already disappearing from his life.
He took another step. *The silence.* The toilet not running. The refrigerator not humming. The cat. *"Dusty!"*

Dusty was in the bathroom sink. Her eyes stared up
at him; her teeth were bared in a pitiful imitation of a
snarl; her throat had been sliced from ear to ear. Every
wall in the room was spattered with her blood.

"No!" he shouted, shutting his eyes, and he
slammed his fist against the wall. He could feel the ancient plaster crumble beneath the blow. When he finally
opened his eyes he saw what his mother had predicted:
his left hand, in front of his face, streaked with blood. He
lowered the hand and started to cry.

Chapter 7

The Prudential Center garage seemed like the right place to be: dark, subterranean, impersonal, a place where machines dwelt, where people were uncomfortable, on edge. Was that distant echo the squeal of brakes or the shriek of a woman being raped?

Alan had started out looking for Julia's Volkswagen, but it wasn't there—if it ever had been. He asked his gift nicely to help him out, hummed whole movements of piano concertos, but it was off somewhere, exulting in his pain.

He had stopped noticing the cars now and was simply walking, level after level, breathing in the exhaust fumes, vaguely expecting the security people to pick him up. Was that fellow in the white socks an absent-minded professor searching for his car or a cold-blooded fiend stalking his next victim?

No one bothered him. Who could be afraid of Alan Simpson?

Il mio tesoro intanto
andate a consolar . . .

Nothing.

He had long ago come to the conclusion that his gift had a consciousness of its own and was determined to be perverse. The worst possible frame of mind was to care about what it gave him.

He recalled the time he had volunteered for a psi

experiment at Harvard. He was a freshman, and temporarily in love with rationality. Surely ESP was the next great frontier of science, and surely he could help to conquer it. And if it helped him to understand himself, so much the better.

The researcher was a middle-aged psychology professor who, secure in his tenure, had evidently tired of running rats and wanted to dabble in the occult. In this experiment, a computer randomly generated simple drawings. The subject sat in a booth and tried to reproduce the drawings. Nothing could be easier. Alan sat down and drew better than he had ever drawn before. The images flowed easily and vividly: a cow crossing railroad tracks, two black boys listening to the radio, a vase of roses lying on its side . . . When he handed in his booklet he was grinning with delight. *You're onto something now, Professor,* he wanted to say.

Then he waited. If the professor was onto something, he wasn't letting Alan know about it. Finally Alan camped outside his door during office hours and managed to get a few minutes of his time.

"Simpson, Simpson . . ." The fellow poked around his desk, littered with blue books and overflowing ashtrays, until he found Alan's folder. "Ah, yes. A. Simpson. Chance level. Some interesting drawings, though."

It took a moment to sink in. And as it did he was inside the professor's mind for an instant of utter clarity: *God, I'm tired. Maybe that sweet little thing with the black tights will show up. Dental bills. A Cognitive-Affective Theory of . . . Perhaps you'd like to discuss your paper over a . . .*

Chance level. *I should mention the black tights,* Alan thought. What were the odds on that?

But then he realized what his gift was up to. *If I mention the black tights, they'll probably be wrong too.* And Alan started to laugh. "Sorry to bother you," he said. "Just curious."

He didn't feel like laughing now. No VW, no Julia, no cat—but he knew the gift remained, lurking in the shadows of his psyche, waiting to play its next trick. Alan kicked an empty motor-oil can and headed for the exit.

Jim Kelliher stood in the bathroom and looked at the bloodstained walls. "Bad business," he murmured sympathetically. "I wish I could do something, but—" He shrugged. "Can't exactly put out an APB on a cat killer."

"It wasn't her, I'm sure of it," Alan said. "It was somebody else; his first name is Seth. He was behind the kidnapping too. He's incredibly evil—and dangerous."

Kelliher looked at him, and Alan could tell he was stifling an *I told you so.* "I can't do anything, Alan. I'm sorry."

"Well, what am *I* supposed to do then?"

"Maybe you should get another cat. They say—"

"Fat chance. Get another life, more likely."

"Are you, uh, feeling better, Alan?"

"Yes, Mr. Phipps. A temporary ailment."

"Things have sort of piled up here while you were out."

"I'll take care of them."

"I would have worked on some of them myself, but you know how debilitating these mundane matters can be for someone of my sensibilities."

"I'm sure they're quite a strain."

"You are, uh, rarely sick, Alan."

"I know."

"It was very quiet here without you."

"I didn't realize I made much noise."

"Oh, you know, footsteps, typewriter; the sounds can be quite . . . reassuring."

"Well, I'm back."

"Yes. Indeed. Perhaps we could work on Chapter Seven then."

Feeding pigeons. They milled around his feet, pecking at the peanuts, flapping at each other as Alan dropped sprays of food on them. A proper old lady walking her Dalmatian stopped to berate him: pigeons were a nuisance, a health hazard. They should be exterminated like rats. Would he throw food to rats? He stared at the ground and told her to fuck off.

Where do all the pigeons go when they die? he wondered. Millions and millions of pigeons. Occasionally you see one run over in the street. What happens to the rest? Perhaps other animals eat them: but then where are the bones?

He imagined a pigeon graveyard in some lost corner of the city, where the birds instinctively flew when the end was near. Over abandoned playgrounds, glass-strewn alleys, depositing their pitiful dying droppings on the roofs of burned-out three-deckers . . . And suddenly, there in front of them . . .

He had wrapped Dusty in a towel and thrown her out with the trash. He couldn't think of anything else to do with her.

When the peanuts were gone he went back to his empty apartment and listened to Siegfried's Funeral Music.

Enough. Put it behind you; life goes on. Get up and watch the sun rise. Read *The Forsyte Saga*. Try all those new beers that're on the market. Go to graduate school. Get married.

Alan did none of those things, but he went to work, kept his apartment clean, took long, mind-numbing walks. And in the *Globe* one morning he read that the son of Senator Hodkins from California was missing—probably kidnapped. He stared at the paper for a while, then called Mr. Phipps and told him he had suffered a relapse.

Chapter 8

Alan felt out of place in Charles River Park. A gorgeous young woman in a suede jacket and silk blouse hurried past him as he entered, a pinstriped banker eyes him disdainfully as he studied the apartment buzzers. What would the banker think of Alan's mother? He stabbed a button.

"What?" a foggy voice asked over the speaker.

"I've got to see you."

"I'm busy."

"I'll wait."

There was a pause, and then the click of the inner door being unlocked

Alan took the elevator up to the eighth floor and stood in the tastefully lit corridor. Two children in tennis outfits walked past him, talking about how positively *dreadful* the courts were on the Vineyard. After a few minutes a tiny lady in a black suit came out of an apartment, glanced at him, and hurried toward the elevator, her head down.

His mother stood in the open doorway, wearing a hideous kimono. "Madame Zelda at your service," she said with a smile, and there was a flash of the old-time closeness: us against them. She beckoned him in.

Her apartment was worse than he remembered it. It was dark—heavy draperies covered the doors to the balcony—and it smelled strongly of herbal tea and her cheap perfume. A long strip of peeling white paint hung down from the ceiling like a sword of Damocles over her faded chintz sofa. But it was the books that held his gaze: thousands of them, stacked in cartons, heaped onto tottering bookcases, spewing out of file cabinets and desk drawers, piled on the floor next to the sofa. Alan picked up a few at random and blew the dust off them: *Proceedings of the Theosophical Society, The Morning of the Magicians, Psychic Discoveries behind the Iron Curtain, The Ancient Alchemists* . . .

He knew all too well how these books had accumulated. His mother would haunt secondhand bookstores, buying everything she could find that might give her an explanation of why she was the way she was, hoping that some forgotten old treatise (or ignored new one) would contain the wisdom she needed to understand her life. She would lug them back to her apartment in a shopping bag, open each one with a twinge of excitement, skim for thirty pages, then toss it aside, another failure, another key that didn't fit. The size of her library was a measure of her unhappiness.

He wondered if she had any of Pottston Phipps's books.

He wondered what he would do when she died, when all the books—all the unhappiness?—became his. Pitch them into the Charles? Or start looking through them himself, searching for clues his mother might have missed . . . He smiled. "Haven't they managed to evict you yet?"

"No, child, but they keep trying. Sit Would you like some tea?"

"Lord, no." He sat. "Is that little old lady in the black suit going to take a sea voyage and meet a handsome stranger?"

His mother sighed and descended to the sofa. "She is an ex-nun with cancer of the bowels. I fear I did not have good news for her. Another client gone. The truth is hard." She shook her head sadly and lit a cigarette.

"How many remain?"

She gestured about her. "The rent gets paid."

"What would you tell me if I were your client?"

"First I would say: If you haven't followed my advice in the past, why pay me to get more?"

"Perhaps I'll follow it this time."

She shook her head, her jowls wobbling slightly. "You don't want my advice. You want facts."

"Can you give me facts?"

She exhaled a cloud of smoke and closed her eyes. "So much harder. The handsome stranger's name. The date the cancer finally— . . . Sometimes impossible."

"Is it impossible this time?"

"This time, perhaps not. If I wanted to."

"What does that mean?"

"The facts are no good without the advice."

"But it's my money."

"And it'll stay your money if I refuse to accept it."

"Let me put it this way: if you don't give me your facts I'll move to Cleveland and you'll never see me again."

His mother laughed. "An idle threat. I can see you out there rooting for the—the Redskins."

"Indians."

"Whatever. Alan, do you think I have shit for brains?"

"No, ma'am."

"Then don't trifle with me. Are you sure you wouldn't like some tea?"

"You won't get rid of me with that poison."

She heaved herself up off the sofa and went to make some for herself. This wasn't going well, Alan thought. Maybe if he offered to clean up the apartment for her. Jesus, nothing was worth that. Which left him only one option. "Ma, I'm in love," he called out.

"Can't hear you, child," his mother responded from the kitchen.

"Damn," he whispered, and he tried to hold on to his courage until she returned.

"I'm in love," he repeated when she had settled herself on the sofa once again. "I'm in love with the girl who was staying with me. I don't know why you can't tell from just looking at me; I suppose you're blocking it out. Anyway, she's gone, and I have to find her. You're the only person who can help me. Please."

She stared at her tea, carefully spooning in three sugar cubes. "Love sucks," she said finally, not raising her eyes. "You ought to thank God she's gone."

"Oh, come on, just because you're old and love-scarred doesn't mean I have to act that way too."

"I'm trying to spare you the pain, child."

"Don't bother. Just help me. Who else in this world do you have to help?"

She looked as if she might cry. Alan didn't think he could stand it if she cried. She waved one pudgy hand vaguely. "Nothing is clear. I have no facts."

"How can you get them?"

"Not here."

"Let's go then."

I'm afraid, she said, and it took him a moment to realize she hadn't spoken. Just like in the old days, the words had simply appeared in his mind.

I'm afraid too, he thought to her, *but I've got to do this.*

His mother sighed, gulped down her tea, stubbed out her cigarette in a filthy ashtray, and stood up. "How will we get there?"

It was Alan's turn to sigh. "Cab, I guess. Never taken so many cabs in my life."

They were both silent during the cab ride. Alan had an inkling of what was to come and would have given anything to be at work, in a coal mine, anywhere but entering this apartment building with this person. It must have been worse for his mother. She was the one who would have to use her powers; she was the one who would have to experience it.

The change came over her as she walked up the stairs to his apartment. Nothing obvious: the muscles in her face seemed to tighten, her eyes became brighter, her back straighter. But suddenly it was not his mother standing next to him outside his door. It was Seth, and Alan was terrified.

Seth knocked. Alan inserted the key and opened the door. "Hello, Julia," Seth said to the thin air. "Nice of you to invite me over." The voice was deep and loud; it was the voice Alan had used in the rooming house.

Seth moved inside. His gaze swept the place quickly. "What a hole," he murmured. He walked over to the window and looked out onto the street, casually twisting the stem of a plant. It had already been twisted. "Get your stuff," he said, and he turned and stared at Alan.

It took Alan a moment to realize what was happening, and then his terror redoubled. He too had a part to play, and immediately he was flooded with emotions too overpowering to sort out. *Oh, Julia.* "What are you going to do?" he asked, and his voice was shaking.

"Get your fucking stuff," Seth repeated.

Alan stood for a moment, uncertain, then went into the bedroom. No stuff to get, but that was beside the point. He waited.

There was a sound of footsteps in the other room, a pause, then—what? a half-muffled whine in the silence? "Nice cat" he heard Seth say.

Alan rushed out of the room. "Oh, Jesus no, Seth, oh please."

An open-fisted blow sent him staggering backward. His vision blurred with pain, he crouched in the living room, whimpering, trying futilely to think.

Seth stooped over and picked up a gray outline of nothingness. "Friendly kitty. Likes strangers. Wants attention. Let's give it some." He walked into the kitchen. Alan heard the rattling of silverware in an open drawer. Seth returned.

"Seth—"

"Shut up, bitch. Blame yourself. Come here."

Alan obeyed—he always obeyed—staggering to his feet and crossing the room, his body trembling, his ears ringing.

"Come on. See what it's like. Experience it."

Seth went into the bathroom. Alan followed. The fluorescent light hurt his eyes. The toilet was running. He thought he was going to throw up. A knife was in his hand.

Seth was bending over the sink. "Come on, God damn it, the kitty isn't so friendly anymore." Alan was next to him. He couldn't look down. He tried to lift the knife, but it was too heavy. "I—I can't," he moaned.

"Do it!" Seth shouted, but the knife was too heavy, all he could do was shake his head, *can't, can't.*

Seth grabbed the knife away from him. Now Alan was leaning over the sink, staring down into darkness, holding on to the darkness, which writhed and scratched beneath him. He didn't dare let go. Then there was a lunge, a flash of light, and the knife was ripping through the darkness, and then everything turned red, his hands, the darkness, the world. He felt life spurting away, and for an instant he saw that it was *good*, this was as it should be. What was this life—any life—compared to the reality of *Seth?* Red was the color of *victory—his* victory—and it should be splashed everywhere to celebrate the triumph.

And then someone screamed.

He looked up into the mirror. It was his mother, standing next to him, hands over her face, trembling uncontrollably.

"Ma?" he said, reaching out to touch her.

She brought her hands down after a while and stared into the mirror. Her eyes were moving slightly, following (he hoped) the traces of the people who had imprinted their presence on his apartment.

His own eyes wandered to the broken plaster next to the medicine cabinet. Why didn't he have the energy to patch it? He waited. Eventually she turned away and walked back into the living room. "Scotch," she demanded in her own voice. She sat down in the wing chair.

"Just beer," he said.

She sighed. He got them each a beer. She swallowed half of hers and then belched softly.

"Facts," he murmured after a while.

"Listen, Alan, you don't—"

"Where?" he said, his voice rising. He didn't go through all of that to get another lecture.

She swallowed the rest of her beer and tossed the can on the floor. She lit a cigarette; her hands were still unsteady. "Old house in the mountains," she whispered. "Not a ranch. Not sure what it is. Two cars in front. A rutted path leading to the gate. *Carmichael* in blue letters on a rusty sign. Not *Carmichael* anymore. A mile or so to the road then a few miles to town. Kincaid. California. America. Earth. Don't go, child."

"How can I stay?"

A tear ran down her cheek. "Alan, if you go, you won't come back."

Alan nodded, unable to think of anything to say. He went into the bedroom and brought her a box of Kleenex to wipe away the tears. "Better call you a cab," he said finally.

His mother flicked her ashes onto the floor and stared out the window.

Chapter 9

Into the Foleys' yard, up onto the roof, or past the asphalt of the driveway was a home run. To the first story on the fly was a double, to the second story a triple. A ground ball flubbed by a fielder or coming to a complete stop was a single. Into the rock garden was no play. Over the fence into the Caseys' yard was an automatic out, and the batter had to shag it.

Alan played with Chuck Foley against Mike and Jimmy Kelliher. They used whiffle golf balls and sawed-off broomsticks. Alan had his own special stick, kept for him rent-free in a corner of the Kellihers' cluttered basement.

"No batter, no batter," Mike yelled, "c'mon, Jimmy, give 'em the old dipsey-doodle. Can't hit the curve, can't hit the curve."

There was a whirl of knees and elbows, and the ball came toward Alan, then dropped as if magnetized. He lunged at it and managed a weak pop-up that Jimmy non-chalanted for the third out. Alan tossed his stick away and trotted out into the field.

"I think that's a spitter," Alan muttered as he passed Jimmy.

"Nah, you couldn't come within a foot of my spitter."

Jim Kelliher came out onto the back steps with a couple of beers. He handed one to Alan. "What's the score?" he asked.

"Don't ask. How're the Red Sox doing?"

"Don't ask."

Alan took a swig and left the can with Kelliher while he played the outfield. Jimmy sent Chuck Foley's first pitch over the roof. Alan sighed and loped after it. It had been a long time since he had won one of these games. Chuck was a good kid and knew the batting average of everyone on the San Diego Padres, but he couldn't play whiffleball to save his life.

Jimmy and Mike could, on the other hand, but perversely they were losing interest in the sport as they got better. Alan detected an air of dutifulness about the way they agreed to play whenever he showed up for dinner now. Sad but inevitable. They were growing up. He had caught Jimmy reading poetry one rainy Sunday afternoon ("Rots the brain," Alan had advised him). And Mike, who had inherited his father's portliness, was a tackle on his junior high football team and was more interested in the Patriots, God forbid, than the Red Sox. It seemed like only a matter of time before the name Carl Yastrzemski would bring nothing more than a puzzled shrug from both of them.

Alan found the ball in the front hedge and brought it back in to Chuck. "Last inning," Connie Kelliher called out from the kitchen.

"Aw geez, and we were just getting ready to make our move," Alan complained.

"Tell me another," Mike shouted.

"Brush him back," Alan advised Chuck. "He needs to be taught a lesson."

Chuck's pitch was straight down the middle, and Mike hit it over the roof.

At the end of the inning Chuck went home, and the rest of them dumped their sticks in the cellar and trooped upstairs for dinner. "I want those hands washed," Connie said as they walked through the kitchen.

"What's the score of the Red Sox game?" Alan asked.

"And turn that TV off. We won't have our Sunday dinner ruined with that foolishness."

Alan washed his hands in the downstairs lav, checked the score of the game before turning the TV off, then went into the dining room where Kelliher was carving the roast.

"Don't ask," Alan said.

"I wasn't about to."

He helped bring in the mashed potatoes, the string beans, the gravy, the hot rolls, the peas, the salad. When the family was all seated he bowed his head while Kelliher said grace. Then he made his usual joke: "I hope you remembered to cook something for the rest of them, Mrs. K."

"I hope you haven't forgotten how to eat since the last time you were here, Alan," she replied, passing him the potatoes.

"I'm certainly out of practice."

Kelliher snorted.

"Hey, I am. Where would I get real mashed potatoes, except here?"

"You *could* learn how to cook, Alan," Kelliher said.

"I'm spoiled, though. I'd never learn how to cook as well as your wife."

"Oh, listen to him," Connie said. She passed him the rolls. Alan hadn't realized he was charming until he had met her and discovered the effect his compliments could have.

"So have you given up poetry yet?" he asked Jimmy between bites.

"Geez, one lousy poem," Jimmy complained.

"That's what dope addicts say at the beginning. One lousy fix, what's the harm?"

"Dad says you read poetry on your lunch hour."

"Only after I've finished the sports page. *I* have my priorities straight."

"I wouldn't be surprised if he *writes* poetry," Kelliher said.

"I tried once, but I couldn't think of anything that rhymed with 'Petrocelli.'"

"What's Petrocelli?" Mike asked.

Alan groaned and stabbed at his string beans.

"Sometimes I wonder if you're a good influence on my boys," Kelliher remarked.

"Tell them to think of me as a reverse role model. Whatever I am, don't be."

"Now, Alan," Connie said.

"Except in my appreciation of their mother."

It was Mike's turn to groan. "Oh, brother."

"Pass the gravy, please."

"So have you found out who killed your cat yet?" Mike asked as they ate their blueberry pie and ice cream.

An awkward silence. "Maybe Alan doesn't want to talk about it, Mike," Kelliher said.

"Dope," Jimmy whispered.

"It's okay," Alan replied. "No, I haven't. Not exactly."

"There's so much crime," Connie sighed.

"If I caught him I'd blow his brains out," Mike said.

"Well, that's the way I felt at first, but maybe revenge isn't always such a good idea."

"It'd keep him from doing it again."

"That's certainly true."

"Anyone want more pie?" Connie asked.

Alan and Kelliher sat on the front porch as darkness fell. The boys were playing Ping-Pong next door; Connie was doing the ironing. Alan's wicker rocking chair creaked back and forth as he watched the streetlights come on. Two young girls roller-skated past; they waved to Kelliher, who motioned with his cigar in acknowledgment. The O'Rourkes' German shepherd was barking across the street.

How had he missed it? What detour had taken him to Marlborough Street instead of West Roxbury? He loved whiffleball; he loved homemade blueberry pie. Can't get them on Marlborough Street.

Creak, creak. Plenty of nice girls. Connie had endless cousins and neighbors' daughters and friends of friends. He had sat next to them at Sunday dinner and felt the awkwardness freeze the smile on everyone's face, felt Connie's silent longing (*oh, wouldn't it be nice . . .*), felt the gap so wide that not even her goodwill could cross it.

One had even liked music. Cheryl Something. Homely, intense, dressed worse than he did. He took her to a performance of *Tristan und Isolde*. She thought Wagner's music was so *sensual*. Afterward she seemed ready for her own *Liebesnacht*, but with no love potion it was a lost cause. He shook her hand and left her in the subway station.

When're you going to settle down, Alan? Connie wants to know.

Can't get any more settled, Jim. That's my problem.

Somewhere a screen door slammed. An old Neil Diamond song floated across the street to them. Kelliher leaned back in his chair and closed his eyes.

"So, uh, this is it," Alan said.

Kelliher opened one eye. "This is what?"

"The turning point or something. I learned the technical term in English 124 once, but I've forgotten it."

"What the hell are you talking about?"

"I'm quitting my job. Going to California. Gonna find the person who killed my cat."

Kelliher opened the other eye. "Are you serious?"

Alan tried to think of a witty reply but couldn't. That answered the question right there. "Yeah," he said.

"Why California?"

Alan just looked at him.

"Oh." Kelliher leaned toward Alan. "But can't you just try to forget that girl, Alan? I mean, she's obviously—"

"Nothing about her is obvious, Jim. And she didn't kill Dusty."

"But she's not worth quitting your job over—or risking your life."

"Maybe not," Alan murmured. "But I can't stay here. I can't pretend nothing has changed. If I don't go I'll—I don't know. Explode."

Kelliher sighed and leaned back. "You're an awfully strange character, Alan."

"That's what people keep telling me."

"I remember the first time you walked into my office. Jesus, what a mess. I thought to myself: 'Oh, God, I'm in for it now.' You don't know how many crazies wander through headquarters."

"Gee, and I dressed up to meet you."

"But the thing was, you came through. All the other crazies start talking about how the CIA's after them, or they're receiving messages from aliens on Neptune, or their next-door neighbor is the Boston Strangler, and you just tell me where to find the goddamn kidnappers. I mean, there was something *real* behind the strangeness. And that's sort of the strangest thing of all."

Alan sighed. "I suppose this disquisition on my strangeness has a point," he remarked.

"Well, I guess the point is that I think you're crazy, but I can't tell you not to go to California. You've been wrong enough times in your life, God knows, but I'm not the one to stop you. Besides, you're the stubbornest cuss in the world."

"My mother doesn't want me to go either," Alan observed. "She says if I go, I won't come back."

Kelliher stared out into the darkness. "I guess she's been wrong too. I don't know, I suppose I should have seen this coming. What's the word?"

"Precognition."

"Yeah. I should've had precognition." He paused. "I've never been to California."

"Palm trees. Dodger blue. I'll send you a postcard."

"Will you be careful, for God's sake?"

"For everyone's sake. Including my own."

They sat in silence for a while. The O'Rourkes' dog stopped barking. Jimmy and Mike came home and ran upstairs to do their homework. It was getting cold.

"Who's gonna tell Connie?" Kelliher asked finally.

"I suppose I'd better." He had known none of this would be easy. And he had barely begun. "Do you think she'd bake me a blueberry pie to take along?"

"I think she just might."

Chapter 10

"'Chapter Ten. Sorrow. The distinction between sorrow and disappointment (see Chapter Six) is a subtle but important one. It is not only a matter of degree but also a matter of outlook. When one is disappointed one thinks, "It could have been better." When one feels sorrow one thinks, "It could not be worse." Disappointment looks to what might have been; sorrow looks only to itself.

"'Sorrow is inevitable; but if we look at it strictly from a utilitarian point of view, it is helpful only to the extent that it does its job and lets us get on with the business of living. Sorrow is the faucet of the soul, letting the waters of emotion run freely; but we must make sure that the shut-off valve works too. When the pipes are clogged, the damage can be tremendous.

"'And who is the plumber? The plumber can be no one but our rational self, saying: "This is enough. Thus far and no further." We cannot forget our pasts, but we must prevent them from destroying our presents and threatening our futures.

"'How does one do this? The first thing to be pointed out is that one cannot ignore sorrow if one is to remain human. One cannot simply take up crocheting, or go to Bermuda. The water must be allowed to run. But there comes a moment—different for every person, every situation—when one either escapes or begins to wallow. You awake, the air is light, the morning is pregnant with possibilities. Do you arise and seize them, or do you remember, and stare sullenly at the ceiling, and curse the malign indifference of the universe?

"'That is the moment of escape. To be fully alive, one must seize it. The alternative is perpetual imprisonment in a past that will not, cannot change.'"

Mr. Phipps laid the yellow sheets down on the table.

"You're on a roll now," Alan said.

Mr. Phipps nodded, his face glowing with pride of authorship. "It keeps getting better, does it not?"

"Where does it go from here?"

"Oh, well, that's a trifle hard to say. You know I don't use outlines. I write from instinct and trust that everything will fall into place. I am rarely disappointed. This time I feel—I sense—that I am leading up to a climactic chapter that will elucidate the ultimate secret, the final wisdom—the meaning of life."

"'The meaning of life,'" Alan repeated.

Mr. Phipps looked solemn. "After that, there may be nothing more to say."

"I can't see how there would be. Would it be possible to give me a sneak preview—to let me in on the secret?"

"Oh, you'll have to await the final chapter just like everyone else, Alan," Mr. Phipps said, his eyes twinkling. "It would lose its effect without the cumulative power of what has gone before."

Alan sighed. "I might have quite a wait, then."

"No, no, you see how fast I'm writing now. It won't be long in coming."

Alan started to speak, then simply nodded and reached out for the sheets of manuscript.

He paced the threadbare Oriental, the worn parquet floor. *The sounds can be quite . . . reassuring.* He ran his hands over the faded wallpaper, looked out at the failed garden. *Not easy, not easy.* To work. He emptied the bottom drawer of his desk into a Star Market shopping bag. Wallace Stevens, Robert Frost, Keats, Tennyson, Yeats, a Red Sox scorecard, Cosima Wagner's diary, *You Can Train Your Cat* (you can't), a Bach Is Beautiful bumper sticker (no bumper to put it on), a very old Hostess Twinkie, a Susan B. Anthony dollar. He closed the desk, drew the draperies over the French doors, and went to find Mr. Phipps.

Mr. Phipps was in the upstairs bathroom. Alan sat down in the dark hallway and waited. He didn't come out. After several minutes Alan became impatient. "Mr. Phipps, come out!" he shouted.

"Use the downstairs," was the muffled reply.

"I have to speak with you."

"Thinking, Alan. Go away."

Alan recalled Charles River Park. Waiting in another hallway, unable once again to get someone to understand. He was serious. He would wait no longer. "I quit!" he shouted.

"Yes, yes, Alan. Go away."

He got up and went over to the door. "I mean it," he said to the oak panels. "I'm going to California. I've prepared a status report on the galleys. I made a list of all the titles and quantities in the warehouse. The Rolodex on top of my desk has the names and numbers of all the people I've ever dealt with here. I typed the chapter on sorrow; it's in the out box. I wrote up an ad for my replacement. All you have to do is call it in to the *Globe*. The number for the classified section is on the sheet. Just call it in. Mr. Phipps?"

There was silence, then the sound of the toilet flushing. Mr. Phipps emerged a moment later, coatless, adjusting his belt. He looked naked without his suit coat. "One can carry a joke too far, Alan."

Alan shook his head. "No joke." He pointed to the shopping bag. "There's my stuff. I'm leaving now. I'm paid through the end of last week. Don't worry about today."

Mr. Phipps looked at the shopping bag, then looked at Alan. "California?" he said incredulously.

"It's a state. Out west. Palm trees. Sunny. You wouldn't like it."

"You can't go. I'll double your salary."

Alan backed away from him and picked up the bag. "Money's no object. Don't need money. I just have to go, that's all."

"What will I do by myself? There are so many problems. One can't be expected—my allergy—Alan?"

"'Life is never exactly what we want it to be,'" Alan quoted. "See Chapter Six." He started down the stairs.

Mr. Phipps rushed over and grasped his free hand. Alan could not remember touching him before. His grip was surprisingly strong. His hands were wet—hadn't dried them in the bathroom. In the darkness he looked like some supplicant ghost, begging for a boon that would release him from eternal bondage. But, damn it, Mr. Phipps didn't want to be released, he just wanted to keep his darkness from being disturbed. *Find someone else*, Alan thought. *I have business to take care of.* He wrenched his hand free. "It'll be all right, Mr. Phipps," he said softly. "You'll see. Run the ad." He quickly continued downstairs. At the bottom, he made the mistake of looking back.

Mr. Phipps was holding on to the banister with both hands, as if he were having a heart attack or trying to prevent his house from collapsing. "I'm afraid, Alan," he whispered.

"I'm afraid too," Alan said, then he turned and walked out of the musty old building into the sunlight.

Alan sat looking out the window. He had thrown away all the plants, and the sill's bareness was strange, disquieting. If he turned his head he knew he could see his bags, packed and waiting by the door. He did not want to turn his head. The street outside was sunny and tranquil. He wanted to close his eyes and doze in the warmth.

He should have been thinking about the future, but it was too frightening. *If you go, you won't come back.* Instead his mind kept turning obstinately to the past, to what he had left, and was about to leave.

He thought of their little house in Jamaica Plain: his father in his brown corduroy jacket, putting up the storm windows while Alan helpfully steadied the ladder; his mother burning cookies in the old-fashioned kitchen, silently giving Alan instructions that he silently obeyed. And then, after his father was gone, trying to be the man of the house himself, breaking storm windows, electrocuting himself at the fuse box. Then college, the house about to be sold, running a yard sale to dispose of their past, fighting back tears that a Harvard man should not shed . . .

And he thought of his gift: the sudden feeling of inexplicable anguish in grammar school one day, so bad he had to ask to be excused, but the puke-green boys' room was no comfort, and it was only later that the principal came around and told them that President Kennedy had been assassinated . . .

Riding on the grimy old Arborway trolley on his way to Latin School and realizing that the cute blonde sitting across from him put out, and not having the slightest idea what to do about it . . .

Eating in the Pewter Pot in Harvard Square, looking at the pinch-faced man at the next table, knowing the fellow would kill him for the pleasure of watching him die . . .

It takes all kinds, Connie Kelliher would say.

And he thought of Marlborough Street: "Come live with me, child." *No, thank you, don't think I will. Time to strike out on my own.*

"It's . . . *interesting*," Agnes Foley, his onetime girlfriend, said as she surveyed the chaos of his apartment and started making other plans for her life.

"Paint, Alan," Jim Kelliher said. "Inexpensive. Easy to apply. I'll help, for Chrissake."

No, thank you, I like it fine the way it is . . .

Lying on the couch with Dusty on his stomach, listening to *La Traviata*, sipping a Budweiser, as content as anyone has a right to be in this life . . .

He was going to hold on to the apartment. It seemed easier than trying to sublet it and figuring out

what to do with all his books and records. He was being inconsistent, of course: after all, he hadn't asked Mr.
Phipps for a leave of absence. But if he were to come
back in a couple of days, his tail between his legs, he
wanted *something* to come back to. No sense in going
overboard on all this.

If you go, you won't come back.

His mother was known to be wrong on occasion. It
was not impossible that he'd come home again.

Alan opened his eyes, looked out on Marlborough
Street, and sighed. "Everyone stay right where you are
in case I return," he murmured and stood up. Bags ticket
travelers checks wallet comb razor deodorant toothpaste.
Lights out refrigerator empty trash gone windows
locked. All set?

On the way out the door he heard the toilet begin to
run.

Chapter 11

Los Angeles.

You simply get on a plane, rent your earphones and
turn on the classical music tape, eat your blueberry pie,
and in half a dozen hours you are there: balmy breeze,
blue sky tinged with brown, straight, flat streets extending for miles through hideous sprawl, huge buildings
named after Japanese banks, billboards in Spanish, palm
trees towering smugly in the dirty air. *Look at how tall
things grow here,* they said, *look at how green everything is.*

Alan was too busy looking at the taxi meter as the

fare mounted like a pinball score on the ride in from the airport. Had to be done.

The hotel, surprisingly, was restrained and tasteful, with parquet floors and elegant Mexican tilework on the walls. Hotels always fouled up Alan's reservations on the rare occasions when he ventured out of Boston, but this time the problem was solved with a minimum of fuss and delay. As soon as he was settled in his bland room he spread out the map he had bought and called the bus company.

His destination was not on one of the more heavily traveled routes, it turned out. He couldn't get a bus until the next day, and even that one didn't bring him really close.

Alan hung up, frustrated and upset. Not being able to drive is no real handicap if the limits of your world are Harvard Square and Fenway Park, but in this new world it was paralyzing. He felt like a freak; and here, more than in Boston, he was one.

He wasted an hour trying to figure out some other way of getting to Kincaid, and then had to get used to the idea that he had an evening to kill in the new world. He began by taking a nap. When he awoke it was still light out, and he was restless and bored. He studied the map; almost immediately he found the answer to his boredom: Dodger Stadium, not more than two miles away from the hotel.

Alan went down to the lobby, bought a newspaper, and found out the Dodgers were playing the Cardinals at home. He had never been to a major league game anywhere but at Fenway. With his trusty map as a guide he set off through the city. He could taste that first ball-park beer already.

His route took him past a vast open-air market, full of strange foods and kerchiefed women haggling in Spanish; then uphill and past the courthouse, deserted now that the workday was done. Soon he was the only pedestrian in sight. He came to an overpass and saw the stadium's light standards blazing on a rise in the distance.

Below him cars streaked by, heading for places with un-pronounceable names like La Cienega and Sepulveda. On the other side of the freeway huge uncultivated palms leaned forward from the slope like sentinels peering at an intruder.

He crossed the freeway and found himself in Chinatown, stared at by surly youths in tight black pants and white T-shirts, passing pagodaed restaurants and record stores with pentatonic music tinkling from their loudspeakers. The light standards were out of sight now. Chinatown trailed off into rows of little frame houses with TV aerials on top. Then the street curved and became a freeway entrance, and Alan faced a sign:

> No Pedestrians
> No Hitchhikers
> No Horses

He turned back and tried to circle around to another route, but there were no signs, and all the side streets dribbled off into more anonymous houses and dead ends.

He thought about asking the tough-looking Chinese teenagers: "How do I get to Dodger Stadium?" But they would just say, "Learn to hit a slider." Or, more probably, they would break his thumbs.

And he thought of taking another goddamn taxi. But what was the point, then? That was giving in to the city, letting it mold him in its image. If he couldn't get there on foot, he wouldn't go. He trudged back toward the hotel.

As he recrossed the overpass he turned and saw the lights still shimmering in the distance, making the sky glow with the promise of magical delights. But not for the likes of him. On the other side of the overpass a black hitchhiker eyed him appraisingly. The palm trees dipped in a sudden cold breeze. Alan returned to his hotel, bought a six-pack of Coors, and watched TV.

The next morning he walked to the bus terminal.

Fat men hosed down the sidewalks in front of their variety stores. Street-corner preachers doubled over with the effort of spreading the Word. Bag ladies argued over territorial rights to a particularly choice location for spending the day. Every other store had radios and tape players and portable TVs stacked to the ceiling amid fit-inducing strobe lights: Phil Donahue smiled at Alan from a thousand flickering screens, contestants on "The Price Is Right" swooned over a washer and dryer. Young men with shirts unbuttoned leaned against traffic lights and drank beer. No one jaywalked.

"The Moonlight Sonata" was playing as Alan entered the terminal. He stopped short, astonished and pleased: a good omen? Then a hundred violins took up the melody, and a snare drum provided the beat, and he decided he would reserve judgment about omens. He bought his ticket and headed downstairs to wait amid the exhaust fumes and the squealing tires.

When the bus arrived eight people got on, all black or Hispanic except for Alan. It wandered through the streets of Los Angeles for a while, then got onto a highway headed north. The white-haired driver whistled "As Time Goes By." One of the blacks played an endless disco tape. A baby cried, and after a while its mother stuck a bottle into its mouth. Alan looked out the window, but the scenery didn't register. *What am I doing on this bus?* he asked himself. No answer was forthcoming.

After a couple of hours the bus reached Alan's stop. He got out in a small parking lot between a gasoline station and a post office. He looked up, and noticed that the mountains around him were the biggest he had ever seen. He wasn't even sure he *had* ever seen a real mountain before. Already it was an adventure. He walked over to the shoulder of the road and stuck his thumb out, more or less ready for the adventure to continue.

"Don't usually pick up hitchhikers, but you don't look much like a hitchhiker, you know what I'm sayin'?"

"Yup."

"I mean, the good Lord put us on this earth to help our fellow man. Not to be at the mercy of kooks and weirdos, mind you, but to do what we can, within our power. You believe in the Lord Jesus, son?"

"Um, I don't know."

"Well, son, you better find out soon, because Judgment Day is nigh, and those that don't believe will be cast into outer darkness, where there is weeping and the gnashing of teeth. Who but God could have created the splendor of these mountains?"

"Don't know, I guess. How soon is Judgment Day, do you think?"

"No one can say for sure, but the signs foretold in the Book of Revelation are all around us, and the wise man should pay heed."

"'Things fall apart. The center cannot hold.'"

"How's that?"

"A quotation."

"Well I'm not familiar with that quote, and I know the Bible pretty well. But the world is in a sorry state, and only the Lord Jesus can take care of it. Beware of the Antichrist, son, beware of the Prince of Darkness, for his power is strong. He will suck your soul right out of you. He will destroy you and leave your bones to bleach in the desert sun."

"Does the Prince of Darkness have a name?"

"He goes by many names. By his deeds will you know him."

"I'll be on the lookout. That's Kincaid up ahead."

"Praise the Lord, so it is."

The dusty blue Toyota came to a stop, and Alan got out with a shudder.

The faded sign on the wood frame building said "Platchett's Gen. Store." Two pickups and a battered Chevy were parked in front. An amber Schlitz bottle lay in the street, waiting to flat a tire. A man wearing a cowboy hat came out of the store, got into one of the pickups, and drove away. There should be a hitching post, Alan thought, a stagecoach rattling by, a dozen extras milling around. He walked through the swinging screen door into the store.

The place smelled of leather and sawdust. Alan took a quick glance around and saw a wall of groceries, an ancient scale on a small meat counter, a hardware section with rakes, shovels, picks, and plumbing supplies, and, behind the cash register, liquor and cigarettes. From the ceiling hung branding irons, spurs, holsters, and a hand-lettered sign that said "Not for Sale." Country music played softly from a transistor radio next to the scale. A weather-beaten man in overalls leaned against the meat counter chewing tobacco and staring at him. Alan had never seen anyone except ballplayers chew tobacco. A fat woman with dyed red hair perched on a stool behind the cash register, reading the *National Enquirer*. "Leading Psychic Predicts UFOs to Invade Earth This Summer."

"Pack of Camels," Alan said to the fat woman, unable to think of anything else to say.

She put the paper down and reached behind her for the cigarettes. Alan laid a five-dollar bill on the counter and she rung up the sale. On the cash register was taped another hand-lettered sign: "If you want credit, you gotta ask Pete." She handed him his change.

"Can you tell me how to get to the old Carmichael place?" he inquired, having now bought cigarettes for the first time in his life.

"How're yer shocks?" she asked him in a rumbling bass.

Alan couldn't make any sense of that. New world, new language. "Pardon?"

"The last bit's pretty bumpy. How're yer shock absorbers?"

"Oh. Well, I'm walking."

She glanced down at his dusty black wingtips. "It's a hike," she said dubiously.

"Do you think I could pay someone to drive me?"

The fat woman glanced over to the man at the meat counter, who was rubbing his nose energetically. "You friends of the folks up there?" the man asked.

What should he say to that? *Yes, Officer, the one with the black wingtips, he was part of the gang too.* "You might say that," he offered.

"What I'm wondering is, why don't you call 'em up, have 'em come to town and get you?"

"I don't think they have a phone," Alan extemporized.

The man nodded. "Think you're right." He rubbed his nose some more. "The thing is," he continued, "people around here aren't too fond of unexpected guests."

"Why's that?"

The man looked at him as if he had just asked why the sun sets over the ocean. "Gold," he replied. "My guess is those people up there are prospecting. With gold the price it is, I've got half a mind to join 'em."

Alan tried to remember his grade school history. "I thought all the gold had been taken out of California."

The man chuckled. "There's just enough left to set people's eyes to sparkling. Some kids got nothing better to do, they hike up into the Sierras and try to strike it rich. After a while they get bored and go back home. Meanwhile they keep me in business."

Not a bad place to be, then, if you didn't want to be disturbed. "Well, I'm not going to be doing any claim-jumping or whatever it is you do to prospectors. And I could still use a ride up there. How're my chances?"

"Oh, I guess Ned Coggins could run you up when he gets back from Palmdale. Couple of hours."

"Any place I can get a room, wash up?"

The man smiled. "You might try Mrs. Kelly's place. A hundred yards down the road on the right."

"Much obliged." Alan was already beginning to talk like them, he realized with a pang.

Mrs. Kelly's place was a small yellow house with starched white curtains in the windows and a tidy vegetable garden off to one side. Mrs. Kelly herself was a white-haired widow with a gold tooth. Alan thought he detected a whiff of whiskey on her breath. "The Match Game" was on the TV in her cozy living room when he arrived. Part of the price of his room, evidently, was listening to her talk.

"Oh, it's not a great room, but many a poor soul has been thankful for it—you know, hikers who wander away from that Pacific Crest Trail and need to rest their feet, or traveling salesmen who want a home-cooked meal, here are your linens, some of them hikers smell pretty ripe when they get here, but all in all I prefer them to the salesmen, you can usually trust the hikers. Oh, I've been robbed, there's danger taking in strangers, no doubt about it. Some people say I'm crazy. But what am I going to do, that Social Security isn't enough to live on, not with prices the way they are today. I have Dial and Camay, most of the men prefer Dial, first thing they want is a bath, it's awfully dusty as it gets toward summer. I wouldn't have to be doing this at all, except my choice of husbands wasn't what you'd call the best. He was working in a gas station in Fresno, could fix anything, when he heard 'the call of the wild' as he put it. Greed is more like it. 'There's still gold out there, Edna, and I'm going to find it.' What he found wouldn't fill that jigger. So he took to drinking—he was Irish, you know—and drinking and prospecting just don't mix. One night he wandered away from his camp, fell into a gorge, and broke his neck. They didn't find him for weeks, of course. By then the buzzards had pretty much taken care of him. If you need an extra towel, there's plenty in the chest there."

The room smelled of some old-ladyish sachet. It was so small he began to imagine that the walls were closing in on him imperceptibly, as if he were in a Poe story. "The Fiendish Widow of the Sierras." Gene Rayburn's voice boomed through the paper-thin walls: she tortured her victims first. Alan threw his bag down and hurried to take his bath. He didn't want Ned Whosis to leave without him.

He ran the water and sank gratefully into the tub. He was already tired, and he hadn't even reached his destination yet. He used the Camay, just to be different. *This is California dirt*, he thought. *Bet it never expected to see me.*

And once you're clean, what are your plans, Mr. Simpson? it asked him.

Headin' up to the ol' Carmichael place, he drawled.

But what are your plans then?

That's a good question, my fuliginous friend. Fact is, I haven't got any.

Doesn't that strike you as a trifle foolish—not to say dangerous, Mr. Simpson?

I've always had this lucky streak, you know.

Not in California.

That's true. Not in California.

Alan ran more hot water to shut the dirt up. If he could think of a plan he'd use it. He didn't need anyone—or anything—else to tell him he was in danger. When he started to wrinkle he pulled the drain plug and prepared to move on. He dried himself, put on a change of clothes, and went out into the living room.

Mrs. Kelly was watching Merv Griffin now. Some hard-looking blonde was singing "The Shadow of Your Smile." "Will you be staying to supper?" Mrs. Kelly asked. "You could pick up another pork chop at Platchett's. Pete charges outrageous prices, but what can you do? You won't get a better meal in Kincaid than here, or a cheaper one. Oh, you'll have to put up with my prattle, but I have this nice fresh blueberry pie, and we might get a pint of Seagram's . . ."

Her words faded from his consciousness. Blueberry pie indeed! Was that some kind of cosmic trick? Next thing you knew she'd be offering to play whiffleball with him. No, it wouldn't do. "I'm sorry. I have to go meet a—an acquaintance."

Her face fell. "Someone in town?"

He hesitated; hell, the whole state probably knew by now anyway. "Up at the old Carmichael place."

"Oooh," she said, raising one eyebrow meaningfully.

"You, uh, know something about the place?"

"Just that it used to be one of them, you know, *houses*. Back when things were really booming around here. That's all over with now, of course."

"Yes, I'm sure there's none of that going on up there."

She wagged a finger at him. "Well, just in case, you be careful." She started to giggle.

"I'll be careful," he promised.

Back at the general store nothing had changed, except that the fat woman's *National Enquirer* had turned into a Los Angeles *Times*. Even the same song seemed to be playing on the radio; but then, they all sounded the same to Alan.

"Ned ain't back yet," the man said. "Sit down, rest a bit."

Alan sat down on a stack of Coke cases and watched the clientele come and go. All had a greeting for Pete, all stared at Alan. "The Carmichael place," he thought he should be repeating. "Waiting for a ride to the Carmichael place. Know someone at the Carmichael place." But no one asked. Pete would tell them soon enough.

A black woman in a nurse's uniform came in and bought a can of tunafish. "Any news about Senator Hodkins' son, Angie?" she asked the fat woman.

Angie shook her head. "Bet it was the Communists that took him," she rumbled. "Mark my words. Should be shot."

"Shooting's too good for whoever did it," the black woman said.

"How 'bout leaving them out in the desert come August?" Pete suggested, spitting out some tobacco juice. "Let 'em broil a bit, give 'em a taste of the hereafter."

"Throw in a couple of rattlers," the black woman laughed. They were having a fine time.

A scrawny man with a cigarette stuck behind his ear came through the screen door. He waved to the fat woman. "Hiya, Angie."

"Hey, Ned."

Alan tried not to look relieved.

Ned picked up a Hershey bar and tossed Angie a quarter. She caught it with surprising agility. "So, Pete," Ned said, unwrapping the bar and taking a bite, "this cardinal goes in to the Pope and says, 'Pope, I got some good news and I got some bad news. Which do you wanna hear first?' And the Pope says, 'Gimme the good news.' So the cardinal says, 'Jesus Christ has come back to earth and he's on the phone for you right now.' And the Pope says, 'Well, that's tremendous. What's the bad news?' And the cardinal says, 'He's calling from Salt Lake City.'"

Pete rubbed his nose.

"Salt Lake City," Ned repeated. "You know, where the Mormons are?"

"I heard of Salt Lake City," Pete said. "It just ain't funny."

"Charlie Tolliver told it to me over in Palmdale. Cracked me up."

"A forest fire cracks you up. Can you drop this fellow off at the Carmichael place?"

Ned glanced at Alan and nodded. "Sure thing. If you're looking for gold you're wastin' your time, because I looked already, and if it'd been there, I'd've found it."

"Some people I know," Alan said vaguely.

"Well, lemme just pick up a few things at this clip joint and we'll hit the road." Ned bought a can of soup, a loaf of bread, and some American cheese. Angie marked the prices down and put it on his account. "Keep smilin'," Ned called out to Pete as he left the store. Pete leaned over and turned the radio up.

Ned's pickup was a gleaming new Datsun with a waving green hand in the rear window and a CB antenna a mile high. Alan climbed in the passenger side, displacing a couple of well-thumbed copies of *Penthouse*. Ned tossed the groceries onto the seat and roared off.

"Where you from?" Ned asked.

"Boston," Alan replied.

"No kiddin'." Ned shook his head and smiled. Alan expected him to say, "It takes all kinds," but instead he asked, "You know any Boston jokes?"

Boston jokes? "Just the Red Sox," Alan offered.

Ned laughed appreciatively. "Not bad, not bad. Hear the one about the prospectors who took turns cooking?"

"Don't think so."

"Well, none of them liked to cook, see? So they had an agreement, if any of them criticized the food, he had to take over the cooking. So this one prospector had been cooking for a while, and he was getting tired of it, so one night he finds some moose shit and fries it up and serves it. So the first guy takes a bite out of it and he's ready to barf, but he doesn't say anything because he doesn't want to cook, right? The second guy eats a little and thinks he's gonna die, but he keeps quiet too. So the third guy takes a bit and says, 'Jesus, this tastes like moose shit—but it's *good!*' "

Alan chuckled. Ned roared with delight. "But it's *good!*" he repeated, and beeped the horn a couple of times for emphasis. "I've got a million of 'em like that," he said, and he started in on them.

Darkness had fallen. The road was steep, and the Datsun bucked and whined as it made its way up into the mountains. The headlights picked out occasional outcroppings of slate rising abruptly from the dry ground. They looked to Alan like ancient tombstones in a deserted cemetery. The air was getting colder.

"I give up," Alan said, barely listening to Ned's riddle.

"Three. One to screw in the bulb, and two to write a book about it. Get it?"

"Yeah. Is it much further?"

"'Bout a mile down that road comin' up on the left. Gets a little bumpy, I'm afraid."

"Maybe I'll walk it. Save your shocks."

"Okay, suit yourself. Watch out for the coyotes."

Alan didn't know whether he was serious and decided he didn't want to ask. He got out and watched the taillights until they disappeared around a bend. Then he trudged off in the direction of the old Carmichael place.

The first thing he noticed was the stars. He had never seen so many stars before. Where had they all been hiding? The next thing he noticed was the noise: croaks, gurgles, whistles, shrieks. What sound does a coyote make? He was an intruder in this world. He should be home watching a documentary about it on public television; he shouldn't actually *be* here. He could see the headline in the *Globe:*

Hub Man's Skeleton Found in California Mountains
What The Coyotes Didn't Want, The Buzzards Took

Was that the worst that could happen to him?

After an endless walk he saw a light in the distance. He was happy for an instant—civilization—until he recalled what the light represented. A couple of minutes later he reached the gate with the rusty sign next to it. A pickup and a car were parked in front of the ramshackle house. The car was a Volkswagen.

Alan walked through the gate. Any tremors of evil—from past debauches or future horrors? His gift slumbered. He thought about trying some Mozart but knew it would be useless. He was on his own.

He advanced toward the house. Maybe he should circle around back. Maybe he should circle back to Boston. He put a foot on the first rickety step of the porch and felt a sudden pressure in his side. He looked down and saw the barrel of a rifle sticking into his ribs.

"Reach for the sky, pardner," a squeaky voice said. "One false move and you're dead. And like that."

Chapter 12

Alan sat on a torn horsehair sofa in as depressing a room as he had ever seen. Long strips of faded wallpaper bowed to the floor, exposing plaster that was cracked or gouged or missing entirely. The lone window was covered by a plastic sheet to keep out the cold. One bare light bulb hung from the discolored ceiling.

He couldn't decide if the person standing in the doorway with the rifle was male or female. It was thin and shapeless, with short hair and small, nervous eyes. The high-pitched voice was no help in deciding: it sounded like a cartoon character, or a tape recorder played at the wrong speed. "Shouldn't be here, shouldn't be here," it kept repeating, its hands twitching at the rifle. "But he can't be disturbed, under no circumstances. Who are you? Who is he?"

The questions didn't seem to be aimed at him particularly, but Alan thought he had better open up some lines of communication. "I'm a friend of Julia's. Could I speak to her, please?"

"Julia?" The tone was utterly uncomprehending, and for an instant Alan thought: *It's all wrong, she isn't here, my mother got her wires crossed.* Then something seemed to connect, and the person called out "Julia!" Alan felt an enormous sense of relief and then thought: *Why should I be relieved?*

There was movement in another part of the house. "What is it?" Julia's voice, annoyed, impatient.

"Caught someone. C'm'ere."

Quick footsteps. The person with the rifle turned and beckoned into the room.

"Oh Jesus God."

She did not look good. She was wearing a man's plaid shirt and dirty dungarees. Her hair was unwashed, and there was a large bruise on her left cheek. She didn't seem happy to see him. "How did you find me— Oh shit, I suppose I know. Go away, Cindy."

"You want the rifle?"

Julia shook her head, not taking her eyes off Alan. When Cindy didn't move she lost her temper. "Go away, idiot. Get. Lost."

"Seth will—"

"I'll deal with Seth."

Cindy looked dubious, then obediently shuffled off.

"What are you doing here, Alan?" Julia asked softly when they were alone. She remained standing by the door.

"I've come to take you home."

"Home?"

"You know, where the heart is."

"You should have just forgotten me," she said.

"You left behind a reminder. In the bathroom sink."

She looked away. "You shouldn't have come. There's nothing you can do. It was all a mistake."

"I quit my job," Alan said. "Came out here into the real world, with rattlers and coyotes. I'm fighting for you, Julia."

She stared at him. Alan couldn't take his eyes off her bruised cheek. "You've already lost," she whispered. "Can't you tell? If you leave now Seth'll never know you were here. I can take care of Cindy. Go home, Alan. We'll both be better off."

Alan sighed and shook his head. Not easy. "I guess maybe it's time I met Seth."

Julia's eyes pleaded with him for a moment, and then she gave up. She left the room abruptly, and Alan was by himself.

You sure you know what you're doing? the strips of wallpaper asked him.

I have no idea what I'm doing.

Well, good luck, then. You're going to need it.

Julia came back shortly, and her face was a blank. "Seth wants to see you. Alone."

Alan stood up. "Lead the way, then."

He followed her through a short dark hallway to a closed door. The madame's room, he supposed. "Go ahead," Julia said. "Alone." He glanced at her, but she had already turned away and was walking off toward the kitchen.

Alan raised his hand to knock, then changed his mind and turned the knob. The door was unlocked. He pushed it open and walked in.

He had a quick glimpse of dozens of fluorescent lights—all aimed at him, it seemed—and then he just stood there, transfixed, like a rabbit caught in the headlights of a car, while his eyes adjusted to the brightness. He heard a low chuckle, and his eyes desperately blinked against the light as he tried to focus on the source of the laughter.

The man was seated cross-legged on a white bed, leaning against a bare white wall. He wore cut-off denims and a white T-shirt. He had thick black hair and the square, open face of a jock. He smiled at Alan. "My name is Seth Stone. I guess I should've been expecting you, Alan."

The voice was familiar to Alan. And the chuckle . . . it echoed in his mind against the background of clinking glasses and screaming women on "Family Feud," of mustachioed children looking up at him and smiling expectantly, trustfully. Beyond the memories was this reality; his gift tossed restlessly in its sleep and said: *This one is like you: you are kin.* And that filled Alan with such horror that he could scarcely breathe.

Stone got up and advanced toward Alan. "You interrupted my meditation, but that's okay. How did you get here?"

"I walked."

Stone smiled again. His body was heavily muscled; his biceps bulged against the sleeves of his T-shirt. He had bright blue eyes that bored into Alan's own. Alan wanted to look away but thought that would be a sign of weakness. A couple of faded scars on Stone's face were the only flaws in the specimen. When Stone had looked long enough his smile faded. "I usually exercise after meditating. Can you do one-handed push-ups, Alan?"

"I have difficulty with the two-handed kind."

Stone nodded, then abruptly dropped to the floor and began pumping himself up and down. *Show-off*, Alan thought. He looked around: the bright lights made everything stand out in absurd detail. All the walls were white, although the paint could not hide the fissures in the plaster. There was a long mirror on a pine bureau opposite the bed; there was a stool in the corner. A window had been boarded up and painted haphazardly. On the floor was a shag carpet that had seen better days. Too many push-ups.

After an eternity Stone arose, not even breathing heavily. "Ought to get in shape, Alan," he said, glancing at himself in the mirror. "Sound mind in sound body."

"My mind is sound enough."

"I'm beginning to wonder, Alan." His blue eyes turned back to Alan and started to probe again. "Have a seat," he said finally.

Alan couldn't think of a reason not to obey. He sat on the stool in the corner, feeling as though there ought to be a dunce cap to go with it. Stone sat back down on the bed. "So you've come to rescue the fair damsel in distress. She doesn't want to be rescued, you know."

"You beat her up," Alan said.

Stone shrugged. "She expected it. She was disobedient."

"You killed my cat."

"That was in the nature of a warning, Alan."

"I took it as a challenge."

"Then your mind is in worse shape than I thought." Stone leaned back against the pillows. "You're such a *type*, Alan. Such a loser. So moral in your petty little way. Helping out the police, sheltering confused young girls. Julia told me all about you. You're not in love with her; you're in love with your own goodness. You think I'm evil, so you have to try to stop me, even though you know you're going to fail. It's really pitiful."

"Try not to think about it," Alan suggested.

A quick smile. "And it's all the more pitiful because you have the power within you. You know what I'm talking about. Only a few of us have the power, Alan. But you choose to stifle it—or dribble it away trying to find two-bit murderers. Such a waste."

"I'm content."

"The point is not contentment. The point is *power*."

"If I had an atom bomb, should I use it?"

"Exploding an atom bomb is not its only use."

"What are you doing with yours, then?"

"I'm still working on it. This is my Manhattan Project." Stone stood up and went over to the bureau, where he began to comb his hair. It didn't need combing. "When the project's over, then I'll decide how to use it."

"Sounds a bit backward to me." Alan could barely glimpse a slanted reflection of himself in the mirror: pale, scrawny, ineffectual. Somehow the debate wasn't getting them very far.

Stone seemed to agree, because he didn't bother to reply. He admired himself for a while and then said: "What am I going to do with you, Alan? You really don't belong here. I suppose I should kill you."

"You seem to enjoy that sort of thing."

"But on the other hand it's so rare to meet someone else with the power. Perhaps I should keep you around, for psychic stimulation. And maybe you can witness the first . . . detonation."

"I guess it's up to you."

"I guess it is. Julia tells me you're a Red Sox fan. What does your power tell you about their chances this season?"

Wait a minute, we haven't finished with that killing business yet. "Bleak, I guess. Don't need to be psychic to figure that out."

Stone nodded. "I'm a Yankee fan myself. The Yankees'll win."

"The Yankees always win."

"You noticed. Tell Cindy you'll be staying the night. I'll think about you again tomorrow."

Alan got up from the stool. Stone was still staring into the mirror. Alan walked slowly to the door. *I won't look*, he thought as he passed Stone, but Stone made him look: at the blue eyes like knife points in the glass, at the taunting smile.

"Not me," Alan whispered. "You won't get me."

"But Alan, I already *have* you."

The smile widened. Alan hurried out of the room.

Cindy was sitting in the kitchen, rifle on her knees. Julia was nowhere to be seen. Dishes were piled high in the ancient porcelain sink. A coffeepot lay disassembled on a small wooden table. Alan thought he could smell beans. Boston baked beans. A window looked out onto utter blackness. He walked over to it. "Seth says to drive me back into town," he said.

"The guy thinks I'm stupid," Cindy murmured to her rifle. Did it talk back? Inanimate objects were quite chatty out here.

"Just kidding. Actually, he wants me to stay the night."

"Now you're talkin', pardner."

Alan had a feeling that sustained conversation with Cindy might be difficult. Also, he didn't like the way she was fondling the rifle. Suddenly he felt too tired to stand up. "Maybe you could, uh, show me to my room."

Cindy seemed to take a moment to process the sentence. "No room," she said finally. Then: "I know," and she got up. "C'mon."

Alan walked back across the kitchen. He heard footsteps on the stairs and saw Julia at the other end of the hallway. She walked toward him, eyes down. He was about to speak when she turned away, into Stone's room. Alan caught a flash of the white light, and she was gone.

"Seth has fucked me too," Cindy said, with the tone of a fourth-grader trying to score a point on her playmates.

"Swell," Alan murmured, and he went upstairs with Cindy following. There was a musty, tired odor on the second floor. The Oriental wallpaper was water-stained and faded. All the doors were closed. "Wanna go wee-wee before I lock you up for the night?" Cindy asked.

"I suppose." They walked to the end of the hallway. Should he try to take the rifle away from her? He didn't have the energy. Besides, she probably knew tai-kwon-do or something. He went into the bathroom. There was an ancient pull-chain toilet and an oversized bathtub with clawed feet. Alan avoided looking into the tiny, spotted mirror over the sink. He hadn't shaved very well this morning. Wee-wee. He was so tired he almost found that funny. "Hey, Cindy," he said when he came out. "How many feminists does it take to change a light bulb?"

Cindy stared at him, uncomprehending. She had a door open back down the hall. "He thinks I'm stupid," she said again, nervously fingering the rifle.

"Never mind," Alan sighed.

She motioned to him to go inside the room. He silently obeyed. The door shut behind him, and he could hear a key being turned. He leaned back against the door and waited for his eyes to adjust once again—this time to darkness. And he heard a low moaning sound that brought him back once again to the noisy bar in Boston. A child's moan, a moan of weary, endless terror. And as he listened the moan turned into words, endlessly repeated: "I don't wanna die, I don't wanna die, I don't wanna die . . ."

The words quickly became a meaningless chant, a rumble and then a squeal, the *die* floating off into the air like a child's balloon. When it had disappeared the rumble started again, hoarse and pleading.

Alan could make out a bed now, and a small figure lying on it. He thought of the rooming house in the South End, the boy unconscious in the dim light. What the hell were they up to?

He walked carefully across the room to the bed. The chant suddenly ceased. He could feel the boy's eyes on him. "He sent you to kill me," the boy whispered.

What was the kid's name? Scott? Jason? Alan was too tired to remember. "No, no, I'm your friend. Is there a light in here? You can see how friendly I am."

"No light, no light. If I see you then you'll be real, and then you'll kill me."

"I'm not a dream, I'm a friend. We're in this together. They locked me up too." He reached out to touch the boy. His face was hot, feverish. The boy shuddered and began again. "I don't wanna die, I don't wanna die, I don't wanna die . . ." Alan could feel the words now beneath his fingers like some obscene tumor. He drew his hand away.

He stumbled over to a dilapidated chair and slumped into it. The chant was awful. It was bludgeoning him, killing him. "Stop it," he moaned, but the boy did not stop. Perhaps if he stopped the killer would get him, just as light would make the killer real. What defense did the poor child have, besides insanity?

Alan closed his eyes. He needed to sleep, but the chant was not going to let go of him easily. When was the last time he hadn't slept in a bed? Waves of self-pity washed over him. Like the boy, he had done nothing to deserve this. Or had he? He at least had had a choice, and by making the choice he had accepted the consequences. Maybe everything had been present in that one vision in the bar, one whole version out of the infinite possibilities of his future, sensed like the salt smell of a distant sea by his feeble gift. And his rational mind had accepted that future when it chose to go off in search of Julia in the South End, embracing the sneering laughter, the hopeless moans, the horrifying rustle (yet to come) of cold wind moving through dark tres.

Why?

The only possible answer—if any were possible— lay even further in the future. Somehow he had to trust that it would appear.

After a while the chant faded from Alan's consciousness, and he could feel sleep coming: relief from the insanity, relief from the consequences of his choice.

But sleep brought no relief: his subconscious was as frightened and confused as his waking mind, and its topic was one that his waking mind had yet to deal with. Stone.

Alan was climbing a mountain. The top was nowhere in sight, and he was terribly tired, but he had to keep going. Maybe there was gold to be found, somewhere higher up, or maybe it was just that if he stopped the coyotes would get him. And then Stone was in his path, arms folded on his chest, grinning like the Jolly Green Giant. *Ho-ho-ho. Thou shalt not pass.* Alan felt himself wearily headfaking, left, right, but the path was narrow and Stone barely had to move to stay in front of him. Alan turned and ran, finally, away from the gold, away from everything. "You'll never get me!" he shouted with false bravado.

"But, Alan, I already *have* you. Ho-ho-ho."

And there was a mirror in front of Alan. He stared into it, and Stone was smiling back at him. Stone's sparkling white canines grew into fangs, and he was a vampire, coming out of the mirror toward Alan, his cape ready to enfold him, his fangs ready to plunge into Alan's neck.

I don't wanna die, I don't wanna die, I don't wanna die . . .

"You're not going to die," Stone whispered. "I'm

going to take your life, your power, into my own." The ground started to tremble, and Alan realized the power was welling up beneath him, the bomb was about to explode. And when it did, he realized it would destroy him, and everyone, and there was nothing he could do about it. *Stop,* he shouted, but no sound came out, there was only laughter, and moaning, and the distant rumble of the coming explosion. He started to tremble, and Stone's cape was around him, swallowing him in its darkness. And Stone came closer, lips parted, ready to plunge . . .

Alan awoke with a desperate grunt. Darkness. He thrashed around for a moment, totally disoriented. Then the outlines of the room came clear, and he heard the boy's regular breathing, the only sound in the sleeping house.

Alan's mind was clouded, cobwebby. *I've got to escape,* he thought, the cape still enfolding him, the breath still hot on his neck. He stood up. His body was stiff and sore from the uncomfortable chair. He went over to the window: darkness. Where had all the stars gone? All he could see was the outline of trees, trembling blackly against the black sky. He pushed at the window; it wouldn't move.

Smash it. Jump. Get out of here. Some semblance of rationality remained, however. Break a window and they'll haul you back inside, or Cindy will get you in the sights of her rifle and fire away. He ran his hands over the sash and found the nails that held the window in place. What else then?

And what about the kid?

Alan tired to imagine waking him up, hearing the chant start again, dealing with a crazy child along with all the other craziness. No, he was not part of this anymore. The kid would have to fend for himself.

He made his way over to the door. Strange, there was an old-fashioned heavy key in it. He turned it slowly and heard the satisfying click. The door swung open toward him, and he took a step forward. It wasn't right. Something about the quality of the darkness. He put his hands in from of him and took another step. Wall. Surrounded by wall. Metal protrusions. He had walked into the closet, damn it.

He retreated and felt his way along the wall until he reached another door. No key in it. He turned the knob. It was open.

But hadn't he heard it being locked behind him? Was this, too, a dream? Or were they setting him up, knowing he would try to escape? But why would they know that? And besides, if they wanted to kill him they could simply kill him. He was too confused to try to figure it out. He just wanted to leave, and this was the way to leave.

He walked out into the hallway. The ancient floorboards creaked under his weight. Surely someone would hear him. But Stone was downstairs in his room, and Julia, Alan recalled with a pang, would be with him. There was just Cindy, then. Was that her rifle aimed at him from the top of the stairs, from one of the rooms across the hall? Better not to worry about anything, just to *leave*.

He moved slowly down the hall, running one hand along the wall, waving the other in front of him. Eventually he reached the banister and descended, willing the stairs not to make any noise. At the bottom, still safe, he thought: *I should kill him*. Find a knife and slit his throat. Let the blood spurt over the white bed, the white walls. The color of victory. Let Julia help if she wanted to. And if she interfered . . .

What? He doubted that he could do it, with or without her help. Stone would open his eyes and smile, and the knife would drop from Alan's hand. Just *leave*.

He slid back the bolt of the front door, opened it, and walked out into freedom. The night had turned cold and overcast. How far away was the main road? Then how far to town? How many jokes could Ned tell per mile? Surely he could find the strength to make it. *I'll tell myself jokes. Did I ever hear the one about the minister, the priest, and the rabbi?*

Past the cars and the gate, onto the narrow rutted path. Stick to the path. Don't miss the turn onto the main road. Coyotes. Rattlers. Buzzards. *Fell into a gorge and broke his neck. They didn't find him for weeks, of course.* The trees shivered in a gust of wind.

I, Alan Simpson, not being of particularly sound mind at the moment, do hereby will and bequeath all my books to my mother, so that she can figure out the mysteries of life and add to the decor of her apartment; my opera records and stereo system to Detective James Kelliher, to give him respite from the sleazy people in this world; my whiffleball bat jointly to his sons, so that they will never grow up; my television set to Mr. Pottston Phipps, to give him a chance to view humanity without leaving his residence and risking brain damage; my second-best bed to Ms. Julia Walker. Literary allusion there. I have only one bed, and she doesn't seem to want that. The remains of my body after the buzzards and coyotes get through with it I leave to medical science in order to study the mysteries of psychic phenomena. My soul I leave to whoever wins the battle for it, a battle that appears to be hanging in the balance right about now. Signed by me this day, whose number I have unfortunately forgotten in the press of recent events.

There, that took care of the formalities. Best to have everything in order. *Have I missed the turn? Was there a turn?*

Alan had only been lost once in his life. His father had taken him to a county fair, far away from the house in Jamaica Plain and all their problems. Somehow they had become separated, as his father looked at the goats or something, and Alan's eye was caught by the crazy rides and the spinning wheels of the games of chance. Before he knew it he was all alone on the midway, with hundreds of people rushing past him carrying cotton candy and Kewpie dolls. His mind reached out for someone familiar, but he was alone. He could never reach his father that way. He gave up after a while and wandered along with the crowd, gazing at the brightly colored booths, the gesturing hucksters, listening to the dopey merry-go-round music, smelling the popcorn and the sawdust and the suntan oil. His father had given him a dollar, and suddenly he itched to spend it. Did he want to knock over milk bottles, or ride the Tilt-a-whirl, or buy a slice of pizza?

He decided he would try to win a candy bar. He loved candy. There was a game where a ball bounced down through rows of metal pins to land on a number at the bottom. If you picked odd or even right you got a couple of candy bars. If you picked the number right you got a dozen candy bars. "Only a nickel here, only a nickel," the fat lady in the booth called out. "You got a nickel, sonny?"

Alan put a nickel on eight, his age. The lady pulled the string to let the ball go. "C'mon, eight," Alan whispered. "C'mon, eight." The ball hopped down through the rows of pins . . . "Eight, eight" . . . and landed on eight.

"Hey, we've got a winner here. Easy to win here. Only a nickel."

Alan collected four Baby Ruths, four Hersheys with almonds, and four Nestlé's Crunches. He put a nickel on three, the number of people in his family. The ball bounced around, headed straight for fourteen, hit the edge of one pin, scooted to the left, and landed on three.

"Hey, he won again. Anybody can win."

He won twice more, with fifteen, the street number of their house in Jamaica Plain, and seven, the place the Red Sox were in at the time. Then the fat lady said, "That's it, kid. Beat it."

"That's it?"

"Only four wins in a row. House rule. I know your kind."

Did she? What kind was that? It didn't really seem fair. But then again, he had enough candy for a while. He turned away, clutching his cartons full of chocolate, and saw his father staring at him with a sad expression on his face.

"You shouldn't've run off like that, Alan," his father said.

Alan wanted to say: *I didn't run off, I got lost*, but his father looked so sad he didn't want to argue with him. Alan often seemed to make his father sad. He tried to think of a way to make him happy. "Want a Baby Ruth?" he asked.

Not long after that his father ran off. Or maybe he just got lost too.

Have I already made the turn and not noticed it? He felt like the ball dropping down through the rows of pins, helplessly subject to the cold, uncaring laws of chance and gravity—or perhaps to the whims of a hungry eight-year-old. *We think we are in control of our lives, we think we make decisions, but they are just the ploings of the pins, bouncing us one way or the other, until we reach our assigned number, the bouncing is over, and the candy bars have been won or lost*. Jesus, he'd have to tell that one to Pottston Phipps, if he could ever find the damn turn.

All this talk about candy bars had made Alan hungry. He realized he hadn't eaten any dinner. When was the last time he had missed a meal? *I could kill for a Baby Ruth*, he thought.

No I couldn't. If you cannot kill for love then you cannot kill for anything, and it seemed that he could not kill Stone to save Julia. Did that mean he didn't love her? What was he doing here if he didn't? But he was running away now, leaving her to Stone. All he had managed to accomplish for quitting his job and trekking across the continent was to show up, say hi to the participants in the drama, get scared, and hit the road. *Love is not love that alters . . .*

Alan stopped. The mountains loomed above him. There was a roaring in his ears. *I have come all this way, and I'm nowhere, and I don't know where to go*. He began to shiver, and the roaring grew louder. *Tell me what to do*, he asked the mountains.

Beats us, the mountains, in their Olympian detachment, replied.

He felt a brightness on his back, and he turned. The roaring in his ears became an engine, the brightness became headlights. The pickup stopped in front of him; Cindy and Stone got out.

Ploing.

Cindy aimed the rifle at Alan. "With practiced eye she raised the rifle to her face and aimed it at the evil hombre—"

"Shut the fuck up." Stone glared at Cindy, then moved his gaze to Alan. "In the truck," he said softly. "If you so much as blink, Cindy will blow you back to Boston."

Alan got in the truck.

Chapter 13

"I locked the door, Seth, I remember turning the key and *everything*." Cindy's hands twitched around the rifle. Stone said nothing. "Are you going to hurt me, Seth? I guess I deserve it. I guess maybe you should."

Stone ignored her. He leaned back against the kitchen table and looked at Alan. Cindy began to cry. "I didn't *mean* to leave it unlocked. I swear, Seth."

"Get lost," Stone said.

Cindy scurried out. Alan sat on a wobbly kitchen stool and returned Stone's stare. Why wasn't Julia part of this tableau? Somewhere a clock was ticking. Alan had no idea what time it was. The smell of baked beans was making his stomach growl. He didn't know if he was more hungry or afraid.

Stone's face was expressionless. It was also clean-shaven, Alan noted. Didn't he need to shave? Or did he shave constantly—another excuse to look in the mirror? *Just the two of us again, and I'm still sitting on the stool*.

It happened so fast that at first Alan was more confused than hurt. Why was he lying on the floor? What was that blur he had seen out of the corner of his eye? Why would anyone punch him? And with the realization that he had been punched came the pain, throbbing through him, forcing humiliating tears down over his cheeks.

The linoleum was cold beneath him. Stone looked like he was a mile tall. The Jolly Green Giant.

"Get up," Stone whispered.

Alan was a loser, but he wasn't stupid. He stayed where he was. Stone reached down with one enormous arm and scooped him up. Another punch sent Alan reeling back against the sink. A dish clattered to the floor and broke. Alan's knees wobbled, but he stayed standing. Why bother?

After the third blow, nothing mattered. All thoughts fled, and there was just the pain. At some point he ended up on the floor again, among the pieces of the broken dish, but he had no interest in whether he was standing or lying. And finally there was Stone's voice—in his ear or in his mind?—soft, calm, terrifying: "Try it again and you'll beg to die like your cat. I have the power."

Then the voice faded, and Alan was alone.

Julia lay in Seth's bed and waited for him to return. She had no doubt that he would bring Alan back, from the instant Seth jerked upright in his sleep, then grimly arose and headed out into the darkness with Cindy. How could she have thought otherwise?

It was torture having Alan here. He was a fool to

have come. She had made her choice; why couldn't he accept it? But even as she thought that, she knew her anger was misplaced. *She* was to blame. She had created all this chaos when she had returned to that rooming house, when she had allowed herself to be saved and then decided she didn't want to be saved after all. Alan's only fault was in loving her. Then again, she didn't see how she could be to blame for *that*.

Seth had been silent for virtually the whole time during the long, horrendous drive back to California. She lay next to him in cheap motels night after night and felt the rage seething inside him. Killing Dusty had done little to soothe it. She longed to explain to someone, anyone, why she had done what she had done, why she was who she was. But Alan wouldn't have understood, and Seth didn't care. So she endured the silence, and, back here finally in the white room, he had hit her once, hard, and the worst of it was over. And when Cindy returned, miraculously successful, things were almost right. Until tonight.

She heard doors slam, then footsteps in the hall, Cindy's whining voice. More footsteps. A thud. A gasp of pain. Another thud. A dish breaking. She buried her head in the pillow. Seth was going to kill him. How could she live with that guilt? Perhaps Seth would kill her too, and she wouldn't have to.

Eventually Julia sensed Seth's presence and she turned over. He was standing by the bed, looking down at her. "Go to him if you want," he said "Make the comparison. See how people like him end up."

"Is he dead?" she asked dully.

Seth took his T-shirt off, revealing his muscular, hairless chest. "No, but he might as well be." He lay down on the bed.

Julia got up and went out into the kitchen, leaving Stone smiling in the white room. Alan was sprawled on the linoleum. His face was a mess. When he saw her he attempted a smile. "Never could stop a left hook," he croaked.

"Oh, Alan." She went around him to the sink and wet a sponge. Then she crouched down beside him and dabbed at his face.

He reached out a hand and started stroking her bare calf. "Nice legs," he murmured.

The sponge was turning pink. She wanted to cry. "Can you stand up?" she asked.

"Don't know. Why don't you sit down here beside me?" She swept away the broken pieces of the dish and obeyed. She couldn't think of any other solace to offer him. "Does Stone know you're out here with me?" he asked.

"Yes, but he doesn't care. He knows I'll come back."

"Lucky him. Will you?"

"Yes, Alan." They were silent. Julia felt she ought to say something in her own defense, but there was only one thing. "I unlocked the door for you. But I didn't want this to happen. I just wanted you to go away and be safe."

"How did he find out?"

"I didn't tell him, Alan. He's psychic. He just knew."

"Does he know you unlocked the door?"

"I'm not sure. If he does, I guess my punishment will come later."

"His punishments certainly are memorable."

"I'm sorry," she whispered. There was nothing else she could say. She put his head in her lap and held it there, wishing she could take his pain upon herself.

Alan relaxed and shut his eyes. But after a minute he opened them again and staggered to his feet. "It's no good, Julia," he said. "I can't just lie there and be comforted while that kid is dying of fright upstairs. What the hell is going on?" He flopped onto a stool and stared at her grimly.

"I can't hope to make you understand, Alan," she said, nervously fingering a shard of the broken dish.

"Just give it a try, okay? I might surprise you."

She doubted it, because she knew she lacked the words to explain. Perhaps the right words did not yet exist. "We are at the dawn of a new age," she began, but that wouldn't work, Alan's eyebrow was already arching suspiciously. Try again. "You know that there are powers in the universe that we haven't begun to tap. You know what it's like to have those powers within you, Alan, to almost be able to control them. Imagine what it would be like if someone actually managed to master them, to use them all the time instead of just on and off."

"If it was Stone that had control of them I'd head for another universe."

"That's because you judge him by the old morality. But why should that morality apply in the new age? In the new age national boundaries will no longer have any meaning, personal identities will be vague and trivial; they may disappear altogether. Everybody and everything will be part of the One, which is where we should be, which is what mankind's striving is all about."

The vision was so pure, so clear to her, yet it was impossible to communicate. Seth could do it if he chose, of course, but he only wanted to reveal it to a few—like Jesus at the start of His ministry. Alan would laugh if she brought that up. She stood. "It's useless, Alan. I can't make you understand."

He grabbed her hand as she tried to go past him. "Tell me about Stone, Julia. Why is he our latest Messiah?"

"Alan, I can't."

"You got me into this. You owe me."

Julia loosened her hand from his grip and sat down next to him. She had never seen him like this before: angry and desperate and confused and in pain. She did owe him. She would tell him what she knew. "Seth has spent his life searching for meaning and purpose in things. In the sixties he was part of the student revolt at Berkeley, the antiwar movement, all of that. He was trying to understand existence from a political and social point of view. But that was wrong, you see, he knew that the changes in the way we exist had to be more radical than even the most far-out thinkers would dare suggest, or the struggle just wasn't worth it. So he concentrated on himself, tried to test the limits of his courage and endurance. He smuggled dope up from South America for a few years, risking death every day. He became rich, but it wasn't really satisfying. I mean, he found some of the powers inside him, but that sort of life is pretty meaningless.

"So he bought a beach house in Malibu and spent all his time there, meditating, searching inside himself, trying to understand what he needed to reach the next level. He had always known that he had some sort of psychic ability, but it was only then that he really worked on it. And as he worked on it he caught glimpses of these immense possibilities—for him and for everyone—if only he could reach the essence of his ability. And finally, after years of meditation and self-study, he felt ready to try and reach this essence."

Alan was staring fixedly at her. No trace of disbelief or amusement. Was she getting through? She could scarcely believe it. She rushed ahead. "I was waitressing at this health food place in Malibu. I don't really know what I was doing there; maybe it was fate. Seth came in one day, and I took his order. He just stared at me. It wasn't sexual or anything, Alan. It was like he was taking an X ray of my soul. I couldn't breathe, I couldn't think. Finally he said, 'Come with me,' and I went. You've looked into those eyes, Alan. You know their power. He took me back to his place. The other two were already there."

"Other *two?*"

"Oh. Heather. She's . . . not here right now. Anyway, we were all he needed, he said. And he told us what he wanted to do."

"Kidnapping?"

"He wants to supersede the old order, Alan. He wants to unite East and West in him. It's sort of symbolic, but the powers operate through symbols—like dreams, you know—not rational thought. It's only by using symbols that Seth can achieve what he wants to achieve. The old morality—"

"But you still have some of that old morality sticking to you, Julia. I saw your doubt; I felt your fear. Part of you still hasn't been captured by him. Has it, Julia?"

"Obviously I am not as purified as Seth is," she responded. "Old habits die hard. I'm scared sometimes and I don't pretend to understand everything. But when I'm with Seth it's all so clear."

"Has he straightened you out about me, along with everything else?"

Julia sighed. What could she say? What comfort could she give him? "Seth says you're a loser, Alan. He says you're taking the easy way out of life, and that's what attracts me to you; part of me wants to be a loser too. But he's not going to let that happen. He told me to come out here and make the comparison."

"And you've made it?"

She stood up and turned away from him, looking out the window at the darkness that was now beginning to lighten. "Oh, Alan, why did you come?"

"Beats me," he replied after a while. And then he was standing next to her and speaking quickly, tonelessly. "I guess maybe I thought I could save you, if by chance you were in the power of some Manson clone who was preying on your guilt and unhappiness, who attracted you because he offered you a chance to lose your identity in his, who might have some powers but whose ideas about them were straight from the junk heap of pop parapsychology. I thought I could help, but I guess I was just taking the easy way out."

She started to cry. "I knew I couldn't make you understand."

"Oh, I understand *you*. It's me that I'm having difficulty understanding. Listen, before you lock me up for the night, would you grant me one request?"

She nodded, wiping her eyes.

"Heat up some of those beans for me. I'm starving."

Then the tears flooded out, and there was no shoulder to cry on.

Chapter 14

No more dreams. Reality now. Wake up, you have dreamed too long. Too long. TOO LONG!

Alan opened his eyes. Reality was a horn blaring somewhere nearby, a headache and a stiff back, clothes that felt as if he had worn them all his life. He shook his head to try to get it working and looked over at the bed; it was empty. He twisted in the chair. The boy was kneeling down and looking out the window, his folded arms resting on the sill. Alan struggled to his feet and went over to him. Outside a young blond woman was talking animatedly to Stone. Cindy was dragging an unconscious boy out of the back seat of a beat-up station wagon. Julia stood to one side, watching.

"They beat you up," the boy said, looking up at Alan. "Are you a prisoner too?"

Alan nodded.

"Looks like they've got another one."

"What do you think they're up to?" Alan asked.

"They're gonna kill us," the boy said matter-of-factly, leaning his chin on his arms.

"Why?"

" 'Cause they're crazy."

That was as clear an analysis as Alan could have produced. "Your name's, uh, Scott, right?"

Scott nodded.

"Mine's Alan."

"Hi."

"I was here last night but you were kind of—"

"Out of it. Yeah. Something weird happens to me when the sun goes down. I keep thinking they're gonna come and get me. This place is really spooky. That guy in the shorts down there is the spookiest of them all."

"I know what you mean."

There were footsteps on the stairs, then the door was unlocked and Cindy entered, the boy slung across her shoulder. She ignored Alan and Scott and dumped the boy on the bed.

"Who's that?" Alan asked her.

She looked at him, and he saw that her face was almost twitching with excitement. "None of your business. Who are you anyway? Tomorrow you'll be nothin'. I locked this door."

Alan shrugged and she turned to go. "Do you feed your prisoners?" he called out to her as she was shutting the door.

"Sleeping Beauty missed breakfast and lunch. This ain't a hotel. Maybe if you're good we'll rustle you up some grub." She slammed the door and locked it.

"Nice girl," Alan murmured.

"What do you think she meant about 'tomorrow you'll be nothin''?" Scott asked.

"Beats me."

Julia brought Alan some food a while later: three peanut butter sandwiches, an apple, and a glass of milk. She too was excited, although she was making an effort to hide it. She avoided looking at the two boys.

"So what's-her-name—Heather—came through for you," Alan said. "What happens now?"

"You wouldn't understand," she said for the hundredth time.

"All right, how about: When does it happen?"

She looked undecided about whether to reply, and then murmured, "Tonight."

"And what are me and my two pals going to be doing tonight?"

She shook her head. "You shouldn't have come," she said, and hurried out of the room.

"I'm beginning to get that message," Alan said, and he took a bite of his sandwich. "You like peanut butter, Scott?"

"I like the all-natural kind. Not that processed stuff."

"Good grief."

Scott went back to looking out the window. Alan turned in his chair and studied him. He was about ten, blond and tan, with wide blue eyes and a slightly pudgy face. California child. The other boy, still unconscious on the bed, was dark-complexioned, with faintly Jewish features. He was wearing corduroys and a soiled Lacoste jersey. Who was he, Alan wondered: the President's nephew? The senator from Maine's son? *Tonight*.

"When I came here, I thought I might be able to rescue you," Alan said. "I didn't do such a good job."

Scott turned around. "Are you a cop?"

"No."

"Then how come you didn't just call the cops?"

Alan didn't have much of an answer for that, so he kept quiet.

"Were you beat up by the guy in the shorts?" Scott asked after a while.

"Yeah."

"You shouldn't mess with him."

"I've gotten a lot of advice on that subject."

"That Cindy's kind of spacey but he's in a whole other dimension, you know?"

"I know. What do you think of the other girl?"

"She's okay, I guess. She got me some Perrier. I like Perrier."

"But she's not exactly letting you go home."

Scott shrugged. "What are you gonna do?" he asked with a world-weary air.

"What do you think's going to happen tonight?"

"I dunno, but I'd sure rather be watching it on TV."

Alan nodded his agreement.

The afternoon limped past. Cindy returned to check on the unconscious boy and let Alan go wee-wee. Through the small window in the bathroom he saw Julia and Heather walking up the steep slope behind the house, carrying something. Back in the room, he and Scott talked desultorily about the difference between the National and American leagues, but their gaze would keep drifting to the boy lying on the bed, and to the sun moving closer and closer to the tops of the mountains, and they would fall silent, and wait.

My last day on earth. Alan tried the phrase on for melodramatic fit. He didn't care for it very much. *Dying so that the new age can be born.* What a load of crap. Alan knew how Stone had worked it out: start from the premise, "I am special, I am different, I am better"; get used to the taste of power—of reading someone's mind, of making the ball *ploing* down onto the number you've chosen; then wonder: if I'm better, why not be best? If these awesome powers have been given to me, why not take some more? You know they're out there, indifferent, waiting. It's just a matter of preparing your mind somehow, of breaking through some perverse barrier that has already been breached, and then everything is yours.

Only trouble was, it wouldn't work. At least, Alan didn't think it would work. How many psychics had tried? His mother had tried, and Stone wasn't fit to kiss the hem of her powers. *The harder you struggle, the worse they become, child. The more you ask for, the less you receive.* Hard-bought wisdom. Stone would do well to heed it.

Little chance of that. What mattered now was not reality, but Stone's perception of it. If he thought this was the way to bring about the new age, then God help those who were in his power.

As the sun set and the shadows lengthened, Scott became increasingly agitated. "I don't like this," he said. "It's going to be worse now. It stinks, it really does." He started breathing rapidly.

"What do you feel?"

"Like—like I'm drowning. Hard to see—everything turning red."

"Red?"

"Like I've been holding my breath too long. Like—I dunno." Scott started to cry. "This stinks, you know?"

"I know." Alan went over and put an arm around the boy. They sat together and watched the room grow dark.

Cindy eventually opened the door. It took her a moment to spot them by the window. "Hey, no screwin' around," she called out. "Seth wants to see you," she said to Alan.

"What about?"

"Don't matter. Seth wants to see you."

Alan got up reluctantly. Scott reached out to him, and then his arms fell back to his sides. "Good luck, Scott," Alan said, but the boy didn't reply. As Cindy locked the door after them Alan could hear it begin: "I don't wanna die, I don't wanna die, I don't wanna die . . ."

He followed Cindy downstairs. Heather was standing in the hallway. She was about Julia's age and had the vapidly pretty face of a cosmetics salesgirl or a small-town beauty queen. "So this is Julia's friend," she remarked. "She got in trouble for *him?*"

"Shut the fuck up," Cindy said.

Heather laughed. "Are you the boss?"

"Anybody could boss *you.*"

"I only take orders from Seth," Heather replied and sauntered off to the kitchen. *A certain lack of team spirit here*, Alan thought. It probably didn't bother Stone a bit, as long as they took their orders.

Cindy brought him to Stone's room. "He wants you," she said.

Like Uncle Sam. Alan went in.

He felt as if he had stepped inside a blizzard. He had been prepared for the dazzling brightness, but he hadn't expected the waves of energy pulsing toward him from the center of the room, swirling around him, blinding him.

"Come in," Stone said. Had he spoken, or had the words simply formed out of the energy?

Alan moved forward. It was all he could do to stay on his feet. Finally he was able to make out Stone, standing in front of the mirror, smiling. The blizzard seemed to subside. Alan couldn't tell if he was getting used to it, or if Stone had simply turned off the snow machine.

"Sit down," Stone said.

"Mind if I stand?"

The smile broadened. "Suit yourself." He stared at Alan, and Alan did his best to stare back. "You noticed our new arrival," Stone said finally. "He is the son of the governor of New York. Now East and West are here, with us. Now things happen."

"Like what?"

"You'll see—if I don't kill you first."

"Do you need some help in deciding what to do?"

Stone ignored him. "I thought about having Julia kill you; after all, it's her fault you're here. But that seems rather trivial, and I want her attention focused on what is going to happen tonight."

"Sounds reasonable to me."

Anger clouded Stone's face momentarily, and then the smile returned. "I know Julia has told you what I'm up to, Alan. I know you think I'm crazy. I know how you think: it's impossible to break through, to get control of the power, of everything. Why even try? Just let it take hold of you when it wants to, and ignore it the rest of the time. You think small, you live small. You're wrong, and you're stupid. Your smug obtuseness annoys me. I thought the lesson had been taught last night, but I guess I'll have to teach it again. Did you ever Indian wrestle when you were a kid, Alan?"

Alan had the feeling he had missed a connection somewhere. "Sure," he lied.

"I think it would be interesting to Indian wrestle with you."

"Gee, I'd love to but I have this trick knee and—"

"It won't hurt your knee. Come here."

Alan obeyed.

"Okay, we stand facing each other, right feet together. We hold right hands and try to push each other off balance. First one to move his right foot loses."

"What does he lose?"

Stone smiled. "It's just a test of strength, Alan. No need to worry." He planted himself, right foot forward, and held out his right hand. "Let's go."

Some test. Alan placed his right foot next to Stone's, then slowly reached out his hand.

Stone's flesh was cold and hard. His hand surrounded Alan's and seemed to draw out of it whatever piddling amount of energy it contained. Alan kept his gaze on that hand.

"On the count of three, Alan. One . . . two . . . Three!"

Alan tired to brace himself for the thrust or wrench that would inevitably send him sprawling. None came. Finally he tried a pitiful little push himself, but Stone did not budge. Their hands remained locked, motionless, between them.

Look at me.

Uh-oh. Alan knew that those words hadn't been spoken; they had simply appeared, clear and powerful, in his mind. Only his mother had been able to do that before. Her presence had been familiar, comforting; the notion of Stone lurking in his cortex filled him with revulsion.

Look.

So that was what the contest was all about: psychic Indian wrestling. The world's most demanding sport. And Stone had the first advantage. The commands throbbed through Alan's brain: *See what you are missing by not using your powers to the fullest. Feel what I can do now, even before the next step; before the detonation. Believe that it will happen, and that the world will change.*

No, Alan's mind responded, but he could barely hear the response. All that seemed to matter was what

Stone wanted. *What is wrong with looking,* he thought, and suddenly he didn't know who was doing the thinking.

After all, if he wanted to survive, he would have to challenge Stone sooner or later, would have to fight it out with him in the only arena where he stood a chance. Why not do it now, get it over with?

Alan couldn't think of a reason. Stone wouldn't let him think of a reason.

Look.

He looked.

Stone's eyes were blazing. They were beyond words, but their message was clear: *power.* The room was white with heat. Alan's hand seemed to fuse to Stone's. The pain was unbearable. Why bear it?

He had always been a stubborn child. His right foot didn't move. He felt his memories, his emotions, being sucked out of him into the vortex of those eyes. Nothing was left of him but his gift. And the gift fought back.

There was not enought left of Alan's mind for him to follow the struggle clearly. It seemed to him afterward that he tried to get past the eyes, to go beneath them, to find a reality that would make sense of the man, make sense of the evil. But the reality escaped him (if it really existed in the first place), and he had to settle for a metaphor, or a dream, or some damn thing that wasn't what he wanted any more than he wanted to be Indian wrestling.

It seemed to Alan that he was standing on a pitcher's mound. The stands were filled. The noise was so loud it seemed to make the field vibrate. He didn't have to look down at his uniform to see what team he was playing for. He didn't have to look up to see who the batter was. He bent over and gazed in for the sign. The catcher wagged his hand a couple of times and then put down one finger. Fastball. Alan had never had a fastball. His gaze moved finally to the batter. Stone looked good in the Yankee uniform, the pinstripes accenting his bulging muscles, the cap low over his fierce eyes as he cocked his bat and crouched at the plate. Alan sighed and went into his windup. The pitch was slow, and straight down the middle. Stone's bat did not move.

"Steee-rike wan!" the umpire bellowed.

The catcher rifled the ball back to Alan harder than he had thrown it to the catcher. Alan reached down and hefted the resin bag, then leaned in for the sign once more. Another fastball. Was there a trace of a smile on Stone's lips? Alan let the ball fly. Stone just watched it.

"Steee-rike two!"

The crowd roared. "Attababy," the catcher seemed to shout above the din and flung the ball back to Alan. Alan didn't need to see the sign this time. Go with your strength.

And then Stone stepped out of the box. The crowd quieted. The smile was obvious now, fearsome. In the silence he took his bat and pointed, Babe Ruth-like, Uncle Sam-like, not at the right-field stands, but at Alan, standing exposed, defenseless, on the mound. Then he returned to the batter's box and swung the bat slowly, menacingly, while Alan fingered the ball.

Alan had no choice but to make the pitch. It was part of the game, after all. He wound up and released the ball and watched Stone's smooth swing make contact. The line drive exploded off the bat directly at Alan, and was blown backward, or upside down, or inside out; the roaring of the crowd retreated inside his head, and the game was over.

Alan shook his head and blinked. Stone was towering above him, his arms folded on his chest. His eyes seemed calm now, but there were beads of sweat on his forehead. Alan was lying on the floor, his right foot trembling, his head aching.

"You moved your foot," Stone said. "You lose."

"Best two our of three?" Alan asked.

Stone chuckled and turned away to look into the mirror. "You've got more in you than I thought," he said. "But it still isn't enough, because you don't know how to use it. You're a loser, Alan, like the Red Sox, even if you do put up a good fight. I think I will kill you, but not before the ceremony. I want to have all my powers first, I want you to feel the full force of them as you die. I think you would make an interesting first victim."

"You're planning on having others?"

Stone shrugged. "I'm sure some will be required."

Alan staggered to his feet. His legs wobbled precariously. He looked in the mirror and didn't like what he saw: greasy hair plastered to a cut and swollen face, two days' growth of beard, rumpled white shirt soaked with sweat. A loser if he ever saw one.

"I want you to watch tonight," Stone said. "It will add a certain flavor to the ceremony."

Alan had never thought of himself as flavoring, but he was too depressed to come up with a snappy reply. He had never thought of himself as a victim before, either. *I don't wanna die, I don't wanna die . . .*

Stone went over and opened the door. "Heather!" he called out.

Heather appeared almost instantly. "Yes, Seth?" she said in a timid little-girl voice.

"Take our guest here up to the altars. Stay with him until the rest of us come. We won't be long."

"What if he tries to escape?"

Stone glanced back at Alan. "He won't go anywhere. Now do as you're told."

"Yes, Seth." She motioned to Alan, who followed obediently.

She brought him out through the kitchen, where she grabbed a flashlight. Alan realized he was hungry but didn't have the strength to ask for food. They went down the rotting back steps and across a small yard overgrown with weeds. It was night, but a full moon was rising, and the narrow beam of the flashlight was scarcely needed. Beyond the yard was a steep dirt path heading up into the mountains. Heather led the way quickly, with the air of someone who was on familiar terrain. She was wearing khaki shorts and a white jersey. "Come on, move it," she said as he struggled to keep up. Her voice was trembling. She was terribly frightened, he suddenly realized. Should he play on her fear, get her to turn against Stone? Fat chance of that happening, even if he could catch his breath long enough to say something.

After a few minutes of climbing the path petered out and Heather turned left through the pines. It is really quite beautiful here, Alan thought, with the moonlight filtering down through the trees, the soft carpet of pine needles underfoot. *If it weren't for us people.*

Heather stopped in a small clearing. "Here," she said. The beam of the flashlight played over two long, rickety-looking metal folding tables, the light reflecting dully off their imitation wood-grain finishes. At one end of each of them was a small pillow; at the other end was a coil of rope. "I can see you spared no expense on your altars," Alan remarked as he regained his wind.

"Shut up," Heather said. She sat down on the ground and stared forward between her knees at the altars. She had reason enough to be afraid. She had already been a kidnapper; it looked as if she was about to become a murderer.

Alan wandered to the other edge of the clearing. She didn't look at him. Easy enough to wander off into the woods and disappear. But Stone knew he wouldn't do that. First, because he was a loser. Second, because he had to be here when it happened. To try to prevent it? Maybe, but he wouldn't be successful. To try to understand it? That too. But would there be anything to understand? Mostly he wanted just to sit and rest, even if it meant earning the privilege of being Stone's first postceremony victim. He slumped to the ground and looked back through the legs of the tables at Heather. A mosquito buzzed in his ear. He slapped at it and waited.

Two dozen mosquitoes later the waiting ended. Cindy and Julia arrived, each lugging an unconscious child. Cindy was grinning delightedly, Scott on one shoulder, her rifle on the other. Julia was completely out of breath. She was carrying her burden in both arms, like a mother with a sleeping infant. *Not exactly,* Alan thought.

They sat the children on the tables and took off their jerseys. Then they each took a coil or rope and tied the boys down. Julia didn't know much about knot-tying, Alan noticed. When they were finished they silently moved back to the edge of the clearing and stood staring at the victims. Heather got to her feet and did the same.

Alan stayed on the ground. He didn't want to stare, but after a while he couldn't help it. Scott's tanned good looks were horribly out of place here. He should have been in a Little League uniform, delivering newspapers, surfing. Only insanity could bring him here, splayed on the table like a laboratory specimen. A surge of anger shook some of the weariness away from Alan. *Damn them*—Julia and all of them.

And what was he going to do about it? Cindy held her rifle loosely by her side, still grinning in savage anticipation. Blowing Alan's head off would no doubt also give her great pleasure. He might still manage to disappear into the woods, but that would not save Scott. He stayed where he was.

The other boy stirred slightly—a mosquito in his ear? Julia made a move as if to go to him, then changed her mind. The tableau was set, ready for the star to make his appearance. Wouldn't want to spoil that. Alan stared at Julia, but she ignored him; he wasn't part of this.

What if he were to shout "I love you, Julia," over and over again, have it re-echo through the mountains and over the altars? Would that get her attention, break the spell? It would certainly get him slapped around some more—if not worse. Besides, was it still true? That was where he had stopped thinking the night before, as he staggered along that road leading nowhere. Maybe he just loved her in the unreality of Boston. Here neither of them was the same person; how could he expect his feelings to be the same?

It didn't matter in any case. He had lost her, and that was that. A loser.

A cold wind sprang up in the darkness surrounding them, rustling through the tall trees. Alan shivered, and normal time slipped off into some more normal part of the universe. He was back in the bar and grill, at the beginning of everything, sensing this moment with perplexity and dread, wondering if he wanted to prevent it. But this moment was nothing, an instant of waiting before the curtain went up. The true moment lay somewhere in the future—perhaps not even in this play. And suddenly he was there too, looking back, still perplexed, but somehow different, somehow . . .

Somehow what? *God damn it*, Alan wanted to shout. *Of course I'll be different. I'll be older. Somehow what?*

Ask Madame Inez, the obnoxious god of psi replied. *She knows all and sees all.*

Who the fuck is Madame Inez?

But the deity had departed, time had returned, and animal eyes glared across the clearing at him, impossibly large, impossibly evil. The first act was beginning.

Stone was naked. A long knife gleamed in his right hand. The moonlight surrounding him had changed to a different, more lurid color. His body pulsed with a scarcely controlled ferocity that seemed ready to split the mountain in two. He gazed slowly around the clearing, fixing each of them with his awful eyes. Alan hugged his knees to his face and took a deep breath.

Stone strode over to the altars and stared down at the faces of the children. And he smiled. He backed away from them and held the knife in front of him like a priest holding a chalice. "Now is the time," he whispered, each word perfectly audible. "Now all is joined in me, and the new age dawns. Come with me into the reborn world."

His three acolytes gazed at him in awe, ready to follow him into any world he chose. Stone continued to hold the knife upraised, motionless. The woods were completely silent. Last night they had throbbed with sound. Had all the animals—except the mosquitoes—

run away? They were a lot smater than Alan was. "East and West become one in me, and all that was, is no more." Stone lowered the sword once over each of the children and stayed staring at Scott. The other boy stirred once again, moaned softly. Stone ignored him.

The air was oppressive; it was becoming hard to breathe. The moon was gone; the night was descending into blackness, except for the gleam of the knife and Stone's eyes, which blazed with their own exultant light. No one moved, until finally Stone lifted the knife over his head, smiled, and—

Alan shut his eyes, gasping in the foul air, biting his arm to keep from screaming or throwing up. When he opened his eyes he saw red, *the color of victory*, the night pulsing with it, Stone smearing himself with it. He heard a feral howl and saw Cindy on the ground in front of the altar, groveling in adoration.

It is *good*, Alan thought wildly for a moment, his heart racing. *Why are we alive, if not for the thrill of moments like these?* And then he saw his mother in the bathroom mirror, trembling uncontrollably; and he saw Scott's glassy eyes, staring uncomprehendingly at a world too evil to understand. And he saw Cindy's rifle, left lying on the ground ten feet away from him. Numbly he crawled toward it.

No one paid any attention to him. Their concerns were far more exalted. Stone had turned with his gleaming red knife to the second boy. Cindy was moaning ecstatically. Alan reached the rifle and picked it up.

He had never touched a rifle before. Its contours felt familiar to him, though, from a lifetime of TV-watching. He raised it to his shoulder, aimed at Stone (looking like some X-rated parody of an Indian, his body streaked with obscene war paint), and pressed the trigger.

The trigger didn't move. Alan stared at it in shock: that didn't happen on TV. Stone's eyes turned to him, startled and, yes, afraid. He said something unintelligible. Time disappeared once again. There was a roaring in Alan's ears; the world was drenched in red. The safety,

God damn it—some sort of catch. Yes. He aimed again at the bastard's heart, and pressed the trigger. The roar became real; the recoil pushed him backward. He stumbled over a rock, and thought: something went wrong. A shadow in the sight.

He scrambled to his feet and saw Cindy grinning derisively at him from against the altar. Blood spurted out from the hole between her breasts. As Alan watched she slid to the ground, leaving Stone still standing behind her.

Alan moved forward, and Stone retreated a step. There was a loud moan, and both of them glanced over at its source. The other boy had come to and was struggling feebly against the rope. Heather and Julia were still standing, shocked, at the edge of the clearing. Alan went over to the boy and with one hand helped him untie Julia's knots. With the other hand he kept the rifle trained on Stone, now about four strides away from him. No one was going to get in the way of the next bullet.

The boy squirmed loose and climbed down from the table. He stayed close to Alan—smart kid. Alan raised the rifle to his shoulder once again. Stone stared at him, and Alan could feel the power still there in the eyes, but there was fear too. It was a fair fight this time, and Stone was going to lose. Alan pressed the trigger.

And nothing happened. He pressed again. The words *bolt action* popped into his mind, but what did they mean, what was he supposed to do? He saw the smile appear on Stone's face, felt the power grow, and Stone was coming toward him, knife upraised.

Alan rammed him with the rifle, wishing it were a bayonet. Stone grabbed hold and jerked it away from him. Alan took the boy by the arm and moved to the other side of the table, next to Cindy's corpse. The boy started to cry. Alan turned and ran, dragging the boy along with him.

He could hear Stone's footsteps behind them. Every second he expected to feel a bullet rip into his back. But they made it into the woods, plunging headlong through the trees. Branches snapped at their faces, roots clutched at their feet, but the savage creature at their heels did not overtake them.

Alan's heart pounded in his throat, his legs were rubbery. He wished now that he had been out there with those masochistic joggers on the banks of the Charles, instead of eating his Cheez-Its and feeling sorry for them. He and the boy half ran, half slid down a steep dark slope and kept going, heedless of everything but the evil pursuing them. The boy lost hold of Alan's hand for a moment. With a yelp of fear he lunged to grab it again but tripped over a rock and went sprawling. Alan helped him up and looked wildly around: no one. No footsteps. No crashing branches.

The guy is naked, Alan realized as he bent over and struggled to give his body the oxygen it was demanding. Didn't matter what shape Stone was in, what powers he possessed; hard to run through the mountains barefoot. That didn't mean they were safe, though. "What's your name?" Alan gasped.

"Joshua."

"Can you go any further, Joshua?"

"I dunno. I don't feel too good."

"Let's try."

They continued to work their way downhill, hoping to spot some sign of civilization. Clouds covered the moon, and the darkness became impenetrable. Joshua began to shiver, so Alan gave him his shirt. After a while Alan remembered Mrs. Kelly's husband, wandering off in the darkness, and decided they had gone far enough. "Let's stay here until daylight," he whispered. That would keep them from falling into a gorge, but what about rattlesnakes and coyotes? "Can you climb a tree, Joshua?"

"I think so. It's awfully dark."

They found a tree with low-hanging branches; Alan gave Joshua a boost, then scrambled up after him. They made their way about fifteen feet up the tree, until they reached a branch that looked sturdy enough to hold both of them. "I'll hold on to you," Alan said to the boy. "Try to sleep."

"Is he gonna catch us?"

"No way."

"He's the craziest-looking guy I ever saw in my life."

"No doubt about it. He's crazy."

Joshua leaned back against Alan's chest. Alan gripped his sides and eventually felt his heart slow, his breathing become regular. Alan was exhausted but totally incapable of sleeping. For one thing, he was as uncomfortable as he had ever been in his life. Last night a chair, tonight a tree; tomorrow night—what? The primeval ooze? He was definitely regressing.

For another, it finally started to sink in that he had killed a person. Now *there* was a regression. Cindy had been a bundle of feelings and memories and firing nerves and muscular responses, and Alan had done something, and all of that had ceased. The reality of the death and its suddenness astonished him but, astonishingly, his role in it did not seem to bother him. In real life, one risked death, and one had to be prepared to inflict death. The closest he had come before to such reality was to nose around it afterward with Kelliher, sniffing at the traces of human lust and greed and evil. Now, simply, he was part of it. He had received his baptism of blood.

The thing that really did bother him was that he didn't know how to use a fucking rifle. If he had known, then he wouldn't be sitting up a tree now, still afraid for his life; and, he felt sure, a lot more people would be in danger because of his ineptitude.

He closed his eyes and listened to the forest sounds: Siegfried by the dragon's cave. His lungs felt raw and abused, his back was killing him. Dawn was probably hours away. Could be worse, could be worse. Joshua was warm against his chest. He was a murderer but he had also managed, fumblingly, to save a child's life.

Time passed, and in the utter darkness it was impossible to say whether he slept or not. The sounds that surrounded him could have been dreams, his dreams

could have been waking visions of his weary brain. His
mother was there in the darkness—but that was not impossible—shaking her head reprovingly. *If you go, Alan,
you won't come back*. And Julia, beautiful and vulnerable in the night breeze. *You shouldn't have come.
There's nothing you can do.*

But, Julia, who has risked more for you in your life?
No reply.

And Cindy, her corpse already rotting, her skull
grinning beneath the flesh: *One false move and you're
dead*. Too bad, Cindy.

And was it real, or was it fevered fantasy, when he
saw the blazing eyes cutting through the night—Stone
coming closer, still naked and blood-smeared, knife at
the ready, stalking his victims? Alan pressed himself
against the tree and held his breath. Stone approached,
and paused, and looked up, but somehow the realities
did not intersect, his gaze passed through Alan to the
darkness beyond, and then he was moving away, fading
into the night. But Alan knew that this reality would not
always be so kind. Stone would be back, if not tonight
then some other time, some other dream. They had not
done with each other yet.

The sleeping boy stirred uneasily, as if he too had
felt the presence. Then all was quiet till dawn.

Alan thought he might never be able to stand up
straight again. Joshua, on the other hand, seemed pretty
chipper after a good night's sleep. "Gee, I never spent
the night in a tree before. I'm starving. Do you know
where we are?"

"Somewhere in California's about the best I can do
for you. And we're not out of the woods yet. Literally."

"Wow."

They started hiking downhill. Alan's feet were covered with blisters. Wingtips were not exactly ideal for
this sort of activity. His beard itched. The day was cloud-
less and already hot. Alan noticed that everything was
going brown with dryness: the meadow grass, the leaves

on the large bushes, the caked clay in the empty stream beds. He began to get extremely thirsty. "All we need is to find a road," he muttered. "Must be one somewhere."

Joshua handed Alan back his shirt; he seemed eager to get a tan, if nothing else, out of the experience. "Do you think there are any mountain lions around?" he asked.

Alan sighed. No one had brought up mountain lions before. "Wouldn't be surprised."

Finally the slope became less steep. They passed a couple of long abandoned cabins; a Pepsi can glistened in the brush. And there was a road. It was narrow and unpaved, but clearly a road. A road has to go somewhere—doesn't it?

But what if Stone was waiting for them around the bend, knowing they'd find this road? Well, Stone wasn't omniscient, he wasn't God—yet. Alan would take his chances.

"How's it going, Joshua?"

"Fine, thanks. Will we be heroes when we're rescued?"

"I don't think there are any heroes in this story, my friend. Let's just get ourselves rescued."

After about a mile the road became paved, and then another road joined it. The heat, rising from the blacktop, baked Alan's feet, shimmered like a dream in the distance. Alan tried to keep from seeing Stone in the dream. They started trudging along the road.

A pickup truck was the first sign of life they saw, appearing out of the heat and roaring past them. "Let's try to flag down the next one," Alan said. The next one was a dusty Jeep that ignored their frantic waves. A few minutes later a bakery truck passed them, then miraculously stopped and backed up. They rushed up to it and leaped in. Alan let Joshua sit next to the driver; he scrunched down behind them amid endless trays of donuts and coffee rolls. His stomach let out a roar of interest. "Much obliged," Alan said to the driver. "Can I buy some of these donuts off you?"

The driver was a young fellow wearing an earring and a red bandana. "Gee, I'm sorry. Company policy. You guys look kinda strung out. Where you headed?"

"The nearest police station'll do. We had a bit of trouble up in the mountains."

"I was kidnapped," Joshua piped up. "This man saved me. He's a hero."

"Oh yeah? You're not the Senator's kid, are you?"

"Nah, my father's a dentist in Albany. But there was—"

"Joshua," Alan interrupted. "Maybe you'd better save that for the police."

"Oh. Okay."

"Holy shit," the driver said.

Alan mulled over Joshua's remark. "Your father really a dentist?" he asked.

"Sure. Dr. Feldman. Best dentist in upper New York State."

"Then why—" Obvious. Heather had kidnapped the wrong kid—or, more likely, had gotten scared and grabbed the first kid who came along. No wonder she was so frightened up there. *You just can't get good help nowadays.* What a farce.

"Hey, maybe you're on the news," the driver said, and flipped on the radio.

"Yeah," Joshua agreed excitedly. "And see how the Yankees are doing, okay? I've been out of it for a while."

"You a Yankees fan?"

"Sure, isn't everyone?"

Alan sighed and leaned back against the pastry trays. That would certainly explain a lot. He listened to his stomach growl hopelessly and wondered what in the world he was going to tell the police.

Madness. There are those who believe that madness is just another way of coping with the rigors of life, no more to be pitied or censured than any life-style that does not harm others. This is a pleasantly liberal point of view, but it hardly squares with the commonsense perception of the problem. The trouble is, crazy people have a very difficult time living. It is all very well to say it is society that is sick, and that in a different world these people might fit in nicely; but this is the only world we have. And in this world, one of the keys to successful living is flexibility: being able to change yourself in response to changes in the world. The insane are stuck in an adaptation that does not work in things-as-they-are. If they do not change, life will crush them like a trash compactor—unless someone in the sick society bothers to pull them out of the rubbish.

—Pottston Phipps
*Thirty-seven Keys to
Successful Living*

Chapter 15

Madness. Her real name was Marilyn, but they called her Madness. She thought she was the Virgin Mary. No one bothered to point out to her that what she did with Clem Perkins in the lav twice a week technically disqualified her from the title. Like most of them, she could have been almost any age but was much younger than she looked. Madness wears you down.

* * *

"What do you think of Madness?"

"She ought to get some teeth. It's disgusting. Just because you're—you know—that's no reason to let your appearance go. You feel as good as you look."

They moved in slow motion, shuffling around the ward in endless, meaningless patterns, rolling imaginary pills between thumbs and index fingers. What else was there to do? Mrs. Garcia put a chair through the TV when they left the protective Plexiglas screen unlocked, and no one had fixed it. They smoked cigarettes, read tattered old magazines, sometimes played cards, and talked—to themselves, to others, but mostly it seemed they moved, as if searching for something they had lost.

The air conditioning didn't work. A big electric fan had been brought in to push the hot air around. It was pointed out that the fan did no good, in fact constituted a danger to the patients. Mrs. Rosenthal's response was that the benefit was psychological. People *think* they are cooler when the fan is on.

Mrs. Garcia liked to take her clothes off in the heat. One minute all would be calm, the next she would be standing in the middle of the day hall, cackling triumphantly, her naked body jiggling with satisfaction. Sometimes it took three aides to subdue her.

"And Mrs. Garcia?"

"She's a pig. Oh, I know I sound harsh but there it is. She's more trouble than anyone else and she's glad of it. If you don't watch out she steals your food. Not that that's any great loss, I suppose. Virgil is bad too. In the OT room once he started smashing all our ceramic dishes—*bam, bam, bam*. They had to put him in seclusion. But he's sorry for it afterward, if he remembers. He offered to pay me for my dish. He doesn't have enough money to make a phone call."

Mornings weren't bad. It was cooler, and there was an illusion of purposeful activity. Patients had to be gotten up, washed and dressed, then herded into the dining room, where they ate their government-issue slop with plastic spoons out of plastic bowls. Then many of them went places, did things. Some had to see Dr. Dugwatti; others had appointments with the social worker, or went of to various forms of therapy. And before you knew it they were back in the dining room for another serving of slop.

Afternoons could be hard. Sometimes there were visitors, and that was exciting for those being visited. But for some of the others it seemed to be a reminder of the world lurking, terrifying and uncontrollable, beyond the locked doors of the ward. The hours till nighttime loomed like mountains that had to be climbed, the heat baked through the tattered brown shades covering the barred windows, and the postlunch torpor turned to restlessness, and worse. Virgil Coleman bellows curses, Mrs. Wilkerson claws at Mrs. Roth, Reynaldo weeps uncontrollably and gibbers in Spanish, and the staff starts earning their pitiful wages.

But sometimes nothing happened, there was only the random shuffling, the glassy stares. To the observer in the proper frame of mind this could be more depressing than the chaos: this too is life, as much as the striving and the planning and the hoping outside. This will continue as long as there is life: the same vacant faces, ugly bodies, filling up space, waiting for death. No hope of cure; only, at best, a lessening of the pain.

"Sandy just sits there. She doesn't bother anyone, she just sits. I've tried to talk to her, get her to take an *interest*, but it's no use. Sometimes I understand that. Sometimes I just sit myself."

"What do you think about when you sit?"

"Freedom."

Dr. Dugwatti knew little English beyond *Thorazine* and *Valium*. The patients—and some of the staff—called him Dogwarty. He was short, swarthy, and heavyset, with Coke-bottle glasses that made it difficult to know if he was looking at you. He would spend a few hours a day at the place, fiddling with doses and making obscure notes in the patients' files, and then he would leave as quickly as he could.

The ability to leave was the most important difference between patients and staff. The nurses and the aides did not take their clothes off in the day hall or mumble unintelligibly about their son Jesus, but they could, if they wanted to, and not much would change. When their shift was over, though, they could unlock the doors and walk away from the sounds of hysteria, the smell of psychosis. Of course the world outside was a much more dangerous place. Rumor had it that Dr. Dugwatti dealt in drugs to supplement the slave wages the state paid him. One day he would end up in jail, probably, or with a bullet in his brain. The charge nurse, Mary DiGregorio, came in with a swollen lip, occasionally, or a bruised cheek; her husband drank and enjoyed getting angry. But Mary would rather be home than on the ward; Dr. Dugwatti was willing to take his chances in the parking lots and alleys. For all its terror the world still offered some control. The patients had left that behind along with their sanity.

"Cassie is so young. She shouldn't be here, I don't think. This ward is for the bad cases—the ones they don't think are going to get better. I guess she's kind of retarded. I showed her how to use makeup once. She liked that; no one had taught her before, or maybe she forgot. I gave her some—oh, some extra things I didn't need. She kissed me on the cheek. But the next day she forgot again—or she just went crazy for a while. She came around with the red lipstick smeared all over her— big red circles around her eyes, made her look sort of like a raccoon. Up and down her arms, everywhere. She started writing on the walls with it, and then the aides took it away and made her clean up. Once she got a hold of the cleaning lady's Lestoil and drank the whole bottle. I don't think she was trying to kill herself, it's just one of her problems. She's about my daughter's age. Did I tell you I have a daughter?"

Everything has levels: levels of control, levels of sanity, levels of freedom. If being outside was better than being inside, being inside was better than being in seclusion. The seclusion room was small and windowless, except for a small Plexiglas square in the door. The walls were padded; there was a filthy mattress on the floor that stank of urine. This was the bottom level, the nadir: mind and body both trapped, alone, helpless. To consider deeply what it meant to be in such a situation would be to risk madness oneself. So in practice it was not considered. Sometimes a patient just had to be put there, and so it was done.

Most patients screamed and cursed, attacked the walls and pulled at their hair (this was the kind of behavior that got them there in the first place). But there is a limit to human energy—even insane human energy—and eventually they ended up on the mattress, dull-eyed, sweat-soaked, their curses now mumbled between gasps of breath, their limbs twitching with memories of their rage. Then they would be taken out of the room, and they would have to try, once more, to live.

"John Huston was in to see me the other day. Did you happen to notice him? Very striking appearance. He lives in Ireland now, but he comes to L.A. a lot, and he always stops in to see me. A very close friend. He sat next to me and took my hand and said, 'My dear, what are you *doing* here? You must get better and come back to us. You are a *very* good-looking woman. There are still roles for you. You must give me a call as soon as you are available.' Such a good man. I just wish I could—you know—I wish—"

"Maybe I should come back later."

"No, no. Sit by me, don't leave me. It's the booze, you know, that put me here. They say it's a disease, so I don't see how it's my fault. They give me that Antabuse stuff—oh, it's vile. If you try to take a little drink afterward you're so sick to your stomach you have to throw everything up. I suppose it's for the best.

"I just know that if I can control the booze my career will take off. Not that it was bad before; I had featured roles in some very important films. But you can't afford to stand still in this business. You can't just disappear and expect people to shower parts on you when you come back. That's not the way it happens. The doctors say I have delusions, you know, but I don't have any delusions. I know it won't be easy. It's never been easy. But thank goodness I have friends. Ray Stark has *promised* to come by for a visit. Do you know who Ray Stark is?"

"No, not really."

"He's just about the biggest producer in Hollywood. He says he knows an exclusive sanatorium that does miracles with people who have my sort of problem. It's just a question of pulling a few strings to get me in. Wouldn't that be wonderful?"

"Wonderful."

Dreams blur the borders between sane and insane, the free and the trapped. In his tiny condo in Van Nuys, Dr. Dugwatti would like to dream of Jaguars and country estates, of sleek Western women, blond hair curving around milk-white shoulders, blue eyes glazed with passion, elegant hands moving over his naked skin . . . But instead he dreamed of dark alleys and hunger gnawing at him like a rat, of steaming heat and the sudden flash of a knife, the taste of fear like chalk dust in his mouth. And he would wake up with a desperate grunt, clutching his sweaty sheet, and he would stare into the darkness at the ghosts that stalked his existence.

Mary DiGregorio sometimes dreamed that her husband had been committed. He wanders around the ward with a dazed expression until, finally, he sees her. Then his eyes take on that familiar look—angry, aggrieved— and his mouth twists into that shit-eating, guess-what- I'm-going-to-do grin, and he advances toward her, fists clenching. And just as he is about to strike, she signals two aides, who grab him and toss him into the seclusion room. He bellows and shrieks and pounds on the door, but no one pays any attention. And she unlocks the medication room and gets a special dose of a special drug. When he is lying exhausted on the mattress, she will give it to him. He will drink it down meekly, and all her troubles will be over.

But in the morning she would not remember the dream, and he would still be snoring gently beside her. He was not too bad, really, in the mornings. And she would get up and cook his breakfast, feeling vaguely guilty, although she didn't know why.

Nights on the wards were filled with groans and shouts and muttered curses. But the meds blocked such things out. If they didn't, you simply got used to the noise. You can get used to anything.

Julia Walker's mother slept deeply and dreamed of when she was a girl: walking down the high school corridor, acutely conscious of every turning head, of every pause in a doorway. She loved it all: she loved being beautiful, she loved the effect her beauty had on others, she loved what her beauty would bring her in life. She saw Mr. Carson glance at her as she passed by the science lab. Mr. Carson, in his tweed jacket and V-neck sweater, smelling of pipe tobacco and Old Spice. Mr. Carson, removing her bra with trembling fingers and gazing in awe—yes, in awe—at her naked perfection. "Holy Jesus, you're going to be something when you grow up." And she was straddling him, feeling him thrust deep into her, hearing the frantically whispered words: "Oh God, you're going to be *great—great—great*."

And the cameras were already rolling, the bright lights shone on her glorious face.

Alan Simpson, psychiatric aide, slept in his bland apartment overlooking the faceless city. In his dream, he is sitting in a tree in a dark forest. Just what he is doing sitting in a tree is outside the scope of the dream. A hunter comes by. He is naked, although his body is covered with red war paint. He carries a long knife. The hunter stops beneath the tree, pauses, and suddenly is staring up at Alan. His eyes gleam in the darkness. And then he grows, becoming impossibly larger until his eyes are even with Alan's.

Alan realizes he has a rifle. He takes aim between those eyes, but he doesn't know how to use the damn thing. Besides, the bullet would only be a minor annoyance to the giant. The giant laughs at Alan's helplessness, and one enormous hand closes around Alan's throat. The knife moves toward Alan's face, he can't breathe . . .

And he woke up to another sunny day. *Good morning, world*. He took two deep breaths, then scrambled to the shower and got ready for work.

Chapter 16

Alan was changing the sheets in the women's dormitory. It was a pleasantly mindless task, except when Sandy had had an accident. Then he would begin to wonder, hardly for the first time, what the hell he was doing here. He usually did her bed first, just to get it behind him.

The nicest part of the task was that he was by himself. All the patients were in the day hall or at their therapy sessions. If they were allowed to, most of them would have stayed in bed all day: the meds drained the energy right out of you. But that would not have helped their "rehabilitation," so the dorms were off limits during the day.

Of course the rules weren't always obeyed. His second day on the job he had come across two women kissing passionately in bed, their legs tangled together, their hospital gowns up around their waists. He reported it diffidently to Mary DiGregorio, who merely shrugged. "A lot goes on here, Alan," she said. "A lot goes on."

This was both true and false. There was plenty of bizarre behavior, there were crises big and small, but after a few weeks it became clear to Alan that nothing much really changed, that time had stopped for these people in their little world as much as it was going to stop for anyone. This was not unacceptable to him at the moment. He stripped the sheets off Mrs. Garcia's bed and dumped them into the laundry bag.

"Hey, Alan, Miz Rosenthal wanna see you. Agnes say fo' me to finish up."

"Okay, Flo. You know what's going on?"

"What's goin' on is fo' you to see Miz Rosenthal."

"Right." Alan left the linen trolley for Flo and headed back through the day hall. He unlocked the door at the far end and walked down a linoleum-tiled corridor to Mrs. Rosenthal's office. He knocked.

"Come in, come in."

Her office was small and cramped but, blessedly, air conditioned. Six file cabinets surrounded a small metal desk. Mrs. Rosenthal was a big woman, and her bulk made the desk seem even smaller. She wore her gray hair in a bun; her reading glasses hung on a chain around her neck and dangled over her ample bosom. Through the window behind her Alan caught a glimpse of the hospital's brown lawn and the high fence that surrounded it.

"Sit down, Mr. Thompson," she said in her deep voice.

Alan sat.

"Do you by any chance suffer from insomnia, Mr. Thompson?"

Alan shook his head.

"Well, I often do. It's a terrible affliction. One thing I like to do when I can't sleep is to read through back issues of *Time* magazine. I'm usually too busy to read

them when their first come out. Last night I found myself glancing through the issues of late May and early
June. And whose picture do you think I came across?"

Alan shifted glumly in his seat. "Beats me."

"Why, yours, Mr. Thompson. Do you think that's
possible?"

"It's not out of the question."

"Well then perhaps I should just start calling you
Mr. Simpson, shall I?"

"Doesn't matter."

"But it does matter, Mr. Simpson. Providing false
information on your employment application is a viola-
tion of state law. You could be sent to prison."

Alan considered. "Still doesn't matter."

Mrs. Rosenthal laughed—a low rumble in her
throat that ended in a hacking cough. She lit a cigarette.
"I knew you were too good to be true," she said. "We
haven't had your kind around here since Vietnam, when
the place was crawling with C.O.s doing alternative service. Now it turns out you're some sort of weirdo psychic
mixed up in the murder of the Hodkins boy."

"The police know where I am. No charges have
been filed against me. I have no record of any sort."

"That's not the point."

"My performance on the job has been satisfactory,
hasn't it?"

"And that's not the point either. Can't you imagine
what the result will be when the patients find out who
you are—which is bound to happen sooner or later?
Imagine that one of our paranoids learns that there's a
psychic working in the ward—someone who can listen in
on his thoughts, discover his darkest secrets. Do you see
the difficulty, Mr. Simpson?"

"I could deny it. It would be just one of many delusions."

Mrs. Rosenthal shook her head and took a deep puff
of her cigarette. Her bracelets jangled on her arm. "Odd
as it may seem, the patients come first here. I can't risk
their peace of mind, such as it is, just to keep you em-

ployed. Why in the world do you want to work here anyway? Clearly you're not in it for the money."

"I came here to escape from the people who seem to think it's all right to pry into my life and thoughts the same way your paranoids might think I was prying into theirs. I have nothing interesting to say, if only people would allow me to not say it."

"All right, take it easy. If you don't want to tell me I don't really care. You've been a good worker, but you can't stay here. So why don't you just finish out the week, all right, Mr. Simpson?"

Alan shrugged and stood up. "What if I become a patient?" he asked. "We psychics are quite unstable."

Mrs. Rosenthal chuckled and stubbed out her cigarette. "You don't belong here as a worker or a patient. My nonprofessional diagnosis is that you're saner than I am, Mr. Simpson."

"Wouldn't want to bet on it."

Alan sat on the parched lawn eating his tuna fish sandwich. It was hot, but he didn't feel like facing the people in the air-conditioned nurses' room. Besides, he was getting used to the heat. He was getting used to a lot of things that might have surprised him a few months ago.

A shadow fell across him. "Mind if I join you?" It was Gail Chalmers' voice, straining to be nonchalant.

He restrained a sigh, and silently patted the grass next to him. Gail sat down and stirred her boysenberry yogurt. "That stuff'll kill you," he said.

"Oh, now, Alan." She grinned delightedly at him and swallowed a mouthful. Alan groaned.

Gail was a year or two out of nursing school, bright and pretty and eager to help humanity. She included Alan in that category. She also included him in the category of eligible bachelors, which was not where he wanted to be just now. One particularly lonely day he had accepted an invitation to dinner at her apartment. There, over a bottle of Riunite, she had offered him her charms. To ease the pain of rejection he had invented (well, not entirely) a tale of a tragic love affair and a resulting search for true meaning in his life. That was why he was working in such a menial job. That was why he could not respond to her advances. She had been more than understanding; he had felt like a total jerk.

"I didn't want to disturb you," Gail said, "but I hate to see you sitting out here all by yourself. I don't think it's good for you to be alone so much."

"Why?"

"It'll make you brood."

"Oh." Alan brooded. He supposed he should tell her. She'd be hurt if he didn't. "Anyway, it's not going to last much longer."

"What do you mean?"

"Mrs. Rosenthal just fired me. Friday's my last day."

Gail looked like she had just contracted boysen-berry yogurt poisoning. "But she can't do that. You're the best aide in the hospital. What was the reason?"

Alan shrugged and tossed out a lie. He was getting good at it. "Some Civil Service rule. I couldn't really follow what she was saying."

"You should fight it, then, you should—" Gail paused to think it through. "You know, maybe this is what you need, Alan, to get your life going again. You can't stay here forever, after all."

"I suppose you're right, but I would've preferred to make the decision myself."

Gail put down her yogurt and laid a tanned hand on his. "All things pass, Alan. You have to get the hurt behind you and go on living."

"I suppose you're right," he sighed.

"It'll be for the best, Alan. I just know it will."

He gazed at her. She was smiling. Every freckle on her face oozed sincerity. She looked like a Coke commercial. Any particular reason why he didn't fall for sincere girls? He reached into his brown paper bag and brought out a Baggy. "Want an Oreo, Gail?"

Her smile deepened, and she squeezed his hand.

* * *

"Alan, Alan, come sit down beside me."

"Good afternoon, Mrs. Walker. Did you have any visitors today?"

He could tell right away she was in one of her bad moods. She pouted and stared at her stained blue pants. Her hands were shaking. "Not one. I can't understand why some of my so-called friends can never find the time to see me. Sometimes I think you're the only one I can trust."

"Oh, I'm sure that's not true."

"You didn't know me before—before this. That's the difference. When you're on top, everybody loves you. When you've slipped a little, they forget you so fast it isn't funny. Bastards," she said, raising her voice. "I'd like to slit their hearts out."

No one paid any attention. "Now, now, Mrs. Walker."

"Well, they are. Why have they left me here like this, year after year, with these—crazy people?"

"The doctors have let you try those halfway houses, haven't they? You just couldn't seem to manage."

She started to cry. "But with a little *help*. A little *help*."

"I'm sure you'll have visitors any day now."

She cried softly for a minute or so. "Perhaps you're right," she said finally. "Perhaps you're right." She reached into the pocket of her pants and produced a quarter. She pressed it into Alan's hand. "Would you do me a great favor, Alan, and call up Charlton Heston? I don't recall his number but I'm sure you'll be able to get it. Tell him my situation. Explain what I need. He's so active in humanitarian causes, I'm sure he'll help. I'd call him myself, but you know how the phones are around here. He'll come through. I know he will, if you talk to him."

Alan stared at her. This probably wasn't the time to bring up his piece of news. He pocketed the quarter. "I'll do my best," he said. "I've got to get back to work now."

* * *

"Take your next left. Remember to signal. Ease up now, ease up. Don't worry about the guy behind you, he'll wait. Go when you're comfortable. Jesus Christ, don't wait all night. Okay, okay, that's good. Now go straight to the next set of lights." Mr. Gorff took a swig of his cough medicine and drummed nervously on the clipboard. Alan, his eyes glued to the road, didn't notice. "Don't jam on the brake. Softly. Anticipate. Okay, take a right. Signal, wouldja? They'll flunk you right off if you don't signal."

"Sorry, sorry."

"You're not doing so good tonight. Something on your mind?"

"I'm losing my job at the end of the week."

"Jesus, that's a bitch. Let 'im honk, he's not gonna do anything. Laid off or something?"

"Yeah, like that."

"What'll you do now?"

"I dunno. Drive a cab?"

"*Watch out for the goddamn*—" Mr. Gorff took another swig of his cough medicine. "Have you considered maybe a desk job?"

In his apartment, Alan turned on the Dodgers game and listened to Vin Scully's soothingly familiar tones while he drank a Budweiser. He hadn't been to Dodger Stadium yet. He would drive there when he went. He glanced at the L.A. *Times*, but there was nothing in it he was interested in except the Red Sox box score, and that was depressing.

His apartment was much nicer than the one on Marlborough Street, with wall-to-wall carpeting and a balcony and a toilet that didn't run. It was much nicer, certainly, than he could afford on a therapy aide's salary, but he had been saving money for years with nothing to spend it on, and here at last was a worthy cause. He felt about as much at home in the place as he did in a doctor's waiting room.

When the ball game was over (the Dodgers won), Alan turned the TV off, popped open another beer, and went out onto his balcony. The huge city twinkled below him. Cars roared past; a plane soared through the night sky; from another balcony came the sound of laughter and clinking ice. He was so lonely he could scarcely breathe. He imagined calling up Gail: *I have to talk to someone about my future, and you're so understanding . . .* imagined her moist-eyed and comforting . . . imagined everything but telling her the truth. Thought about visiting the guy next door, who wore purple eye shadow and played Adam and the Ants albums on the other side of the paperthin wall at two in the morning. *Hey, man, I'm really looking to get into the punk rock scene. Can I borrow some of your eye shadow?* Imagined calling up the airlines and checking on flight times to Logan . . .

No.

Just what do you think you're doing here? the city twinkled up at him.

None of your business, he replied.

And what are you going to be doing next week?

Alan turned his back on the conversation and went inside. He would go to sleep and see what his dreams had to offer in the way of companionship. As if he didn't know.

Alan tried to be in the day hall during visiting hours. Sandy's father came in and sat beside her in the corner, twirling his porkpie hat in his hands. He knew most of the people on the ward and had a smile and a greeting for each of them. He barely glanced at his daughter, but he never left her side.

Virgil Coleman's wife was there for a while, a loud woman with dyed red hair. She hated the place. She kept looking around nervously to make sure no one got the jump on her. Within minutes of her arrival she and Virgil were arguing about when he was going to get himself straightened out, and Virgil's face was starting to twitch with anger. One of the nurses went over and spoke to her; she acted offended and demanded to see the doctor, but the doctor was long gone, and finally she too left, muttering to herself.

A black minister was talking to Mrs. Wilkerson, earnestly jabbing his finger in the air as he made some point. She nodded her head and murmured, "Yes sir, yes sir, that's *so* true, *so* true." He was sweating profusely, drops of moisture beading his glasses, huge wet circles spreading out from beneath the arms of his suit coat. After a while Mrs. Wilkerson's eyes glazed and her hands started to tremble, but the minister didn't seem to notice.

No one came to see Mrs. Walker. She sat by herself underneath the barred windows, glancing through an old magazine. She looked quite presentable, freshly made up, hair washed and combed. But no one cared, and by the end of the afternoon the makeup was streaked with sweat, and another day was gone.

"Doesn't anyone ever visit Mrs. walker, Gail?"

"You mean besides Rock Hudson and Gregory Peck?"

"Seriously."

"I'm sorry, Alan. I didn't mean to be facetious. No one's visited her in the six months I've been on the ward. Poor dear, she must've been quite good-looking in her day. What a mess people can make of their lives. They've tried releasing her, but she gets actively suicidal on the outside. Life is just too much for some people."

"I know."

"Are you busy tonight, Alan? I thought maybe we could have dinner—you know, since you're leaving in a couple of days and—"

"I'm sorry, Gail. I don't think I—"

"Oh. I understand, Alan. It's all right."

Alan sat down in a pink plastic chair next to her. "I've got to be leaving soon, Mrs. Walker."

"What do you mean, Alan?"

"Leaving the hospital—my job. They told me I can't work here anymore. Something about Civil Service rules. Friday's my last day."

Mrs. Walker looked wildly around her for a moment, as if the Civil Service were somewhere in the room, waiting to be challenged. Then, abruptly, she calmed down, and even managed a smile. "These things happen, I guess. The only aides who stay are the bad ones. Will you come and visit me, Alan?"

"Of course I will."

"And you'll still try to help me get out of here?"

"Of course."

Mrs. Walker nodded, satisfied. "I know you will, I know you will." She went back to reading her magazine.

During visiting hours on Thursday Marilyn started acting up. She got it into her head that she was about to be assumed into heaven, and so she had to get outside immediately. Alan and another aide wrestled her down from the window, where she was banging on the bars and screaming to Jesus to help her. It took another fifteen minutes to sedate her and put her into the seclusion room, and it was only when he returned from this that Alan noticed Mrs. Walker's visitor. He stood at the opposite end of the day hall while the two of them chatted, apparently amicably. After a while the visitor's expression turned to shock and, yes, fear. She looked up, and her eyes met his. He walked toward her.

"Oh, Alan, Alan. Julia, this is the man I was telling you about. This is my daughter Julia, Alan."

"Pleased to meet you."

She was wearing jeans and a powder-blue leotard. Her hair was loose, reaching almost to her shoulders now. Her face was flushed, but that could have been the heat. The tension and the weariness had nothing to do with the weather, though.

Mrs. Walker looked enormously pleased. "Sid Caesar once said I had the prettiest little girl in Los Angeles. Didn't he, Julia?"

"Yes, Mother."

"I've often thought she should go into show business, but it's such a tough, tough life I wouldn't put any pressure on her. I've always let her make her own decisions. Haven't I, Julia?"

"You certainly have."

"Well, don't let me interrupt your visit," Alan said.

"That's okay. I was just leaving." Julia stood up.

"Allow me to see you to the door."

Julia glanced at him quickly, then turned back to her mother. "Well, goodbye. I'm glad to see you're getting along so well."

Mrs. Walker grimaced. "Oh, I wouldn't say that. These patients are so disgusting and horrid, and the staff—except for Alan—is no better. It makes me feel so old. So old and ugly. Most of the time I wish I was dead."

"Keep taking your medication or you'll feel a lot worse." Julia hesitated, then leaned over and brushed her mother's cheek with her lips.

Mrs. Walker didn't seem to notice. "When Alan goes, maybe I *will* die. Unless he can help me get out of here. It's so hard. So hard." She started to cry. Julia walked hurriedly toward the door. Alan followed and unlocked it for her. Once she was in the outer corridor she leaned back against the wall and closed her eyes.

"What are you doing here?" she whispered.

"Waiting for you."

"Why?"

"To talk over old times. Why do you think? I have to go back to work now. 3421 San Rafael Boulevard, Apartment 14-G. The name on the buzzer says Thompson. I'll be there about six."

"What if I don't come?"

"If you came here you'll come to my apartment."

"Will the police be there?"

"Don't be silly."

Julia's eyes were watering. "But I don't understand."

"I wish to hell I did. 3421 San Rafael. The name is Thompson."

Alan unlocked the door and went back into the ward.

Chapter 17

Julia waited nervously for him in the lobby. She had braided her hair and put on makeup, but she knew she looked terrible. She felt terrible. Up until the last minute she was convinced that she wouldn't come, but then the same loneliness that had brought her to her mother brought her here. She was frightened, but even fear was better than loneliness. And right now her strongest fear was that Alan would change his mind and not show up.

He arrived ten minutes late. He nodded to her and headed for the elevator. She followed him silently. His apartment was a surprise: modern and functional, with not a trace of his personality. "Where did you get the furniture?" she asked.

"It came with the place." He handed her a beer. "I'm going to take a shower. It gets a bit hot at work, you may have noticed. Make yourself at home. Make supper, actually, if you want to help. I'll be right out."

"Okay." She went out into the kitchen and looked around helplessly. She found some graying hamburger in the refrigerator that she hoped wouldn't kill them and set to work preparing a meal. The domestic chores made her feel a little better. By the time Alan returned, the butcher block table was set and his dinner was waiting on the stove.

He sat down and took a swig of his Budweiser. "Just like old times," he said. "Sort of."

Julia bit back the tears. She was determined not to cry. "Let's eat," she whispered.

They ate in silence. Julia simply waited for him to start explaining. If he didn't want to explain, there was nothing she could do about it. She would take what he gave her.

After dinner they cleared away the dishes and went back into the living room. Alan sat down on the couch and put his feet up on the glass coffee table. Julia sat in a white director's chair.

"So," Alan said. "We're both probably wondering what we've been up to these past couple of months. Want to flip a coin?"

Julia shook her head.

"Well, I'll start then, just to get the ball rolling. As you can see I've got a new job, new apartment, even a new name. Things were really starting to look up for me until my boss found out about my sordid past and told me to hit the road. But I think I may have a future in the mental health profession. I get along quite well with the patients." He paused. She just waited, gazing at him pleadingly. He drummed his fingers on the arm of the couch. "If it hadn't been for the kid sitting next to me at the police station I would've thought I was making it all up," he said, his voice lower. He stared past her, out through the balcony doors into the twilight. "Maybe it all took place in my mind, some weird perversion of my powers. But it was real, all right, real policemen were asking real questions. And I had to decide whether or not to tell them what really happened. I had no particular desire to protect you right then, but it occurred to me that no one else could link you to what happened up in the mountains, besides Stone and Heather. Scott was dead. Joshua never saw you; he was either unconscious or running for his life.

"So I decided to leave you out of it. It was a stupid risk to take, of course, because if they found out I was lying they could nail me as an accessory; it wasn't as if the rest of my story was easy to believe."

"Why did you do it, then?"

"Because putting you in prison wouldn't solve anything. And because I want you to help me find Stone."

Julia shivered. "The police—"

"The police won't find him. You know that."

"But I don't know where he is, Alan. Honest."

Alan shrugged. "You know more than I do."

"Your gift, though—"

"Has stopped giving. Maybe it's the smog."

"But how did you find my mother? How did you know I'd visit her?"

"I found your mother because you gave me an idea where to look. I didn't know you'd visit her. I just hoped you would. After I talked to the police and the FBI and whoever else wanted to question me, I had to sit back and figure out what to do with the rest of my life. All I wanted to do was get Stone. My mother had told me where he was the first time, but she wasn't going to do it again. And I haven't the faintest idea how to be a private detective—as if I could find him that way. My only link was you, and the only link I had with you was your mother. So I came back to L.A. and changed my name and got a job, and waited. I figured: if she comes, maybe all is not lost for her, for us. Don't ask me why I figured that."

Julia got up and went over to the balcony, her arms folded around her. He wasn't the same. He had changed, like his furniture. How could it have been otherwise? What did he mean: all is not lost? *Don't ask.* "You became great friends with my mother," she said.

"I talked with her. No one else was talking with her very much."

"That's because she isn't interested in talking with anyone who isn't a star. Which doesn't give her many opportunities for conversation. Did she talk about me at all?"

"She may have mentioned your existence."

Julia nodded. "She isn't interested in me. She's interested in what Sid Caesar once said about me. Sid

Caesar, for God's sake. She wasn't happy to see me today or anything. Only if I'd become a star."

"But why did she talk to me?"

Julia laughed and turned around. "You don't know? She must be a better actress than I thought. She *knows* about you, Alan. She saw your picture in a magazine or something. She thought you were at the hospital in disguise to help her, the way you helped out on the kidnappings. Simpson's next case. You made her summer, Alan. She told me you were quitting because you were taking the case to the public, exposing the shameful conditions in the hospital. You had listened to her thoughts and determined she was sane. Now whenever I go to see her she'll tell me how Alan Simpson has promised to visit her real soon, how you're going to have her back starring in movies in no time."

Alan considered this piece of information. "Of course I *was* there to help her, if I could."

"There's nothing you or me or Darryl Zanuck can do to help her now. The layers of fantasy are too thick. You either add to them or she ignores you. Either way, you're not doing her any good."

"Then why did you bother visiting her?"

Julia sat back down. She could tell him it was none of his business, but it *was* his business. And what if he told her to get lost, he never wanted to see her again? She didn't want to get lost again. "Because she was all I had left after I got through screwing up my life. A lunatic who doesn't even love me. I figured I might as well start from there."

Alan nodded slowly. "When did it occur to you that you were screwing up your life?"

The answer to that was the price of admission, of course. She didn't know whether she could afford it. "Please, Alan," she said.

He gazed at her for a while, then went out into the kitchen to get another beer. When he returned he paced back and forth in the living room, eyes on the floor. "Tell me what happened."

"Don't want to," she managed to whisper.

"It's not going to start again," he said, pacing. "The mystery, the silences. You owe me. I've got to know."

"Can't we just—"

"*No!*"

She had never heard him raise his voice before. She wanted to shrink inside herself and hide from him. But she had been hiding too long. She would do her best and hope it was enough. "It was cold," she said, not looking at Alan. "We stood there for a while—Heather and I—shivering. We thought we should do something about the bodies, but we were too scared, without Seth. Finally we just walked back down to the house and sat there until Seth came back. It was nearly dawn. He was dirty, and limping; his feet were all cut up. He was carrying that damned rifle. 'Get the bodies,' he said. 'Get the altars. Get everything.' So we dragged them all back to the house. The bodies were becoming stiff, and Cindy wouldn't stop grinning . . . it was awful. Then we had to go back and cover up the footprints and everything, while Seth got dressed. And then Seth waved at the house and said, 'Burn it.' So we put some clothes in the cars and moved them out of the way, and we soaked the place with gasoline and set it on fire."

"Damn near burned down the whole forest too," Alan remarked.

"We didn't stay around to find out. You were probably talking to the police about the same time. We each drove one of the cars to L.A. and ditched it. We met downtown and bought a used car at some sleazy place and drove away."

"Where were you going?"

Julia closed her eyes. "East."

"That narrows it down."

"We were going to get another politician's son and complete the ritual," she explained softly. "Unite East and West, in Seth. He wasn't scared or anything, just angry—at himself, really, for not killing you. It was a weakness, he said. It wouldn't happen again."

"I'm sure it won't," Alan sat down. "So what brings you back to L.A.? Seth isn't in town, by any chance, ready to finish me off?"

She shook her head. "I don't know where he is. I—I left him. Somewhere in—I don't even know the state."

"Why did you leave him?"

"Can I have a beer?"

"Tell me first."

Don't cry, she thought. *Just don't cry.* "We heard the news reports on the radio—about how they were looking for a man and a girl, about how a dentist's kid from Albany had escaped unharmed. That's when we discovered that Heather had chickened out of kidnapping the governor's son."

"Sort of like you."

"Except she tried to trick Seth. And except he was angry anyway. She told him she had made a mistake, but he knew better."

"What happened?"

Julia didn't think her voice would work, thinking about what happened, but she forced it to. "It was night. We stopped at a rest area on the highway. Heather was crying. We walked into the woods—maybe a couple hundred yards. Then Seth stopped and took a knife out. We were both holding Heather. She struggled a bit, and she was trying to scream—but nothing came out, only this kind of strangled moaning. Maybe she was just too scared—or maybe Seth took her voice away from her. But her eyes were open. She saw. She understood when Seth brought the knife up to her throat, when . . .

"We covered her up with branches and rotting leaves. Then Seth and I walked back to the car and drove away. Nobody said a word the whole time."

Alan heaved himself up off the couch and got a beer for her. She swallowed half of it and set the can down on the gray carpet. Now what? The story needed an ending. Did she have one? "We stopped off at a motel that night," she went on in a dull monotone. "When Seth was asleep I took all his money and the keys to the car and left. I drove until I couldn't drive anymore, then I left the car and took a bus back to L.A. I've been living in a seedy hotel near the bus terminal ever since, just waiting for something to happen. But the police didn't come, and Seth didn't come, and—and you. I sat in my room day after day, and I thought I'd either go crazy, like my mother, or just start over. So finally I started over, and this is where I ended up." She picked up the can and finished the beer. The empty can crackled in her grip afterward like distant gunfire.

"Why did you leave Stone?" Alan asked.

Julia lowered the can slowly to the floor. Good question. "Same reason I holed up in the room in Boston, instead of driving back to California, I guess. There's a part of me that resists him. I just didn't want to face any more death. Could we talk about something else now?"

"You don't know where he might be?"

"I only know he was heading back East. I'm sure he made it, even without money or a car. Please, Alan—I don't want to think about him."

"But wasn't this our problem in Boston? His influence on you doesn't go away by trying to ignore it."

"Would you still have—have fallen in love with me, if I had told you about Seth?"

Alan pondered the question. "I think so, Julia."

Julia's body tensed. "Do you love me now?" she whispered.

Alan paused a moment, then reached over and picked up the bent can she had placed on the carpet. He looked at it. "Love is like a beer can, my former employer might say. Easy to bend and twist and crush, damn near impossible to destroy completely. My love is bent and twisted and crushed."

Julia got up from her chair and knelt at his feet, laying her head on his knees. "Can I stay?" she asked softly after a while.

Alan put one hand tentatively on her hair. The other held on to the beer can. He too was tense, afraid. Did he want to start over as well? "Yes," he murmured finally. "Yes."

She lay in his arms and listened to his heart thud. She knew he was awake, eyes open, staring into the darkness, but she could think of nothing to say. If she cried, would he be able to comfort her? Would he want to? She longed to burrow into his warmth and hide there forever. Life was too hideously complicated; he was the one simple, straightforward thing she had known. And now that was gone. The complexity had infected him too; the warmth was a mixture of colds and hots and luke-warms. If only she had stayed . . . but if she had stayed, it would not be over yet.

As if it were over now.

She closed her eyes and tried to sleep.

Chapter 18

Gail baked Alan a cake, and Mary DiGregorio, against all regulations, brought in a bottle of wine. The staff sat in the nurses' room, sipped Lambrusco, and talked about freedom.

"No more cleaning up after Eddie Keenan or Sandy when they have an accident."

"No more grabbin' Madness down off the windows."

"No more chasing Mrs. Garcia when she's running around in her birthday suit."

"No more listening to Mrs. Walker talk about her bigshot Hollywood friends."

"They's crazy people all over," Flo said.

"But at least Alan won't have to look after them," Mary replied.

"Still has to look out for them."

"Have you decided what you'll do?" Gail asked, bright-eyed, sympathetic.

Alan shook his head. "I've saved up so much money while I've been here I thought I might just retire."

"You've got to think about settling down, maybe going back to school," she said, ignoring his feeble joke. "You're too intelligent to just drift along."

"Intelligent people make the best drifters."

"But you're wasting your life, Alan."

"It could be worse. At least I'm not going around shooting people or something."

Mary filled his coffee mug with wine. "And at least you don't believe you're the Virgin Mary."

"Yeah. Look on the bright side, Gail."

"If you're happy, Alan, I guess that's all that matters."

"Happiness is another piece of that cake."

Alan sat down by Mrs. Walker. "I guess I've got to go now," he said quietly.

Mrs. Walker said nothing for a while, merely stared at her hands. She looked very old. When she smiled, it was the smile of insanity, and Alan wanted to look away. "It's best that you go, Alan. Your talents are wasted here."

"That's what people keep telling me. My talents aren't large enough to be wasted, I'm afraid."

Her smile broadened. Would there be a conspiratorial wink too? She reached out and covered his hand with hers. It was hot and trembled slightly. "You're too modest. We're going to meet again, aren't we, Alan? Only under far better circumstances than these."

"I'm sure we'll meet again, Mrs. Walker." He let her gaze drink in his smiling, lying face and after a moment gently withdrew his hand.

He walked to the door, then stopped and looked around the day hall at the barred windows, the useless fan, the overflowing ashtrays, the faded linoleum floor covered with spilled coffee and gum wrappers and Styrofoam cups. Then he looked at the people, wondering how long they would stay in his memory before they faded like the linoleum beneath the unceasing tread of existence. He had changed here, but he wasn't quite sure how. He would miss the place, but he wasn't quite sure why. He unlocked the door and walked out.

He handed in his keys at Mrs. Rosenthal's office. She glanced at him quizzically. "Are you sorry to be leaving, Mr. Simpson?" she asked.

"If the air conditioner had been working, it would have been heaven."

She blew a cloud of smoke in his direction and smiled. "No hard feelings?"

Alan shrugged. "I have no hard feelings toward anyone."

Mrs. Rosenthal stared at him for a moment, then shrugged in turn and put the keys in her desk drawer.

Gail was waiting for him outside in the corridor, looking shy and worried. "Alan, I hope you don't think I was being too critical of you at the party," she said hurriedly. "It's just that I want so much for everything to work out for you."

"Of course, Gail. And I know you're right. It's just that—"

She put her hand to his lips. "I understand." And then she was embracing him. Her body felt magically cool and antiseptic in the heat. It conjured up visions of split-level ranches and station wagons, of freckled-faced kids whose ideas of psychic powers were limited to Mary Poppins and Tinker Bell. He thought of lying awake in the darkness with Julia, tension and fear living presences alongside them, and took another shot at trying to understand himself. No luck. He patted Gail's crisp white uniform and disengaged himself.

"I'll be fine," he whispered, wondering if that, along with everything else, was also a lie. He hurried off to his driving lesson.

Julia had moved her few possessions into the apartment and had made an attempt to give the place some life: a bowl of flowers on the coffee table, a Van Gogh print in the bedroom, a Sierra Club calendar in the kitchen. Her scent filled the air. She had a let-me-show-how-good-I-can-be expression on her face that Alan found both appealing and exasperating. She broke out into a grin when he told her where he had been. "Why are you learning to drive?"

"Can't get around this city without a car. No way to get to the rifle range unless you drive there."

Her smile faded. "What are you going to do at the rifle range?"

"Practice being a target. What do you think I'm going to do?"

"Alan, knowing how to shoot a rifle isn't going to help you against Seth anymore."

"Can't hurt. Besides, you can never tell when it'll come in handy. What's for supper?"

Julia closed her eyes, and after a while found her smile again. "Fried chicken," she said. "And beer."

"I like the sound of that." She was trying hard. They would both have to try hard. Alan wished he could see inside her mind. But he could no more do that than he could understand himself.

They developed a tolerable illusion of domesticity. In the morning they would jog together. Alan could go about a mile before his lungs cracked and purple spots started dancing in front of his eyes. Julia stayed beside him, murmuring encouragement, as long as she could, and then she would take off through the park, her long legs gracefully moving over the asphalt. In the afternoon they would drive their rented car, Julia tensely supervising Alan's progress through the Los Angeles traffic. Usu-

ally they went to the rifle range: Julia would stay in the
car while Alan poured bullets into his target. Occasionally she would prevail on him to cease his self-improve-
ment for an afternoon and go to Knots Berry Farm or
Disneyland, where they would go up the Matterhorn
and pretend they were tourists from Dubuque spending
a few precious days in the magic kingdom before returning to their workaday lives.

But tourists do not have men in white shirts and
sunglasses following them. At first Julia kept this information to herself, sure it was her own incipient insanity
that made her see these faceless creatures. Finally she
decided the insanity could only get worse if she didn't
say anything, so she brought it up. "Over there, just behind Goofy," she murmured, but they had vanished by
the time Alan looked back. He shrugged uneasily.
"Probably just . . ." But he couldn't think of any way to
finish the sentence.

Julia drove home. Did she see a green Chevy once
too often in the rearview mirror? By the time they got
back to the apartment she could barely function. "I just
don't want to go crazy," she said. "I can stand anything
except going crazy."

Alan paced through the living room for a while, then
picked up the phone and dialed a number. "Henshaw?
This is Alan Simpson."

"Hello, Alan. Nice to hear from you." Henshaw's
voice was perfectly neutral. "Do you have anything for
us?"

"I'm just living my life here, Henshaw. Are you having me followed?"

There was a brief pause. "It's as much for your own
protection, Alan, as anything else. If he comes after you,
we want to be there."

"I can take care of myself."

"Alan, knowing how to shoot a rifle—"

"Yeah, yeah." Alan froze as something else occurred
to him. "Have you bugged my apartment too?"

"No, Alan. Should we have?"

"It's a matter of privacy. You may have noticed I have someone living with me now."

"Yes. I'm told you have good taste."

"You're wasting your time with me now, Henshaw. I'm not involved anymore."

"Just let me do my job, Alan. You got yourself involved; it's not up to you to decide that it's over."

Alan sighed. "You're not going to find him, you know."

"Is that a psychic prediction, or just an opinion?"

Alan hung up and sat down in the director's chair. "The FBI is following me," he said. "I guess they've been doing it all along, and I never noticed. What an odd feeling."

"Do you think they suspect you?"

"I don't know. I could never decide how much Henshaw believed when he interrogated me. I guess he isn't bugging the place, or we both would've been arrested by now. Or he could be waiting. I don't know."

Julia stared out at the city. "Maybe I should just turn myself in and get it over with."

"That wouldn't do me a whole lot of good. And I don't think that would end it for you, either."

"But it isn't—" Julia groped for the words, and couldn't find them.

"No, it isn't."

They both became more withdrawn with the specter of the FBI stalking them. When they jogged they would glance over their shoulders and wonder which of their fellow masochists was watching them. At home, at night, watching television and drinking too much beer, they would think of something they wanted to say and then stop short, uncertain, afraid. When they made love they did it silently, mechanically. And at the height of their limited passion Alan would think about Stone, and Julia would think about Alan thinking about Stone.

But if the present was illusory, thinking about the

future was intolerable. "You should go back to Boston," Julia said in the park one morning. The air was cool and soft, and she felt strong enough for once to consider Alan's plight in addition to her own.

"My mother said when I left that I wouldn't come back."

"You haven't always gone along with what your mother says."

"That's true. Of course, every time I talk to her now she tells me to come back. Says I'm in over my head. Says the worst is yet to come."

"Do you believe her?"

"I don't think about it. She wants me to come back and help her with her clients. I guess my notoriety rubbed off on her, and business is booming. Her land-lords aren't too happy, but they've never been happy with her. She's moving the whole operation into more suitable quarters."

"Then if you went back, you'd have a job too. Your money isn't going to last forever out here."

"Nothing lasts forever."

The present felt like it might last forever, though. If it did, at least it was better than the past for Julia. Better illusion than horror. Better the memory of horror than the experience of it. So, when she could, she put on her happiest expression and made their life as tolerable as she could. She didn't really want him to go back to Boston.

Alan went for his driving test in their rented car. The prospect of it took their minds off other things. "I haven't taken a test in years. What if I fail?"

"So what? You take it again."

"But I've never failed a test. What will that do to my self-esteem?"

"You can't fail. You've driven all over Los Angeles. You're a good driver—well, a fairly good driver."

"One missed turn signal and it could be all over,

though. Machines and I don't get along. The car is liable to turn on me, you know, plow into a pedestrian. What if the examiner just had a fight with his wife?"

"Then I'll give him my sweetest smile and he'll do anything I say. Now come on."

The examiner turned out to be a woman, squat and nasty. She took an immediate dislike to Julia's trim good looks, and Alan's sweetest smile provoked nothing more than a snarled order to start the vehicle.

She put him through his paces, barking commands in a hoarse drill sergeant's voice. "Next left! Proceed to the intersection! Go halfway up the hill and turn the vehicle around! Next right! Park behind the red Mustang! Secure the vehicle!"—all the time making inscrutable notes on her clipboard. When the car was safely parked she flipped her clip-on sunglasses up and trained her gimlet eyes on Alan's sweating face. "You pass," she said grudgingly, like an atheist who has just witnessed a miracle.

Alan sighed with relief and swallowed an impulse to ask the creature for a date.

Instead he celebrated as he had always intended to celebrate: by driving to Dodger Stadium to see a night game. "Do you think she had Prussian ancestors?" he asked Julia as he maneuvered expertly into a parking space.

"Maybe she just had a fight with her husband."

"If I were married to her I'd goose-step into a locked garage and breathe exhaust fumes for an hour or two. Do you think my turns were okay? A couple of them were a bit ragged, I thought."

"Nonsense, they were better than I could do."

They got out of the car and headed for the Stadium. "Really? I think I might learn how to do a tuneup. They say you can save a lot of money if you do routine maintenance yourself. Anyway, I'll change my own oil."

"You'll have to buy a car first."

"Details, details."

Alan felt a bit light-headed, to say the least. He

thought he had proved something by finally driving to the ball park, although he wasn't exactly sure what. He explained to Julia about his previous attempt to see a game there.

"I guess it means you're growing up," she said.

"What an awful thought. Do they serve beer here, you think?"

Watching a game at a ball park other than Fenway was an unsettling experience, like eating food that had been dyed blue—Dodger blue. Not unenjoyable, but certainly not what he was used to. As beer followed beer, however, the differences seemed to matter less and less.

"You think our buddies from the FBI are enjoying themselves?" he asked Julia. "Maybe we should buy them a beer."

"I'm sure that's against regulations."

"Poor guys. But heck, they're getting paid to go to the ball game. Nobody ever paid me to go to the ball game."

"Maybe they're just waiting in the parking lot."

"Well, that would be stupid. Stone could be anywhere, even here."

"Could you please be a little quieter, Alan?"

"Even here," he whispered and grinned. The crowd leaped politely to its feet as a Dodger hit a double. Alan cheered with them and then got another beer. "Remember that night at Fenway?" he asked, gulping it down. "I bet I never should've told you I loved you. Prob'ly scared you to death. Prob'ly should've said: 'I like you *enormously*' or 'You're a good egg' or 'Can I take you home to meet Mother?' You'd like my mother. She's a good egg."

"I didn't really mind it," Julia said.

"Well, that's good. I never did that before, and I'd hate for it to have had, uh, untoward consequences. I'd hate to think there was a correlation between that and"— he waved his hand vaguely—"certain other events that shall remain nameless."

"Please try to be quiet, Alan."

"My lips are sealed." Another Dodger doubled, and

Alan let out a roar of appreciation. "Want another beer, Julia?"

"I don't think so."

The Dodgers won easily, antiseptically. Alan bought a cap at a souvenir stand on the way out. "I have changed allegiance," he announced proudly. "I bet these guys never lose. Who wants to be a loser?" Julia steered him toward the parking lot. He looked at the car silently for a while, swaying slightly. "The ultimate challenge," he said finally. "*Anyone* can drive sober. A *monkey* can drive sober. A raving *lunatic* can drive—"

"Maybe I'd better drive," Julia said.

"Maybe you'd better."

Alan leaned back against the headrest, the baseball cap low over his eyes. He was humming "California Dreamin'." "Life could be worse, Julia." he said after a while.

"Could be worse," she repeated, and she felt herself starting to believe it. Maybe they would both get jobs and move into someplace, well, homier. The FBI would get bored and go away. They would buy a car and Alan could change the oil. They could get season's tickets to the Dodgers. In the off season they would go to the opera—there had to be some around somewhere. She would teach him to surf. Maybe they would even get a cat—or was that carrying the fantasy too far? They would live in a world of sunshine and sparkle. They would make such good magic that no evil could enter their lives. In California anything was possible. She started to sing softly along with Alan:

All the leaves are brown and the sky is gray
I've been for a walk on a winter's day
I'd be safe and warm if I was in L.A.
California dreamin', on such a winter's day.

"They don't write 'em like that anymore," Alan mumbled and fell asleep.

* * *

She managed to wake Alan up enough to get him out of the car and into the apartment. He grinned dopily all the while and passed out again as soon as he reached the bed. He lay there, eyes closed, dopey grin meta-morphosed into seraphic smile, totally helpless. She struggled to get his shoes and socks off. Damn black wingtips. They would have to go if he were to become a Californian.

This is a change, she thought. *For once I'm the one in charge, doing the helping.* And then she realized something that made her drop the shoes and stare at Alan as he snored softly on the bed. It is difficult to love someone when all he does is go around saving your life. Your feelings for him get all mixed up with gratitude and relief and dependence and other messy emotions. When he's dead drunk and you have to put him to bed, things become more equal, and the feelings become clearer.

She stretched out beside him and lay her head on his chest. "I love you, Alan," she whispered. "I never said it before because I guess I didn't realize it. We'll be all right, as long as we're together."

Alan's snores became louder. Julia smiled and took off his baseball cap. "You're a good egg," she said and kissed him on the forehead.

Chapter 19

When Julia awoke Alan was already up, moving busily in the living room. "Morning," she called out sleepily

"Good morning," he replied. He came into the bedroom and set a suitcase down next to her. "Up and at 'em, we're taking a trip"

"A trip?" she repeated groggily.

"To New York City."

She sat up and looked at the suitcase, trying not to understand. He tossed a newspaper on top of it. She stared at the headline:

NEW YORK CITY MAYOR'S SON KIDNAPPED
LINK TO HODKINS SLAYING FEARED

"Oh, no, Alan," she whispered.

"It was just a matter of time. The time has come. Hurry up."

She laid her head on her knees. "Please, Alan, the police'll—"

"The police haven't got a prayer. If we get a flight right away we can be there tonight. It might not be too late."

She frantically tried to think of an argument that might move him, but it was useless. All that came into her mind was that stupid song: *I'd be safe and warm, if I was in L.A. . . . .* She knew the depth of his obsession by now. Didn't he know the depth of hers? She began to cry, shaking her head slowly from side to side. "I can't go," she sobbed. "I can't go."

"You have to go."

She picked up the newspaper and flung it across the room. "Don't you see? Don't you see that if I go it'll start all over again? His power is too strong, Alan. You've felt it. You know."

"But you broke free of it before—when you left him in that hotel room."

She stared at him, then looked down at her own naked body. How could so much unhappiness find room to hide in such a small thing? "You're a lousy psychic," she said softly. "Getting worse all the time. I didn't leave, Alan. He threw me out. The police were looking for a man and a woman. After he killed Heather, that was us.

He decided he'd be safer without me. He said I was lucky he didn't feel like killing me the way he'd killed Heather. I begged him to let me stay. If he'd let me, I'd be in New York with him now. I would've done the kidnapping for him, just like last time. If you take me there I'd go back to him, if I could find him—if he'd have me. You still think I should go?"

Alan picked up the newspaper and placed it in the wastebasket. "All the more reason," he said. "You think you could possibly be happy here with that hanging over you?"

·   "I don't think I have any alternative—that you'd approve of, anyway."

"Help me kill him. That's the only thing that makes any sense."

"You're not going to kill him, Alan. I *know* him. Do you think it was an accident that Cindy got in your line of fire, that you couldn't figure out how to reload the rifle? Do you think he's just been lucky to avoid being captured when every law enforcement agency in the country is looking for him?"

"I know he's stupid enough that Heather could kidnap the wrong kid and he didn't realize it. I know he's fallible enough to let me screw up his goddamn ritual sacrifice, and then not be able to find Joshua and me. He's got powers all right but he's not omnipotent. He can be defeated."

"What makes you think you're the one who can do it?"

"If I can get a driver's license I can do anything. Get dressed."

Alan started pulling clothes out of the dresser and sticking them in the suitcase. *Men don't know how to pack*. Julia rubbed her face on the sheets and then swung her legs onto the floor. She had to go to the bathroom. She saw Alan's Dodgers cap on the floor by her feet; she picked it up. "I think you're condemning me to death," she said as he continued to stuff the suitcase. "Maybe you have that right. But I wonder what you'll think of yourself if you end up killing me instead of Seth. Is that how you express your love?"

"If I can't kill him, you're probably better off dead. Everyone's probably better off dead. You want to visit your mother before we leave?"

"No."

"We can probably squeeze in a visit before the plane leaves. I'll drive."

"Why don't you fly the plane too?" Julia got up and went into the bathroom.

Gail's heart sank when she saw the girl with Alan. Of course she was pretty, but—*Now be careful*, she thought to herself. *Don't let jealousy get in the way of the truth*. Still, she did look, well, surly. One of those gloomy types who, no matter what you do for them, how well you treat them, always seem to be thinking: *Is that all?*

Probably she was Alan's great love, the one who had dumped him before. Probably she came back when she realized that she wasn't going to get a better man, not in this world anyway. But why was he bringing her here? *None of my business*. It didn't matter about the girl, anyway. What mattered was Alan.

And she had never seen Alan happier. Not happy so much as, well, *alive*. It was as if he had been sleepwalking before and now, suddenly, had awakened in a bright new world. Love will do that to you, Gail reflected. She could feel his energy, his confidence, clear across the day hall. She wanted desperately to speak to him, to tell him how happy she was for him, but that wouldn't do, not with the girl looking like she wanted to shoot everyone in the ward. Best to just go about her business. It would be enough that he was the way he was. Who could ask for more?

It seemed that everyone there wanted to cause her pain: the patients, the aides, the nurses, the social workers. She hated them all. Why was she subjected to such torture? What had she done to deserve this? She wanted to be like Bette Davis, to challenge them all, expose their evil, force them to let her go.

Or maybe not. Maybe like Audrey Hepburn—patient, forgiving, knowing that eventually justice would be done, eventually Gary Cooper or Gregory Peck would come to rescue her. Audrey Hepburn movies always had happy endings.

And wasn't this just like a movie? The mysterious stranger comes and befriends her and disappears as mysteriously as he came. Her role is simply to hold on, smile, take her meds, be a model patient, and when he returns . . .

"Mrs. Walker?"

"Oh my. Alan. You're back." With her daughter. Now why—Of course: the love interest. She was pretty enough, certainly. Alan glowed with confidence. Could he read her thoughts? Could he sense her confidence too?

"Julia and I are going away for a while, Mrs. Walker. But we'll be back. We just wanted to make sure you were all right."

Going away? That couldn't be. But then again, it shouldn't be too easy. The plot had to have complications: evil doctors, actresses jealous of her talent. There would be obstacles to overcome, probably even dangers. "Oh, be careful, Alan."

"I'll be careful."

He seemed to be bathed in a golden light as the sun poured in through the barred windows: a good effect by the director there. He looked like a knight in shining armor, going off to battle the dragons of modern life . . .

"Well, wish us luck then."

"Good luck, Alan. Don't be afraid of anything. I'll pray for you."

"Goodbye, Mother."

"Yes, Julia."

. . . He was Gregory Peck in *Roman Holiday*, Gary Cooper in *Love in the Afternoon*, Humphrey Bogart in *Sabrina*. He was going to save her. He was going to save us all.

Revenge. Everyone gets angry; only the person who cares seeks revenge. The desire for revenge is the most dangerous of emotions because it requires the most effort. Anger must be nurtured, its fires must be stoked; on its own it can only die out, be washed away by the current of passing time. To seek revenge a person must feed the fire, must will it to continue and to grow. And then he must burn someone with it.

How many of us, really, have carried out an act of revenge—have bided our time, waiting for the right moment, then repaid our enemy tenfold? It is not easy. Many lives are frittered away with casual anger; only a few are wasted on purposeful revenge.

The waste, of course, is in the eye of the beholder. To the person seeking revenge there is nothing more important: the scales must be balanced, the fire must be put to use. But in the abstract usually nothing is gained, except relief for the one seeking revenge. The itch must be scratched.

—Pottston Phipps
*The Twenty-four Deadliest
Sins and What to Do
about Them*

Chapter 20

After midnight in New York City: the cab streaked past whores in doorways, drunks in the gutter, joggers wearing earphones and dayglo shorts, cans of Mace bulging in their pockets. Steam rose from manhole covers like smoke out of the pits of hell; sirens wailed in the distance like the souls of the damned. The cabbie was stoned. He played the disco version of "Night on Bald Mountain" over and over on his tape deck and mumbled to himself about killing the fucking bitch. Alan and Julia sat rigidly in the back seat, trying to think of a suitable prayer to say.

Alan relaxed when they got into the hotel room. But even there Julia sat on the bed and stared at the door, as if at any second a pack of demons would tear through it and possess her.

"Can you feel it?" she asked. "If I can feel it, it must be overpowering for you."

"It's just the city," he murmured.

"You know it's not," she replied, "you know it's not."

In the darkness they lay next to each other, not touching, jet-weary but unable to sleep, listening to the taxi horns and bus brakes, silently awaiting daylight. *If this is hell*, Alan thought, *then I'm in the right place. Let it begin.*

It began with a knock on the door. Alan groggily looked at his watch—ten o'clock—and stumbled out of bed. "Don't," Julia whispered, clutching his arm. He shrugged and broke away from her.

"Who is it?" he called out.

"FBI, Mr. Simpson. Please open up."

He pulled on his pants and opened the door a crack, leaving it chained. Two badges flashed at him. "Henshaw send you?"

"He'd like to see you, sir. As soon as possible."

"Gimme a few minutes. I'd invite you in, but—"

"We understand, sir."

Alan closed the door and went to take a shower. When he came out of the bathroom Julia was still in bed, blanket wrapped tightly around her. "Wanna tag along?" he asked her as he got dressed.

"Please don't make me," she said.

"You'll have to get up sometime."

"Please don't leave."

"I'll be back. You'll be safe. Everything'll be fine."

She didn't reply. When he was ready to go, he kissed her forehead. She didn't respond. He sighed and walked out of the room.

The two FBI men were handsome, bland, forgettable. They looked at home in the hotel corridor. "We meet at last," Alan said.

"Yes, sir. If you'd come with us, please."

They drove him downtown in a bland gray Ford. Alan tried a couple of surefire conversation openers, but nothing worked. If they were the guys who were trailing him in L.A., they must have been heartily sick of him by now, he realized. Eventually he just sat back and watched the drizzle.

They brought him through the rear entrance into a bland gray office building, up twenty flights to a floor that was aswirl with activity: teletypes clacking, phones ringing, smartly dressed people striding purposefully here and there carrying manila folders and computer print-outs. A colored map of New York City dominated one wall. *All a waste,* Alan thought. He was ushered into Henshaw's office.

Henshaw looked harried. His silk tie was already loosened, his California tan seemed pasty in the fluorescent light, the age lines that had appeared distinguished out West were now ruts of worry and uncertainty. Or maybe that was just what Alan wanted to believe.

"I'm not surprised you've joined us here in New York, Alan," Henshaw said in quick, clipped tones that really didn't reinforce Alan's first impression. "The question is why."

"I'm here to help."

"Just like before? Or were you planning to contact the authorities this time around?"

"It was the first thing on my agenda. Your men showed up before I had a chance to demonstrate what a good soldier I've become."

"Oh, I'm sure." Henshaw leaned back in his chair;

his cold gray eyes stared at Alan. Alan found his attitude totally opaque. He could believe everything Alan said, he could believe nothing. "You had no inkling of this happening beforehand?" Henshaw asked.

"Not a clue. My psychic powers seemed to be on vacation out in California."

"Are they working now that you're close to home again?"

"Can't tell. Have any evidence I can handle?"

"I'm afraid not. The kid was jogging through Central Park after school with a friend. They split up when they reached the West Side; the friend headed uptown, Bobby said he was going back to catch the subway at Columbus Circle. That's the last anyone saw of him. Any ideas?"

Alan shrugged. "Show me where he was last seen. Maybe something'll come to me."

Henshaw was silent, appraising Alan. *You've got nothing to lose*, Alan thought. *You're getting nowhere on your own.* Henshaw leaned forward; his gray eyes seemed to want to overpower Alan. Alan was not impressed; he had psychic Indian-wrestled with the best. "Don't mess with us, Simpson," Henshaw said quietly. "I don't like that rifle business out in Los Angeles. I don't have to be psychic to figure out that you're still itching to settle this yourself. Forget it, or so help me you'll be so deep in shit you won't be able to move. Clear?"

"I just want to help," Alan said, oozing sincerity.

Henshaw looked unconvinced. "You know, if the people in Boston didn't have such good things to say about you, you'd probably be under arrest right now."

"I'm really a wonderful person."

Henshaw stared at him. "I'll get a car and driver," he said finally. "There won't be much to see."

It was raining harder. Alan sat in the back seat with Henshaw while the driver leaned on the horn and fought his way uptown. Alan felt cramped and uncomfortable, but his mood was good. Henshaw's welcome could have been a lot worse. Once they were on their way, Henshaw began to look positively affable. Or was that just what Alan wanted to believe?

"We took a lot of heat for buying your story," Henshaw remarked.

"You didn't have much choice. It was the only way the thing made sense."

"As if any of this makes sense."

"Not to you, maybe." As if it made sense to Alan. *We know more but we do not understand more.* Alan looked out at the rain. "I didn't bring a raincoat," he murmured. "I forgot the weather was different here."

The car pulled to a stop on Central Park West, by the American Museum of Natural History. School buses were lined up in front of it; a lonely hot dog vendor was getting soaked.

"They split up here," Henshaw said. "Columbus Circle is about twenty blocks south. The kid probably jogged along this sidewalk. Could've been grabbed as he ran, or it could've happened somewhere else entirely. Hard to believe anyone could've kidnapped him *here* without being spotted, but stranger things have happened."

Alan got out and stood on the cobblestoned sidewalk. Cars swished by on the street. A bearded jogger passed him, black hair plastered to his face, looking as if he were about to expire. Alan recalled standing on the corner of Clarendon and Newbury, eons ago, waiting for something to happen. What aria had he hummed to make it start?

Somebody began to sing "Batti, Batti, O Bel Masetto." *No, that wasn't it.* But wait a minute; the singing was inside his head. It was all inside his head. He closed his eyes. The rain was gone, and the sweat felt good on his face. He thought: *Why stop jogging now?* No reason on earth. He opened his eyes, and started to run.

Light-years behind him Henshaw was shouting something. He paid no attention; that was somebody else's problem. *Flick, flick, flick* over the cobblestones, his Adidas chewing up the distance, arms and legs swinging through the sunlight in perfect harmony. *I'm Alberto Salazar, making his final kick. And there's the finish line, up ahead. Ladies and gentlemen, this could be a new world's record* . . .

He veered into the park at top speed, and abruptly everything changed. The day was dark, the pathway deserted. To his left a playground stood empty in the rain; the twisted bars of the jungle gym were like the passages of time waiting to be sorted out in his mind. He took a step; his black wingtips squished with water. Damn.

He was breathing hard, and it was not only from the sudden exertion. This was a new one. This was not just following someone through the past, this was . . . The thought faded as a new one crowded in and demanded attention: Julia. Still in bed back at the hotel, wearing only a T-shirt and panties, the nipples of her breasts erect under the taut white fabric, the darkness of her crotch showing through the pink silk: Julia, waiting for him, moaning for him. Eyes glazed with passion, legs spread, hands reaching down to massage the moist warmth . . .

Jesus God, what was going on now? He was as aroused as he had ever been in his life. His erection felt as if it were going to explode. He took a few more steps, past the playground, over a bridge, her image still clouding his mind. Was that rain on his chin, or was he drooling? Why was he here and not in bed with her, on top of her, inside her?

And there she was.

No.

Coming out of the shadows of an intersecting path, abruptly stumbling so that he crashed into her and they fell in a heap on the ground. *No, not Julia, but—* Her skin was warm, her legs long and tanned, her golden hair fell down below her shoulders. "I think I've twisted something. Can you help me?" He put his arm around her waist and they got up from the pavement. She leaned against him; her thigh rubbed his. She smelled of bedrooms and secret pleasures. Her hand moved over his side. "You're cute," she whispered. He tried to say something, but his tongue wasn't functioning, only one part of him was functioning, so hard now it was almost painful. "If we go into those bushes there, no one will see." Her hand moved lower. *Am I dreaming? This can't be real.* They moved slowly toward the bushes, green and thick and private, doorway to every pleasure, answer to every mystery. The girl gently pushed him forward—

And there was the answer, smiling at him, blue eyes devouring him. *Ho ho ho.*

Alan screamed.

Henshaw's face was in front of him. Beads of water dripped down over his cheeks, onto his raincoat. He too was breathing heavily.

"How old was the kid?" Alan asked when his heart had slowed a little.

"Thirteen."

"They grow up young around here." Alan sat on the wet ground and put his head between his knees. After he had recovered he explained what happened, and they searched the bushes. A Michelob bottle, a used condom, soggy pages from an old *Daily News*. Henshaw went off to call for a lab man.

Waste of time. Alan prowled around the area, humming "Batti, Batti," but that was a waste of time too. It was gone, and he knew it. Poor girl. Was there an endless supply of them? Poor boy. Meeting Stone was not what he had in mind when he went into those bushes. Poor everybody. Alan wandered back to the street. The FBI car was at the entrance to the park. Henshaw was inside it, giving orders over the phone.

"You want to describe the girl for us?" Henshaw asked when he hung up.

Alan did the best he could.

"You got anything more?"

"I'm surprised I could give you this much."

"No secret clues you're going to track down all by yourself?"

"When am I all by myself? Or have you called off your bloodhounds?"

Henshaw shut his notebook. He looked harried once again. *It may already be too late*. "You're a pain in the neck, Alan."

"Did the people in Boston tell you that?"

"Yeah, but I've found it out for myself too. You want a ride back to the hotel?"

"No, thanks. I've got an errand to do first. I'll be in touch."

Alan got out and walked off in the rain. Probably catch pneumonia. He didn't feel like going back to the hotel. His thoughts of Julia were all confused with his thoughts of that other girl, and he had to get them straightened out. Something about the girl still niggled at the edges of his consciousness, even though the unreality had sunk back into the nameless roiling depths of his psyche. Something that made the confusion of identities unpleasant, ominous. It was not just the embarrassing memory of the adolescent lust he had experienced. It was just that she was—

Doomed. He stopped in the middle of Broadway as the word tolled in his mind. The girl was doomed, and he didn't want to go back to the hotel, because Julia was so much like her, and he didn't want Julia to be doomed too.

He quickly crossed the street and tried to reason it away. It was not Julia who was doomed; he had never had that word flung at him from the future about her. But that didn't mean anything. Since he cared about her, there would be all the more reason for the frolicsome god to keep it secret. Logic didn't operate here; nothing could be proved. All he had was his fear.

Doomed. He thought of Heather, rotting in the woods, waiting for lovers or picnickers to stumble onto her. She had taken a wrong turn somewhere and had paid for it.

No, not really. Julia had just been waitressing, and the guy sat down at one of her tables. And Alan himself had just dropped into the middle of it all, trying to do a favor for a friend. Life—and death—come looking for you; you don't have to seek them out. Which was why he and Julia might just as well be in New York City as in L.A. If they too were doomed, why not go down fighting?

Alan finally noticed with some amusement where his soggy shoes were taking him: Mecca. Gleaming through the fountain spray, tall and majestic, the Metropolitan Opera. The interior was a bit too New York-grandiose for Alan's taste, with its crystal chandeliers and red velvet wall coverings and gold drinking fountains, but one could forgive a lot for opera. It was just about the only reason Alan had ever come to New York, till now. He studied the poster outside the huge glass façade. *Don Giovanni* tonight. That seemed an apt choice. *There are more things to be done*, he thought. But he didn't know what they were, and he didn't know how to do them. He went into the box office and bought a pair of tickets.

When he came out the rain had stopped, and he felt somewhat better. He wandered through the grounds of Lincoln Center and finally sat down in a little courtyard in front of the Vivian Beaumont Theatre. The only other person occupying one of the puddle-soaked benches was a kerchiefed black woman reading *The Metamorphosis*. *I wonder what you're thinking*, he thought.

Nothing.

Still, his gift had made a comeback of sorts. And it seemed to be stronger than ever. He couldn't recall having experienced that total identification with another person before, that utter loss of conventional reality. Was it being back East? the thrill of the chase? getting in shape for a rematch? Who could know? It was hardly worth thinking about. Too much introspection can be a disease, Mr. Phipps had written. Alan Thompson had tried to follow his advice; perhaps Alan Simpson should do the same thing.

But he couldn't stop thinking, really, any more than he could avoid using his gift, if the god of psi decided he needed a dose of the paranormal. Here he was, after all, thinking about his thinking—and that was an example of thinking about thinking about thinking. Jesus, time to go dry off.

One last thought, though: Would Julia still be there when he got back to the hotel?

Chapter 21

Julia listened to Alan's story in silence. She was not surprised by it. She supposed she would not be surprised by anything that happened now. Alan became quite agitated, though, when he talked about the girl and his sense that she was doomed. "I suppose I shouldn't try to understand," he said, pacing back and forth by the window. "I suppose it's not the kind of thing that it's possible to understand. By why you and she and the others would drop everything and follow him, like he was the Pied Piper or something—" He gestured futilely, waving the sentence away.

Not worth finishing because he knows the answer, Julia thought, *even if he can't put it into words.* Even in his little apartment he had learned enough about life to understand. We are all looking for a way out: her mother had found hers; Stone was Julia's. Perhaps Alan wasn't looking, but that was only because he hadn't lived enough yet.

In the good moments when she was with Seth she had felt as if she could conquer death itself; certainly the grungy everyday problems of living became transformed into something special, because they had a purpose. When he made love to her, she didn't care that he seemed unaware of her existence as he communed with his own pleasure somewhere far beyond her—because his being out there made the act more exciting. Perhaps someday she could get there too. "When you are with me," he had told her that first day, "the Universe will be transformed." And, for at least some of the time, he had been right.

With Alan it was different. Alan, she knew, would have to slog through life day by day, even with his gift, even with all his wonderful qualities, and she didn't know whether she would be able to slog through it with him.

But she didn't feel like saying all that to Alan, not now. Instead she asked him mildly, "Why do you say 'drop everything,' Alan? I had nothing to drop."

He continued to pace, in silence.

Julia let Alan talk her into going to the opera. She could see he had been prepared for battle and was surprised at her quick capitulation. But Stone would not be there, and Alan would. If she could be safe anywhere in New York City, that would be the place.

"But what will I wear?" she asked.

This cracked Alan up. "Here you are supposedly fearing for your life and you want to know what to wear. Wear anything. There'll be Juilliard students there that'll make you look like you just stepped out of *Vogue*."

"You're a man. You wouldn't understand."

"Just hold on until the music starts, and then you'll forget about everything else."

She settled on her blue denim skirt and a pink blouse. They had room service bring up dinner, although Alan almost gagged at the prices. She ate hungrily: it was her first food since they had arrived in New York. Alan, for a change, only picked at his meal. It was clear that the more he thought about his experience, the more it depressed him. *I should comfort him,* she thought. But she didn't know what to say. When they left she huddled close to him. The evening was damp and raw; they let the doorman hail a cab for them, and Alan didn't even make a remark about it.

Julia looked out at all the busy, well-dressed people hurrying past the skyscrapers. "I've never been to New York before," she murmured.

"Kind of intimidating, huh? Still makes me feel like a rube."

"I've always wanted to come. Now I'm here, and I don't like it."

Alan pressed her hand. "These aren't the best of circumstances. We'll come back someday and have a ball."

Someday. She was just hoping to be alive tomorrow. She felt the tears pressing against her eyes and willed them away.

Lincoln Center reminded her a bit of the Music Center in Los Angeles. Perhaps all these arts centers looked the same, impersonal mixtures of fountains and marble and glass. Her mother had taken her to the Music Center once to see the stars arrive for the Academy Awards. *Look, there's Steve McQueen. Look, there's Raquel Welch. Look, I don't know who that is, but isn't she beautiful?* So many famous, beautiful people. Steve McQueen is dead, and Raquel Welch is washed up. But that other one, in the gold dress with the scoop neck—surely she was famous now, someone her mother could envy. There would always be someone. Had her mother ever been to New York?

They joined the flood of beautiful people heading into the opera house. Alan was right, of course: some of them weren't quite so beautiful: a bearded scarecrow in jeans and sandals, a fat girl with a blue sweatshirt that said "Roman Polanski Was Raped". . . Julia felt a little better. They made their way into the lobby and up the Grand Staircase—and up, and up. "Our seats are in the seventeenth balcony," Alan said. "It's a big place."

He exaggerated, but they *were* high up—high enough to look down on the chandeliers hanging like bursts of sunlight over the orchestra. She began to get excited, gazing at the huge stage, listening to the buzz of the crowd, the random tunings of the instruments. Alan stuffed a libretto into her hands. "Read it. You can't tell the players without a scorecard."

She glanced through it, but the plot barely made sense on the printed page. There had to be more to it than that; the scorecard wasn't the same as the game itself. "Alan, why doesn't the woman recognize Don—"

"Just listen," Alan said.

The lights dimmed, the chandeliers ascended into heaven. The conductor appeared out of nowhere, smiled, and bowed, and the music began, swirling quickly into a scene of darkness, confusion, and death. *Oh Alan, I don't need this*, she thought. And the woman and her boyfriend were swearing revenge for her father's death, and she became uneasy. Did Alan have a purpose in bringing her here, besides getting her out of the hotel room? Or were her own obsessions simply seizing on the simpleminded story? Don Giovanni, of course, was Seth, larger than life, flouting convention, eager to kill. And the hapless boyfriend was Alan, vowing vengeance against a man who could swat him away like a fly. And the woman: well, wasn't she at least attracted to the Don for a moment? And, as the opera progressed, weren't all the women attracted to him? Even the young peasant girl coming from her wedding became unsure of herself as he sang to her. By the end of the first act they were all banded together against him, but he remained beyond them—out there—untouchable. Julia shivered as the curtain went down.

The audience clapped perfunctorily as the singers made their bows. "Weak cast," Alan muttered. "Let's get something to drink." They battled their way out to the bar and had a beer. They were both silent; was he feeling the same things she was? Or was he simply waiting for her to state the obvious? Finally she had to. "Do you think, Alan, that Don Giovanni is a lot like Seth?"

Alan looked at her for a moment, then burst out

laughing. "But that would make me Don Ottavio; he's too much of a wimp, even for me. If you want to play that game, I'd see it as just the opposite: *I'm* Don Giovanni. He strikes out with every broad he chases, but in the end he doesn't back down from the fight of his life."

"I didn't get that far in the libretto."

"Stick around. The ending's a corker."

This isn't a game, she wanted to say, but as usual she kept it to herself. That was why he liked opera, she supposed. It, like baseball, was divorced from life; to make it relevant was just a game, a silly exercise in finding parallels. She knew he was wrong, but she wasn't smart enough to be able to argue with him. For her, nothing could be more important than that game.

The notion of Alan being Don Giovanni was almost ludicrous, but then—Alan knew the ending. As she watched the second act, it started to make sense. No matter how much he ranted and schemed, the Don was a loser, and the world was closing in on him. But when the Commendatore's voice came booming out of the graveyard, he didn't give in. And wasn't it just like Alan to invite the murdered man's ghost to dinner? The final battle was unequal—how can life hope to defeat death?—but it was still a battle. The stage darkened, then filled with an eery red light. The Don staggered back before the Commendatore's outstretched gray arm, invisible hands seemed to clutch at him, to drag him into hellfire, but he never changed, he never repented, and his image was a more powerful presence at the end than the rest of the cast, standing out there singing about how happy they were that he was dead.

But who was he?

"The story falls apart in the second act," Alan said as they filed out. "They've got nothing left to do until the Commendatore shows up."

"Please don't analyze it, Alan."

Alan smiled. "You're absolutely right. Mozart should be sung, not analyzed."

Julia looked around her, at the jewels and tuxedoes

and occasional sweatshirts. Was it a game for all of them? *A weak cast, the story falls apart.* Maybe she took everything too seriously. She couldn't help it; this *was* serious. "Do you think we'll know when Seth kills the boy?" she asked. Alan.

His smile faded. "I don't know. I wouldn't be surprised. Let's see if we can get a taxi."

They walked across the plaza toward the street. It was still cold and misty; autumn was around the corner.

"I didn't know you were an opera fan," Alan said, suddenly slowing down.

Julia looked at him. His eyes were on a burly man in a raincoat leaning against a placard for *Rigoletto*.

"I'm not," the man said. "Just passing by."

The man nodded to her, and she recognized him with a shudder. Alan's friend the detective, who had gazed at her across Alan's apartment and had known she was guilty. His gaze was just as knowing now.

"Where're you headed?" Alan asked.

"Home. I'd like you to come."

"Sorry. I've got some business here."

The detective shifted uncomfortably. Kelliher, that was the name. "Can we go someplace and talk?"

"How'd you find me?" Alan asked.

"Your mother."

Alan mulled that over, then smiled and shrugged. "Sure. Let's talk."

They walked in silence until they found a Burger King. Inside, a policeman slouched against a wastebasket and gazed out onto Broadway. Four black teenagers were sitting at a table, talking loudly and unintelligibly. A red-eyed derelict stared into his coffee cup.

Alan had regained his appetite. He bought two cheeseburgers and a Coke; Kelliher had a cup of coffee. Julia didn't want anything; the detective made her too nervous to even think of food. They sat down at a corner table, and Alan attacked his first cheeseburger.

"Your mother wants you to come home," Kelliher said. "She called me up in a panic this afternoon. Said you were in grave danger, told me where you'd be, begged me to come and bring you back. She sounded very scared, Alan."

"What kind of grave danger?" Alan asked.

"She didn't say. She just said you were going too far, and it was almost too late."

Alan sipped his Coke. "Clichés. She doesn't know anything, she's just scared."

"She knew where I'd find you."

"But that isn't where the danger is, obviously."

"Alan, she cares about you. I care about you. We don't want to see you hurt."

"I care about me too. I'm very solicitous of myself."

"Then what are you doing going all over the country tracking a mad killer?" Kelliher glanced at Julia, then sighed and crumpled his napkin. "I know you when you get like this, Alan, with the flip answers and the obstinate attitude. You're so stubborn a bulldozer wouldn't move you. Your mother figured you'd be like that. So she made me promise to stay here with you. I don't want to have to do that, Alan. I've got my own life to lead, I've got my own crimes to solve. But, Jesus, it seems like someone's gotta look after you."

"Join the crowd, Jim. I've got the FBI tailing me already. I'm sure if Seth Stone comes at me with a butcher's knife they'll know what to do."

Kelliher looked around. Nobody in a business suit and sunglasses. Did he think Alan was lying? "Maybe they will," Kelliher said. "But you're still gonna need all the help you can get."

Alan started on his second cheeseburger. "Go back to Boston, Jim," he said quietly between bites. "Say hi to Connie and the kids, have a piece of blueberry pie for me. I'm grateful that you've come after me like this, but I'm not going back, and you can't help me. How's that for stubbornness?"

"Us Irish cops can be pretty stubborn too," Kelliher replied. "Especially when we make a promise to a guy's mother."

They stared at each other stubbornly, then Alan stood up and walked quickly out of the restaurant. Julia hurried to catch up with him; Kelliher was not far behind, but he made no effort to join them. After a minute Alan slowed down a bit. "No sense giving him a heart attack," he muttered. He didn't look back.

"He thinks it's my fault," Julia said, out of breath. "He thinks I made you come to New York."

"What he thinks won't do you or me any harm."

"I don't think you should be here either."

"Yeah, but you're no bulldozer. You're hardly even a pickup truck." Alan sped up again as the hotel came into view on the next block. Julia let him go on ahead. Might as well join the crowd following him. Alan was the Pied Piper too, just as Seth was, just as they were both Don Giovanni. No wonder she was confused.

Alan stood staring out the window. Julia lay on the bed, vague, drowsy memories flitting through her mind, until one stopped and said: *Think about me*. Stephen Patterson. The boy who gave her her first real kiss. He wanted to be called Steve but everyone called him Stevie, because he was small and shy and his glasses were always slipping down over his nose. But he was kind of cute—at least to Julia, in the sixth grade. So when he asked her, voice shaking, to go to see a movie with him, she had said okay, even though she had already seen the thing with her mother (*what in the world was it?*). Afterward they went to a Burger King (*ah, there was the connection*) and spent forever sipping their Cokes, saying nothing. He walked her home through the warm summer night, and she thought idly about inviting him inside—she knew her mother wouldn't be there—to do the kinds of things some girls she knew claimed they were already doing. But she was still a good girl, and Stevie Patterson just wasn't the kind of boy you thought of in that way. They stopped at her front door, and she knew what was coming. She wasn't particularly excited, but it had to come sooner or later, so why not now? He put his hands on her arms very firmly and pulled her toward him. She didn't resist. Up close she could see the blond hairs of his not-quite mustache, the blackheads on his chin. She shut her eyes and puckered. His lips were dry and warm and not unpleasant. She was just beginning to respond when he pushed her gently back, and it was over.

"Thank you for a lovely evening," she said. *(What was that movie?)*

"Thank *you*," he said. And then he gazed at her for a moment longer and whispered, "I would die for you."

Or did he? An instant later he had disappeared into the night, a shadow, a memory. She went inside and waited for her mother to come home, drunker than usual, raging at the injustice of life. Julia was not interested.

She never found out the truth. It's not something you can ask a person about. Stevie never asked her for a date again. Maybe it was just her imagination and he really didn't care for her. Or maybe he had said it and was too embarrassed by what he had done to face her again. His family moved away the next spring, and that was the last she saw of him, except in her dreams.

I would die for you. She had felt that way about Seth, a lot of the time; had felt that totality of love and trust, that letting go of will and self. He would sit, lotuslike, on the beach, eyes closed, and she would want nothing more than to be a part of the darkness behind his eyes, part of his power, his ferocity. She had never felt as alive as when she touched his solid flesh and realized that there were mysteries and truths beyond Hollywood and craziness, that this man saw things she could never hope to understand.

But what had Stevie Patterson seen in her? If she could understand that, then perhaps life would not be so terribly frightening; perhaps Stone would lose his hold on her. But Stevie had probably died of a drug overdose, or become a Scientologist; or (more likely) he was engaged to a nice girl from Encino and wouldn't remember Julia, or that evening, or that quickly whispered sentence.

"Come to bed, Alan," she murmured. "You won't discover anything looking out the window."

"I wish I could see him," Alan said. "I hope he's not going to wait outside in the rain all night."

"Don't be silly."

"Maybe we should invite everyone up here, have a party."

"Please come to bed."

He came, finally, and lay next to her, cold and tense. She caressed him for a while until she felt him relax. "Would you die for me?" she whispered.

He chuckled. "I've done my best."

She smiled and moved on top of him. "Much better to live," she said. She kissed him, and guided him inside her.

"Much better," he agreed.

When they were finished she nestled in his arms and tried not to think about tomorrow. "*The Return of the Pink Panther*," she said suddenly.

"Wha'?" Alan murmured, half asleep.

"A movie I saw once."

"I saw it too. God, we've got a lot in common."

He fell back to sleep immediately. Julia fell asleep too, and in her dreams Stevie Patterson's words gave way to the ominous music of the last scene of *Don Giovanni*, and his dim streetlit face disappeared in the red glow of hellfire, leaping forth to claim the Don as its own.

Chapter 22

Alan's dreams started with Inspector Clouseau, bumbling victoriously where Henshaw and all the rest failed. "The kidnaper, he is here," he said with a twitch of his mustache, and pointed—where? It was too dark. Cats' eyes glowed out of the darkness at Alan, and he turned away . . .

. . . to see his mother, her hands covered with blood, reaching out to him, begging him to stop. He ran, but he could hear Kelliher behind him, stalking him through the night, determined to make him fail. He turned to face Kelliher finally, to have it out with his friend, and it was his father who was following him.

Alan was angry—at his father, at the dream. He was scared too, because in dreams you have even less control than you have in real life.

"I've been trying to catch up with you for a long time, son," his father said. He never called Alan "son."

"Bullshit," Alan replied.

"I know how you must feel about me, but believe me I left for everyone's good."

"I don't feel anything about you. Go away. Get out of my dream."

"Of course you feel something, son. I abandoned you, left you to your crazy mother—"

"She's not crazy."

"—took away your chance for all the good times a growing boy has with his father. Remember that Red Sox game I took you to—"

"*They lost!*" Alan shouted. This was intolerable.

"Well, of course they lost, that's not the point. Remember how good a time we had, taking the rickety old trolley down Huntington Avenue, and buying peanuts in Kenmore Square and sitting in the rightfield grandstand—everyone banging their seat to try and get a rally going—"

"It didn't work! Malzone struck out!"

"—and I bought you a badge with Dick Stuart's picture on it—"

"Good old Dr. Strangeglove," Alan said, softening. *Watch out now.*

"—and those old guys were sitting in front of us, betting on every pitch, and that evening we played catch in the backyard, and you pretended you were Dick Radatz—"

"—the Monster—"

"—striding out to the mound to whip his fastball by some helpless batter—"

"—I never had a fastball—"

"—and the shadows were lengthening, another summer was drawing to a close. In the air was the smell of grilling hamburgers, the distant tinkling music of an ice cream truck. And we felt the sudden, intense closeness that only a father and son can share—"

"*Wait a minute!*" Alan screamed. "You never talked like that in your life. You're not real."

"Of course I'm real. I've grown since I left you. We've both grown."

"We've grown apart, that's all."

"That's why I've come back."

"I don't want you back. Go away!"

His father moved a step closer, reached out his hand. Alan watched in helpless horror as the hand closed around his elbow; then he looked up and saw the smiling face appear out of the darkness, the blue eyes, the black hair—"

No!

Alan was sitting up in bed, gasping for breath. He

must have lunged forward at the end of the dream. A bit too much confusion of identity going on around here. He glanced at Julia; she was breathing evenly beside him. He got out of bed and groped his way to the bathroom.

The dream certainly hadn't done anything to relieve his feeling of uneasiness. He avoided looking at himself in the bathroom mirror. Hotel mirrors were unforgiving; they added ten years to his face. Now his old mirror in Marlborough Street.

I want to go home.

He came out of the bathroom and stood in front of the window. No sign of Kelliher, of course. *Please God, let him have enough sense to go to bed.* Taxis and trucks still raced by down below. A few lights were on in the hotel across the avenue. Perhaps in one of the darkened rooms someone was standing, staring out into the night, staring at *him*.

So many people. He tried to imagine himself knowing every person in the city, every unspoken desire, every furtive joy and evil, every pain. His mother said she had such experiences, moments when the whole world seemed to be inside her mind, all the struggling, dying souls bursting through her brain at once. When the moments passed, it was all she could do to regain her sanity. Would his mind explode from the variety, he wondered, or be crushed by the sameness?—everyone drinking Coke, taking aspirin for a headache, driving cars, watching ball games. Some people drink Tab and take Tylenol; big deal. So many people. You've got to narrow things down if you want to keep your sanity.

Not too narrow, though. He thought of Julia's mother, just sitting in the day hall day after day, turning the same thoughts over and over in her mind until they weren't thoughts anymore, they were the pulse that kept her alive.

Were his thoughts too narrow? There was just one person in the city that mattered to him. Was that what was keeping him alive? *You're out there somewhere. Let's get on with it. Let's finish it off.*

The city stared back at Alan, uncomprehending. Then he felt a searing pain in his throat. He dropped to his knees, gasping for air. His forehead pressed against the cold window. He felt the life dribble out of him, but it wasn't *his* life—*oh Christ, let's get this straight*—and then his mind ripped itself away from him: out through the window, through the cold dark city, past the Tabs and the Tylenol, to its horrifying heart, the chilling corpse, the grim, satisfied smile.

Alan groaned. His head was splitting. *I want to go home*. But he couldn't remember where home was. He forced himself to stand up and search through the darkness for his clothes. His legs could barely support him. He glanced at Julia: still asleep. Let her rest. When he was dressed and ready to leave he realized he still had his headache. He went into the bathroom and took two aspirin; he was no different from anyone else. He looked in the mirror and didn't like what he saw. He hurried out of the room.

Outside the hotel he stood at the curb and tried to flag down a taxi. None seemed interested in him. *Damn them to hell. When this is over I'm never*— Finally a guy wearing a Mets cap and chewing bubble gum pulled over. Alan hopped in. "Where to, pal?"

Alan had no idea. "Just drive for a while; I need some air; I'll tell you while we're going."

The cabbie turned and looked at Alan with a world-weary expression. He blew an enormous bubble that miraculously did not splatter all over his face. "Twenty bucks up front if you don't have a destination," he said. "This time of night you gotta have a destination. Company rule."

Alan fumbled in his wallet and produced two tens. "Just need to ride around for a while," he muttered. "Head downtown, will you?"

Shaking his head, the cabbie complied.

Where to, pal? The god of psi did not respond. As usual Alan was stumbling along behind, confused and uncertain. If his body could have flown out across the city along with his mind . . . But he wasn't Superman, he was just a poor schmuck who liked to get into trouble.

The cabbie was telling him his life story. He had a Ph.D. in English, but that didn't buy any groceries. Best he could find for a job was teaching at a Catholic girls' school in Queens, which allowed him to buy milk and bread. He hacked a couple of nights a week so he could afford hamburger once in a while. Sure it was dangerous, but everything in the city was dangerous at night, and hacking paid better than pumping gas. Actually, what he really wanted to do was become a writer. He'd written a few stories that he'd sent off to *The New Yorker*, but they—

"Turn right," Alan interrupted softly. "Now left."

He didn't know where he was—somewhere on the West Side, maybe. He didn't want to know. He had picked up a fragile scent—a blood scent—somewhere in his psyche, and reality might simply overpower it. He was getting close; he couldn't lose it now.

They stopped at a light, and Alan wondered if he should get out and run, sucking in the night air, footsteps echoing along the deserted sidewalk. No, this morning was enough exercise. His damn body wasn't ready yet: he'd keel over before he got there.

Two blocks later it hit him: the smell of death. Too close. He leaned forward and groaned, fighting off a wave of nausea.

"You okay, pal?" the cabbie asked.

"Drive," Alan gasped.

"I'm driving."

His heart was racing, a cold film of sweat covered him. Damn it, how much more could he— *"Right!"* he screamed, and the cabbie swung to the right.

"Jesus Christ, look at that," the cabbie said. Alan raised his head and took a look at reality. A dozen police cars and ambulances littered the street, their blue and red lights flickering over the gathering crowd, giving the onlookers the jerky movements of a silent film.

"This is my stop," Alan said and staggered out of the taxi.

Everyone's attention was focused on a dingy gray apartment building. Its companions on either side were boarded up and ready for the wrecker's ball, and it looked as if it would soon join them. Across the street was an entrance to the Lincoln Tunnel, still busy despite the godforsaken hour.

Alan made his way through the crowd until he reached a burly black policeman. He hesitated for a moment, then tried to walk nonchalantly past him. "That's far enough, buddy," the cop said.

"But I live here."

"Could I see some identification, please?"

"I know Agent Henshaw will want to see me. He's in charge of the investigation. If you could send someone to tell him I'm here—"

"Why don't you just stand back, okay, buddy?"

Alan stood back, but being outside was intolerable, he had to get it over with. "Henshaw!" he shouted desperately. "Henshaw! Lemme in!"

"Can it, fella, you'll wake up the neighborhood."

"There is no fucking neighborhood. *Henshaw!*"

Suddenly someone grabbed his arm from behind. Alan looked back and recognized one of his bland escorts of the morning, still immaculate in a three-piece suit. With his free hand the man held up his badge for the policeman. "FBI," he said. "I'd like to take this man inside."

"Go right ahead, sir."

There was another policeman at the entrance to the building. The badge did its trick on him too. They walked into the vestibule. Doors were open, people were being questioned. A dog was barking angrily. They started up the stairs and had to retreat as two pairs of medical technicians came down, each bearing a stretcher with a sheet-covered body. The technicians did not look to be in any hurry.

"You can let go of my arm now," Alan said to the agent.

"Of course."

The stairway was painted a dismal shade of turquoise. It stank of stale urine. Someone had printed "Blowjobs, one flight up" in pencil on the wall. Alan stopped on the third floor. At the end of a short hallway Henshaw was talking to a fat, white-haired policeman. He didn't look surprised when he noticed Alan. "We beat you to it," he said.

"But you weren't in time either." Alan walked down the hallway. The two men were standing by an open doorway. Alan looked inside.

The apartment was floodlit. Alan hadn't seen a place this bright since—He suppressed the memory. The details of the scene leaped out at him in the intense light: the dirty blue paint peeling from the walls, the *New York Post* lying next to an overturned Styrofoam cup on a metal TV table, a man with forceps patiently picking through a raunchy horsehair sofa, another man carefully brushing a dark powder onto a dirty glass.

The taped outlines on the floor.

The blood spattered everywhere.

Someone was taking pictures.

"Your description of the girl was quite accurate," Henshaw said.

"How did he do it?" Alan asked.

"Their throats were slit."

"Any idea where—"

"You tell me, you tell me. We got a report from a neighbor thought she heard a scream. Couldn't've missed him by more than ten, fifteen minutes. We'll get him."

"No you won't. Can I go inside?"

Henshaw nodded. "Stay away from the taped areas. Don't touch anything."

He stepped into the room. The men looked at him, then continued about their business. The room smelled of sweat and sour milk. His stomach lurched with disgust. The lights were hot. There was an oddly familiar sound. He stood still until he could place it: the toilet was running. He went into the bathroom and looked at it. The seat was cracked, the inside of the bowl was orange with rust. He wanted to jiggle the handle, but he wasn't supposed to touch anything. Life is like a running toilet, he thought Phippsishly, but he didn't feel like expanding on the simile. He looked at the shelf above the toilet: Crest, Ban, tweezers, Tylenol (oh, one of *those* people), Irish Spring, Band-Aids. The window was open. He looked out: people entering the Lincoln Tunnel could watch you taking a leak, if they cared to. He sighed and walked out of the bathroom. "Have you got the knife?" he asked Henshaw.

Henshaw motioned to one of the men, who opened a satchel and gingerly took out a sealed plastic bag. He cut it open and held it out to Alan.

It was heavy in Alan's hands. There were traces of dried blood on the blade, remnants of the fingerprint powder on the handle. Alan thought of the schoolbook that had brought him into this whole business. What had it been called? *Our Friendly Neighbors? Our Neighborly Friends?* He remembered the smiling faces on the cover: black, brown, red, white . . .

We're counting on you, Alan. Save us from Stone.

Don't be absurd. He's just a guy. He did what he said he was going to do, and the world hasn't come to an end.

Then how come you're so scared?

Purely a rational fear. He's after me.

Rational, bullshit.

I'm not going to talk to you if you're going to be vulgar.

The knife, unfortunately, had nothing to say to him. He handed it back to the agent, who put it in the bag and resealed it.

Henshaw looked at Alan inquiringly.

"Nothing."

"You're sure?"

Alan suddenly felt like smashing the floodlights and casting everyone into eternal darkness. Then he felt like crying. He was a baby, with a baby's powerlessness.

Once the bouncing ball has landed, the number is determined forever. The dead will not rise, the past will not change. Doomed. "Have you found out anything about the girl?" Alan asked.

Henshaw shook his head. "Working on it."

Alan closed his eyes. "I think I've gotta go now."

"Take him back to the hotel, Pete," Henshaw said to the agent. "We'll get him, Alan," he added.

"You better start praying he doesn't get you."

Henshaw chuckled humorlessly and turned away.

Alan felt somewhat better in the agent's gray car. The nausea was gone, but the fear remained.

Pete seemed determined to cheer Alan up. "Every law enforcement officer in the Northeast will be looking for this guy," he explained pleasantly. "The only way he can avoid immediate capture is by not going out in public for even a minute—and that just delays the inevitable. It's not like he has the Radical Underground or something to take care of him. He's on his own, and that makes it just about impossible for him."

"He made it across the country without too much trouble."

"His luck is about to run out."

Alan let the assertion stand; it wasn't worth arguing over. Pete dropped him off at the front entrance to the hotel. The black security guard in the lobby stared suspiciously at Alan until the elevator doors closed. The hotel was silent.

Julia was still asleep. Night was ending, and in the grayness he could see her light brown hair splayed across the pillow like a promise of sunshine. He undressed quickly and got into bed next to her. She stirred but did not waken as he put his arm around her waist and buried his face in her neck.

This hotel room was home now, and he never wanted to leave.

Chapter 23

The sound of the TV awakened Alan. The events of the night, recounted in the announcer's portentous voice, now seemed unreal, a nightmare become a TV show. Julia was sitting cross-legged on the floor in front of the bed, watching the tapes of the bodies being hauled out to the ambulances, the angry press conference with Henshaw, the tearful spokesman for the mayor, and then the photograph of Stone, taken back in his radical student days; his hair was longer but his smile was the same, his blue eyes were just as evil.

Julia turned around at the commercial and saw that Alan was awake. She came back and lay on the bed beside him. "They say you were there last night," she murmured.

"Yeah, well, I thought I'd mosey on down and see what was what. Turned out I didn't have much to offer anyone so I just moseyed on back."

"It must have been horrible. The girl was my age. Graduated from NYU last June. She was beautiful."

"Stone knows how to pick 'em. Any leads?"

Julia shook her head. "They don't know."

"Of course not."

Alan got up and went to the bathroom. The sky had cleared. The wall-to-wall carpet felt good between his toes; he was getting used to such little luxuries. In the bathroom he looked in the mirror and sighed. Better get used to that too. His fear had not disappeared overnight. He hurried back to Julia. She had switched off the TV and was lying on the bed, staring at the ceiling. A chambermaid was wheeling her equipment down the corridor and talking to someone in machine-gun Spanish.

Alan sat down. "What do you think happens now?"

"I don't know," Julia said.

"Stone talked to me about a—a detonation. Like an atom bomb."

Julia nodded. "I don't think he knew himself, really. He just had this . . . rite of passage to go through, to unleash his powers. He talked a lot about uniting everyone with them, but I don't know how he was going to do it. I don't think he knew. It was just talk, I guess. Maybe nothing will happen. Maybe he just wanted the . . . joy of killing."

"I don't believe that," Alan said. "He's unleashed the powers, and now he's sitting around somewhere, trying them out. Maybe he's searching for a victim."

Julia reached out and put her arms around Alan. "Let's stay right here," she pleaded. "Let's just watch TV, make love. There's nothing outside we want. Let's not be his victims."

"We have to leave sometime," he murmured.

"Then let's give ourselves today. If he's got the powers, we can't stop him. If he hasn't got them, what's the harm?"

The logic was irrefutable; the fear was inescapable. He embraced her, and they held each other tight against the world and all its evil.

They left the do-not-disturb sign on their door and watched TV: 10:30, "Gomer Pyle"; 11:00, "The Partridge Family"; 11:30, "Beverly Hillbillies"; 12:00, "Bewitched." The chambermaid came and went in the corridor, muttering darkly. Room service brought up lunch, and Alan ate most of Julia's. Each time they heard footsteps they would tense, but nothing happened: the hours passed, and the world went about its business, ignoring them and their little drama. "If only 'Gilligan's Island' were on, this would be a lot easier," Alan said.

Julia laughed. "It must come on sooner or later."

A news update reported no progress in the massive manhunt.

The phone rang. They both stopped breathing for a moment. Alan closed his eyes and picked up the receiver. It was Henshaw. "Just checking to see if you've got anything for me."

"No, I'm just sitting here catching up on my TV-watching. Saw your press conference. I admire your, uh, poise."

"Thanks." He sounded tired. Who wouldn't be? "If you do come up with anything . . ."

"Of course. You know me." Alan hung up. He stared at the TV screen for a while, and then said, "You know, if I had stayed in Boston I would have found out the meaning of life by now."

Julia turned down the sound on "The Brady Bunch." "What do you mean?"

"Mr. Phipps had figured it out. It was going to be the last chapter in his new book. He wouldn't tell me what it was, though. Wanted to keep me in suspense, I guess."

Julia smiled. "Do you really think he knew?"

"If anyone could figure it out, Pottston Phipps would be the man."

"Well, we can always buy the book."

"Yeah, I guess we can do that."

On TV, a woman silently battled ring around the collar. "Do you regret it all?" Julia asked. "Meeting me, coming out to California?"

Alan shrugged. "What's the use of knowing the meaning of life, if you're not really living?"

"What's the use of knowing it if you're going to get killed?"

"This philosophizing is giving me a headache," Alan said with a smile. "Let's watch the Tylenol commercial."

"I'm sorry, Alan. I don't think I ever told you I was sorry."

"Well, don't let it happen again."

No, never again, she thought, but that didn't undo

what had already been done. The choices she had made had brought her to this dreary room, fearing for her own life and that of the only person she truly loved, the only person who truly loved her. And she couldn't let it happen again because she wouldn't have the chance. "Take two," she wished the director would say. "This time, Julia honey, try to act a little more sensible."

"Hey, no reason to cry, Julia. We'll try another station. I'm sure we can find 'Gilligan's Island.'"

"Can't you ever be serious, Alan?" she sobbed.

"I tried being serious in California. It was depressing. If I were serious I'd be crying too. I don't want to cry. I don't want to watch 'The Brady Bunch' either, but it's better than crying." He went over and shut off the TV, then sat on the carpet and watched the tears pouring out of Julia's eyes. He wasn't entirely sure he was right. Maybe there was some relief to be had from tears; certainly "The Brady Bunch" offered none.

When Julia was finished she went into the bathroom and blew her nose. "Show's over," she said when she came back. "I'm sorry."

"Did it make you feel any better?"

She shrugged. "I don't know. What do we do for excitement now?"

"I thought I might go get a newspaper."

"But—"

"I won't go further than the lobby. If I don't do something I'll probably exit via the window and they'll have to scrape me off the pavement—which might be what Stone has in mind for me."

"Please be careful, Alan."

He kissed her forehead and left.

The lobby was filled with tourists and conventioneers and stacks of luggage. Alan bought a *Post* at the newsstand ("Horror in Hell's Kitchen—Psychic Slayer Baffles Cops") and threaded his way back toward the elevators. He almost tripped over Jim Kelliher, ensconced in a leather chair, a crumpled *Daily News* on his lap. "I was beginning to think you'd never come downstairs," Kelliher said.

"I had a late night."

"So I see in the paper. Guess I should've stuck around."

"We've seen enough corpses together, Jim. These two wouldn't have taught you anything new."

"Still, I'm not doing a very good job of keeping my promise to your mother."

"Dead people aren't dangerous—except in *Don Giovanni*. I can beat most of them in a fair fight."

"What are you going to do now?"

"Read the paper."

"And after that?"

"Watch reruns of 'I Love Lucy.' I'm not going anywhere, Jim. Honest. I have no idea where Stone is, so there's no place for me to go."

"You could go home."

"Maybe I will—tomorrow. I could be playing whiffleball in the afternoon."

"Season's about over. The kids were throwing the football around the other day."

"I'll go straight from the airport, then."

"Can I buy you a drink?"

"I'd love that, but someone's waiting for me."

Kelliher grimaced. "Alan, haven't you protected that girl enough? For God's sake, you don't owe her anything."

"True, but I'm in love, and there's just no arguing with love. I guess I'll be seeing you around."

Alan left Kelliher shaking his head and hurried back to his room.

Julia had taken a shower while he was gone and was drying her hair in the bathroom. "I met my guardian angel in the lobby," Alan said.

"It's nice to know we're being watched."

Alan lay down. "I was thinking maybe we should go back to Boston tomorrow. This is kind of ridiculous."

Julia stopped toweling her hair. "I would like that," she said.

"We might not be any safer, but I'd sure feel better."

She came out of the bathroom and kissed him. "I think it's a wonderful idea. You've made me very happy." *Girls wearing nothing but panties are awfully sexy,* Alan reflected. He grabbed at her. "Not after I just got washed," she said with a laugh and backed away from him. "Save it up for later."

"Sure," he said, "you'll have a headache later." She blew him a kiss and returned to the bathroom. Alan picked up the newspaper. He skipped all the stuff about the crime: the photos, the interview with the girl's uncomprehending parents, the outraged editorial; he didn't need any of that. He checked the TV listings. "Hey, 'Gilligan's Island' is on in fifteen minutes."

"My happiness is complete."

He grinned and turned to the sports section, which was filled with stories about the Jets and the Giants and advice on how to bet Sunday's games. Football was such a dreary sport. And there was one short article: "Yankees–Red Sox: Not What It Used To Be."

No, the writer said, the drama of bygone days would be missing when the two teams met at the stadium tonight. The Yankees had already clinched the divisional crown in the American League East; the Red Sox were mired in fourth place. The Red Sox said they were playing for pride, but who cared about Red Sox pride? Think of the history of the rivalry, though. Remember signing Luis Tiant away from the Sox? Remember the great series in '79 when the Yankees took four straight and left them for dead? Remember the playoff game in '78, Bucky Dent's homerun? Remember Roger Maris hitting his sixty-first homerun off Tracy Stallard? Remember Allie Reynolds pitching a no-hitter against the Sox to clinch the 1951 pennant? Ah, remember Babe Ruth?

Alan remembered it all. He set the paper down. Julia was putting on her makeup; her cute behind stuck out as she leaned close to the bathroom mirror. He let his mind go blank and simply enjoyed the sight. Then she started to hum "Il Mio Tesoro," and that was too much. *Nobody said this was going to be easy.* He tried not saying what he had to say, and that was worse than saying it. There was just nothing he could do. He opened his mouth, and set his tongue in motion. "I know where Stone is," he said.

Julia put her eyeshadow down. "What do you mean?"

"I mean, not exactly. I know where he's going to be. Tonight. At the Yankees–Red Sox game. Plenty of good seats still available. Want to go?"

She stared at him. "Why do you think he'll be there?"

"Because he's a Yankee fan."

"But that's absurd. His picture's all over the city—all over the country. He wouldn't dare."

"His picture's been all over the country for some time. That hasn't stopped him from doing what he wanted to do."

"But it's silly. He may be a fan, but the Yankees can't mean that much to him. He's got a lot more important things on his mind than baseball."

"You just don't understand fans, my sweet."

Julia came out of the bathroom and sat on the edge of the bed. "You don't really want to go, do you, Alan? What about Boston—going home?" Her voice was beginning to shake.

"Boston will still be there tomorrow. I hope. I simply have to do this."

She stared at him long enough to worry him, but it simply took her that long to regain control. "Has anyone ever called you stubborn before, Alan?" she managed to say finally.

"The word may have been bandied about in connection with me."

She stood up. "Go to the game. I'll stay here and pray for you."

"And the Red Sox."

"I'll pray for everyone."

Julia finished getting dressed, and they watched "Gilligan's Island" together. It had been too good to be true, of course—and the dream of returning to Boston had died faster than her dream of living with Alan in L.A. She didn't dispute that Alan would find Stone at the ball game; her feeble arguments were only rational, after all. And she knew that when Alan found him, something terrible would happen. But somehow she had run out of tears to cry over such a thing. If it was going to happen it would happen, and she could only be a spectator.

It was not so different from the way she used to feel about her mother, drinking herself into insanity. You just get used to it, finally: my mother is a crazy alcoholic who's destroying herself, and me. Repeat that often enough, and there is no response. She couldn't help her mother; she couldn't help Alan. *God help all of us.*

"Will you let them follow you?" she asked in the middle of "Hogan's Heroes."

"Not if I can help it."

"They might come in handy, you know."

"You don't really think so, do you?"

"I don't know. One bullet—" She gestured slackly and fell silent.

The rays of the setting sun slanted through the skyscrapers into the room. Alan got up and put on a sweater and a jacket. "Get there early enough, I might catch batting practice," he said. "Wish me luck."

Julia embraced him, pressing her head against his chest. "Good luck," she whispered. "Please be careful, Alan. I love you."

He broke free and stared at her oddly for a moment. "Well, uh, I'll call if the game goes into extra innings."

She smiled and turned quickly away.

Alan got off the elevator at the second floor. He found the stairway and walked down a flight, where he was faced with two doors: "To Lobby" and "Employees

Only." Feeling like a criminal, he opened the latter.

He descended a short flight of stairs. In the distance he heard clattering pots and shouted Spanish; he smelled onion soup, and his stomach started to growl. A young black man passed him in the corridor, wheeling an overhead projector on a squeaky cart. Alan walked by an empty locker room. On the wall was a sign that said: "Management Not Responsible for Lost Valuables. Lock Your Locker." *I want you to go out and win this one for management.* He sped up when he saw a door marked "Security." Finally he saw an exit. Next to it were a time clock with racks of time cards and a small glassed-in office in which an old man sat reading *Penthouse*. The man looked up as Alan approached. Alan simply waved and headed through the door.

He found himself in an alley next to a huge, foul-smelling dumpster. He chose a direction and headed for the street. Then he cut away from the hotel and walked rapidly toward the subway stop.

It was a warm evening, and autumn had not yet found its way down into the subway. Alan took off his jacket as he studied the tangled system map and tried to decipher a route to Yankee Stadium. Finally he swallowed his pride and asked. On the platform, he looked around for Kelliher or Pete or other minions of the law. No one. He imagined he was the guy in *The French Connection*, suavely moving in and out of the train until he shook Gene Hackman. He couldn't pull it off. When the train came in he boarded it meekly; if anyone wanted to join him, they were welcome. He had done his best.

The train was long and dirty and fast. Every surface was covered with black spray-painted graffiti. Alan stared at a hemorrhoids ad in Spanish and tried to concentrate on what he would do when he got to the stadium. But instead he found himself thinking about Julia, and the last words she had whispered into his chest. He wished he knew for sure what they had been. They would have meant a lot to him tonight.

Chapter 24

Alan came up from the subway into a tangle of blue gird-
ers on 161st Street. The stadium stood right beyond the
elevated tracks, massive and smug. A large crowd had
turned out for the meaningless game. The plaza surrounding the stadium was filled with people eating pret-
zels and hot dogs, scalping tickets, looking for pockets to
pick. A fat woman pushed a little boy in a wheelchair
who bravely waved his Yankee banner. Had Dave Winfield promised to hit one out for him? A man in a business suit was explaining the mathematical possibilities in
the AL West to a woman who had the resigned air of a
prisoner with a life sentence.

Alan followed the stadium around to the front. He
could tell it was the front because the name of the place
was emblazoned across the façade in blue neon. Was that
really necessary? He sat down by a huge flagpole in the
shape of a Louisville Slugger and watched the people
queuing up at the ticket booths. He'd only have maybe
thirty or forty thousand people to look through before he
found the one he wanted—who was probably in disguise. Best get busy then. He got in line and bought a
seat in the grandstand.

Once inside, he decided he needed some fuel for
his search and bought a beer and two hot dogs. He tried
to look at everyone he passed—black hair? blue, evil
eyes?—but it seemed rather absurd, now that he was
actually here. It seemed even more absurd when he

stood in the runway and looked for the first time at the stands. The place was immense. He could imagine searching the lower level, and even the loges, but the vast expanse of the upper deck depressed him. And what if Stone were sitting in the bleachers, which Alan couldn't even get to from the grandstand? But Stone wasn't the sort to sit in the bleachers. He would be somewhere in the huge horseshoe, daring Alan to find him.

Alan went to his seat and watched the Red Sox take batting practic. As usual, they looked great. If there were ever a championship for batting practice . . . When they left the field the scoreboard showed a dismaying film of great moments from Yankee history: Babe Ruth rounding the bases on his matchstick legs; DiMaggio during his hitting streak; Larsen pitching his perfect game. Frank Sinatra was up next, as the loudspeakers blared out "New York, New York" over the desolation of the Bronx. Then the starting lineups, intoned by a P.A. announcer with the exaggerated diction of an old-time radio actor. It was wrong, all wrong. Even the national anthem was over-orchestrated, offensive. Alan finished his second hot dog as the Yankees took the field. He searched his mind for any random psychic debris: a section number, perhaps, the color of the guy's socks. Fat chance. He left his seat after the first pitch. Time to go to work.

First row? Nothing. Second row? Nope. Third row? Good-looking girl, but no Stone. *Just trying to find a friend of mine, Officer*. He trudged up the stairs. At this rate, it should take him till shortly after the beginning of the next century, he calculated. And what if Stone saw him first, ducked into the men's room? *But it's more likely that he wants to be found*.

Stone, Seth Stone? Paging Mr. Stone. Candygram for S. Stone.

Alan tried not to pay any attention to the game, but that was impossible. It was so typical that he thought it might have been a replay from earlier in the season. The

Red Sox went ahead early, looked unbeatable just long enough to suck you in, and then started to unravel: a walk here, an error there. Alan knew what was coming, the way he knew Tosca shouldn't be so smug about Cavaradossi standing in front of the firing squad. Real bullets were waiting to be fired.

So many people. And none of them Stone. He started separating people into aspirin users and Tylenol users. That guy there, wearing rimless glasses and a peacoat, he probably reads *Consumer Reports* and buys generic aspirin for next to nothing from a mail order outfit in New Jersey. The fat lady with bleached hair and a bowling jacket thinks aspirin will give her cancer and takes about twenty Tylenol a day for the stress headaches she gets working at the dry cleaner's. *Excuse me, ma'am, have you seen a guy with eyes the color of cold fire, with a laugh that causes spontaneous abortions? Well, sorry to bother you then*.

In the fifth inning, with the score tied, Alan went up to the loges and worked his way through the crowd there. He could no longer concentrate on individual faces, he just scanned each section, hoping something would catch his eye: an arrow pointing down from the sky, perhaps, or a glow of radioactivity. The organ boomed out Mexican hat dances and "Charge" trumpet calls to get the fans cheering—as if the Yankees needed any encouragement. Alan bought another hot dog.

Anybody here seen Stone? S-T-O-N-E.

Dondé está Señor Stone?

He ascended to the upper deck, finally, gasping for breath in the thin air. The crowd was also thinner here— and more raucous, throwing peanuts at each other and yelling obscenities at the vendors. Moths fluttered in the light standards. The players far below looked like toys, chessmen moving around a diamond-shaped board. Perhaps Stone might prefer it up here, where the game lost the reality of the living struggle: the grunt of the batter as he swung and missed, the strain on the pitcher's face as he released the fastball, the grimace of the sliding runner. Here the game was nothing more than a game, or perhaps less—a fantasy, a dream, an idea.

Alan climbed to the last row and looked over the top briefly, then thought better of it and descended. He moved into the shadows behind home plate, where there were no light standards to brighten the stands. *This might be a good place*, he thought. *In darkness, far above everyone—*

And then he stopped thinking. Fifteen rows up, all by himself, munching a Yankee Frank, sat his father.

Alan sat down himself and gripped the railing in front of him. When his mind sluggishly resumed work, it tried to think logically (which part of him knew was not the right way to be thinking just now). *Either that was my father or it was not* was what his mind managed to come up with. Either it was an absurd coincidence or his eyes needed examining. *Look again*, his mind suggested to his eyes. They looked and eliminated the second possibility: this was the guy from the old photos, the memories, the dreams; note the curly brown hair, the sleepy eyes, the long, sloping line of the jaw . . .

Coincidence, then? His mind started to wake up as it mulled that one over. *Unacceptable. Intolerably arbitrary. Try again.*

He took another peek and felt old, unused emotions stirring. *Look at that damned corduroy jacket.* His father had owned one just like it twenty years ago. Alan remembered holding his hand as they walked through the Arnold Arboretum, looking at the foliage, wading through the fallen leaves, secure in the warmth of his hand, the grown-up smell of his pipe tobacco. When he got tired his father hoisted him up and he leaned his head against the rough corduroy . . . Oh no. Not that stuff again. *Why have you come back?* his mind shouted. *Go away. Get out of my—*

Dream.

It's the same fucking jacket, his mind told him angrily. The brown hair should've gone gray by now, there should be wrinkles on his smooth face. *This is and is not your father,* it reported helpfully. *It is the father of your dreams.*

And when his father reached out to touch him in the dream his hair had been black, his eyes blue, and he had been smiling.

Alan's grip on the railing tightened. The new age had dawned.

"Well hello, Alan. Fancy meeting you here."

Alan looked up in terror. Jim Kelliher loomed above him in the aisle. He shut his eyes and begged his heart to slow down. *This one is real, isn't he?* He had better be, because if he wasn't Alan thought he might just as well hang up his cleats. He moved over and let Kelliher sit next to him. "How'd you know I was here?"

"Oh, psychic powers."

Alan stared at him, "Julia told you."

Kelliher chuckled. "The girl is not as bad as I thought, maybe. She's worried about you. Anyway, I've spent a long time tracking you down in this monstrosity. Why are you sitting way up here?"

"I wanted to be alone with my grief—hint, hint."

"Oh, I'm a blunt Irishman. I don't take hints."

"Then how about: 'Go away'?"

Kelliher shook his head. "I may already have mentioned I'm stubborn too."

Alan considered. It didn't seem as though Kelliher knew exactly *why* Julia would be worried about Alan going to the ball game. At least she had been that loyal. And Kelliher certainly wouldn't know that Stone was sitting fifteen rows behind them, munching a hot dog. Conceivably Kelliher would see his *own* father if he were to turn around, but Alan couldn't figure out the point of that. He felt sure the show was for him alone, created out of the memories and images Stone had sucked out of his mind during their bout in California.

What he wasn't sure of was whether Stone knew he was here. It seemed hard to believe that Stone wouldn't be aware of him, but it was at least possible, and that would give Alan a tiny bit of an edge. What in the world could he do with it, though? *Say, Jim, just lend me your gun for a second till I plug that guy back there who looks like my father.* Forty thousand witnesses didn't matter to Alan, but the consequences of missing surely did. He would have to wait, then. He would have to figure something out. Glumly he sat back to watch the ball game.

The Yankees were threatening in the bottom of the eighth. The score was still tied. The organ was thumping away. Dave Winfield came up, and the crowd sensed blood. Alan thought of the kid in the wheelchair, probably screaming obscenities at the Red Sox pitcher now.

Winfield took a mighty swing and missed, rocking the stadium. The pitcher threw a couple down and in, then Winfield swung again, carving an incredibly high foul behind the plate into the stands.

Alan observed its approach with something like amusement: the white sphere, moving through the darkness, aimed at him. *You're the one*, it said. *Be thankful I'm not a hand grenade.* He reached out and caught it. It stung a little in his bare hand, but he held on. The crowd applauded the nice catch. Alan looked at the ball, felt the familiar pattern of its stitches, and shoved it into the pocket of his jacket.

"You son of a gun, I've never gotten a foul in my life," Kelliher said.

"I'm so lucky it frightens me sometimes."

On the next pitch Winfield hit a weak ground ball to the second baseman. It went right through his legs, and two runs scored. The crowd went wild.

"The bums," Kelliher murmured. The next batter popped out to end the inning. "Wanna leave now, beat the rush?"

"You do what you want. I'm sticking around."

Righetti came in to pitch for the Yankees, and the Red Sox were overmatched. A pop-up, a routine fly ball, and a called third strike. *As it was in the beginning, is now, and ever shall be* . . . Frank Sinatra put in his two cents' worth over the loudspeakers again, and the crowd headed for the exits.

Alan stood up and waited. Kelliher looked at him expectantly. "Game's over, Alan. They could play all night and not score off that guy." Alan put his jacket on and felt the round bulge of the baseball in his pocket. Stone walked past them. Was he smiling? Kelliher didn't notice a thing.

"Let's go," Alan said.

They wound their way down the crowded ramp. Alan kept Stone in sight, afraid he would lose him in the throng, afraid Kelliher would interfere, afraid Stone knew everything and was just reeling him in.

"Going back to the hotel now?" Kelliher asked.

Alan didn't answer. They rounded the final curve, and he saw the plaza looming ahead of him. He hadn't the ghost of an idea what to do. *You got me into this*, he screamed at his gift. *You tell me*.

Simple enough, came the reply. *If you care to do it*.

He didn't; it stank. Besides, he didn't know if it was possible for him. Bouncing balls were one thing, human minds quite another. But now it suddenly seemed that anything was possible, the night was charged with obscure energies, nameless powers. All he had to do was summon one. He had run out of alternatives. He had to try. He tried.

Give me your gun.

Kelliher slowed dow, a puzzled look on his face.

Give me your gun, Jim.

Kelliher reached inside his raincoat and produced a revolver. Alan silently took it away from him and stuck it in the other pocket of his jacket. No one in the crowd said anything about the transaction; this was New York. *Don't follow me. Stay here. Go away*.

Kelliher stared at him. Alan prayed he hadn't done any damage. "Sorry, Jim," he whispered. Then he walked quickly away and the crowd surged around the confused detective.

Stone was making his way across the plaza toward the elevated tracks. Alan struggled to keep the corduroy jacket in sight as it moved past the pretzel vendors and the policemen and the drunken fans. Across 161st Street, past the subway stop, and suddenly all the crowds were gone, there was just the jacket and Alan, moving swiftly along the sidewalks lined with garbage, past the storefront churches, the Puerto Rican families sitting on stoops, the variety stores with cracked Coca-Cola signs, past the young punks lounging outside bars in white shirts and tight black pants, past the abandoned cars, tires flat, windshields smashed.

Shoot him. Catch up with him and shoot him. But Alan knew that wouldn't work, any more than it had worked in California. Something more was required.

So Alan kept pace with the figure, past empty lots and boarded-up buildings, past prostitutes who asked him for a date, a heap of rags that could have been a sleeping wino or a corpse, an old man in a woolen cap who shuffled along muttering curses . . . Was that steam from a distant manhole, or smoke from another building about to be boarded up? Was that a kitten moving through the rubble, or a large, unfriendly rat? It seemed as if he had been chasing phantoms forever, and they just kept leading him deeper and deeper into the darkness. And now he was too far in to ever find his way out.

Please be careful, Alan. I love you.

He was sure she had said it, damn it. What else could it have been?

Stone cut through a playground: broken glass glistening in the moonlight, weeds growing in the cracks of the asphalt. The basketball rims were bent so that they looked like sad giants, heads bowed in acceptance of their fate. There were four broken swings, seats hanging uselessly inches from the ground. Alan had been afraid of swings as a child, afraid of going too high, of that instant when the chain snaps and you are catapulted out into the world, where the only possible outcome is an abrupt crash and fierce pain. He remembered his father's strong hands on his back, pushing, pushing. "Not too high, Daddy, not too high."

"Aw, shoot, it won't hurt you. Don't be a scaredy-cat."

But Alan was a scaredy-cat, always had been. Swings were dangerous; life was dangerous. Maybe if his imagination had been less vivid it wouldn't have bothered him so much; but as the hands let go he could already feel the ground rushing toward him, and the pain had its arms outstretched, waiting. *The unexamined life, Mr. Phipps—much to be preferred.* "You've got to learn to play with pain," his father would say. But then it isn't playing, is it?

They were on a narrow side street now. The streetlights were out. Every other building was boarded up. In the windows of the occupied buildings TV sets flickered like vigil lights. On the corner two stray dogs were fighting over a bone. A mournful Spanish voice sang about lost love or death or something equally unpleasant. And Stone wasn't there.

Alan rushed ahead. Where the hell had he gone? The building Alan was standing in front of was empty, burned out. There was a dark path next to it. Alan took out the revolver and walked slowly down the path. At the rear of the building he saw a board pried loose from a doorway.

Was Stone somewhere behind that door? Of course he was. Where else would he be but in a place like this?

Go in and get it over with.

Get what over with? My life? Alan was at the top of his swing, looking down at the ground—no, farther, the chain had already snapped, he was flying through the air, helpless, the illusion of freedom past, and gravity was about to claim him.

Please be careful, Alan. I—

He shook his head and leaned back against the fence that separated Stone's dwelling from the next heap of rubble. After a while he put the revolver away and walked slowly back to the street.

I want to go home. He went around the corner and stopped in front of an all-night drugstore that must have been robbed twice a week. They'd probably see the bulge of the revolver and call the cops on him. He realized his head was aching from the strain of what he had done to Kelliher. His mind slowed down once again.

You can't go home, it managed to decide.

You can't go into that building.

You can't go back to the hotel.

You can't stay here, in the pits of the city, waiting for enlightenment.

"Thanks a lot," Alan murmured. He went inside the drugstore, and did the only thing that made any sense.

Julia watched the game on television. She was so sick of the TV she wanted to heave it out the window; but she was so lonely that the silence would have killed her. So she watched.

She didn't see Alan, or Kelliher, or Stone; all she saw was the kind of game that had helped shape Alan's personality. It relieved her that nothing spectacular happened, but that only meant the waiting was not yet over. Past the postgame wrap-up and the beer commercials, past the interview and the highlights, past the eleven o'clock news ("Law enforcement officials report no progress at this hour in the search for the alleged murderer of . . .")—listening for the footsteps in the corridor, the reassuring movement of the key in the lock; hearing only the announcer's meaningless drone, her heart pounding in her chest. And when the phone rang, she almost screamed. She managed to answer it on the second ring.

"I—uh—is he there?"

It was Kelliher. But was it her strained senses that made him sound so odd? "No. Didn't you find him?"

"Yeah, I found him but he, uh, got away after the game. I guess I . . . lost him."

"Oh, how could you; don't you have any idea where he is?"

"No, no . . . I'm still at the stadium here. Maybe I should— I don't know."

"Please, please find him."

"Yeah, well, I'll try. I . . ."

He hung up, and Julia shut her eyes. Stone had done something to the detective. It had started.

"In sports tonight, the Yankees defeated the Red Sox, five to three. This was their seventh consecutive . . ."

And it was up to her. To do what? She tried to be psychic. Surely this was the kind of situation in which even normal people had visions: your lover is in distress, great catastrophes loom, and you sit at home alone, worried, helpless. Surely she would go insane if she didn't at least try. *Tell me where you are, Alan. Please, let me know what to do.*

Please, Alan.

Please.

For some reason that aria from *Don Giovanni* flitted through her mind. *Il mio tesoro* dum dum de dum . . .

And the phone rang again.

"It's me, I'm in Colson's drugstore on 135th Street. I've found Stone but I need your help. Please come."

Alan's voice was trembling. "Where is he?" Julia asked.

"He's in one of these burned-out apartment buildings up here. I was going to go in but I lost my nerve. You've got to help me."

"Call the police, Alan. Call Henshaw. We can't do it alone."

"That's the only way we can do it. But I'm scared."

"Alan, please. Just walk away from it. You'll be humiliated but you won't be dead. Just come back."

"Take a cab, Julia, if you can find one that'll bring you here. I'll be in the first-aid section. Colson's. A hundred and Thirty-fifth Street. If you love me."

The phone went dead. Julia quietly hung up and leaned back against the pillows of their bed. *Welcome to the wonderful world of psychic experiences.* She could still call the police, of course. But look at what she had done to Kelliher by getting him involved. Ultimately this was her fight—not the police's, not Kelliher's, not even Alan's.

But how could she hope to win it? If Alan was a loser, she was even more of one. And the consequences of losing were as horrifying as ever. She knew she could accept death. But to come under Stone's spell once again, to carry out his commands like a priestess to some awful pagan god—that possibility was unthinkable, because to think of it was to feel again the old twinge of excitement deep inside her.

And then she thought of Alan, waiting in the drugstore, frightened, alone. All she had ever been able to do for him was to take off his shoes when he was drunk. *If you love me*. She got up and turned off Johnny Carson. Time to show her love.

Chapter 25

Julia found Alan in the magazine section reading *Playboy*. "Hi, glad you could make it," he said when she kissed him silently on the cheek. "Some excellent short stories in this magazine. Do you think I look suspicious? The cashier's been eyeing me. I guess I *have* been in here for a while. I'm going to get this flashlight; it might come in handy. And a knife for you; I've got Kelliher's gun. This is really a very well-stocked drugstore. They even have pointed sticks, wooden mallets, and silver crucifixes, but that's not quite the kind of enemy we're up against. I don't think I'll get this magazine. You're better-looking than anyone in it. Braver too."

"Let's go, Alan," she whispered.

"I need to get some Tylenol. I have a splitting head-ache. And some candy bars, for quick energy. You want a Baby Ruth?"

She shook her head.

"You scared?"

"Of course."

"So am I, in case you hadn't noticed. I caught a foul ball tonight. Do you think that means good luck?"

"I doubt it."

"So do I. Let's get out of here."

When they were outside he gave her the knife and gobbled down a few Tylenol along with the candy bars. "How did you get Kelliher's gun?" Julia asked.

"I don't want to think about it. We're going just around the corner here. I have a feeling he may be expecting me, but I don't really know. Whatever you see, whatever he looks like—don't believe it. It's him, all right."

"I understand."

They turned the corner, and Alan gestured at the building. "Not very pretty, huh?"

She shook her head.

He sighed. "We've both grown up a lot in the course of the season, wouldn't you say?"

"I wouldn't have thought it possible in spring train-ing."

He smiled, took out the revolver, and flicked off the safety. When they reached the dark pathway beside the building he shined the flashlight on the ground in front of them. McDonald's wrappers, cigarette butts, a faded flyer advertising Madame Inez, fortune teller . . .

She knows all and sees all.

Who had told him that?

Any advice, Madame Inez?

She nodded her turbaned head. *Work on your fastball.*

Alan sighed. He had never had a fastball. The mournful Spanish voice started singing again somewhere behind them. Her heart was obviously broken, her future a blank. The acrid smell of charred wood stung their nostrils. Alan led the way to the back of the building.

He gestured with the flashlight at the loose board in the rear door, then turned the flashlight off and put it in his pocket. "Ready?" he whispered.

Julia nodded, then leaned close and whispered something he didn't quite catch. Just his luck. He took her hand and led her over to the door. He squeezed through first, and Julia followed.

The darkness was total. Alan was afraid to take a step in case the floor was missing. The burned-wood smell was almost overpowering now. Something scurried near their feet, and Julia's grip on his hand became bonecrushing.

Mind, do your thing.

You'll have to use the flashlight, it offered. *Listen for sounds of breathing. Perhaps he's asleep.* Alan could feel the sweat running down the back of his neck. *You are terrified, but you will do your—*

And then Dusty's face appeared in front of him. Julia screamed. It could have been five feet away, it could have been fifty; Alan had lost all perspective. It was perfectly visible in the darkness: tilted head, eyes half closed as if in contentment, the red line of the knife gash extending from ear to ear. He had to make the face go away. He disengaged his hand from Julia's and aimed the revolver.

Couldn't do it.

He lowered the revolver and took out the baseball. He pitched from the stretch: not enough room for a full windup. *Work on your fastball.* He let the ball go, and the face exploded in a shower of red sparks that momentarily illuminated twisted beams, piles of rubbish, a blackened chair with springs sticking out.

"Strike one!" Stone's voice called out, echoing all around them.

Julia clutched at Alan's arm. She was whimpering.

Then Alan's father appeared, with an expression not unlike Dusty's, only this time the gash was new, the blood was still spurting out. And this time Alan didn't hesitate. He raised the revolver, made believe the face was a target at the shooting range, and fired.

The noise was deafening. The bullet went straight through the face, which fell like a discarded mask to the floor.

"Strike two!" Stone said, laughing wildly.

And then Alan faced himself—as he looked on the worst of days, in the worst of hotel mirrors: bleary-eyed, unshaven, tufts of hair sticking obstinately out from his scalp. The ultimate loser. "I want to go home," he sniveled, but which *he* was it? And as he watched he lifted a knife to his throat and plunged it in. Gasping for breath, he aimed and fired. Right in the heart. It was dark again, and he heard himself slump to the floor, and Julia's whimpering had turned to a low, feral moan.

"Strike three!" Stone said. "You're out!" A hand grabbed him by the collar and jerked him into the air as if he were a Little Leaguer being plucked away from a fight. He was pitched aside and fell against something hard. He lost his grip on the revolver, and it skidded away in the darkness.

"Welcome home, Alan," Stone said, and the lights came on, and it *was* home. He was sitting on the floor of the old dining room in Jamaica Plain, where he and his father would try to eat his mother's feeble attempts at a Sunday dinner. The room brought back memories of leathery pot roasts, of turkey still cold in the center, of mashed potatoes with lumps the size of golf balls. There was the mahogany sideboard with the tarnished silver serving dish in it. There was the dismal Rembrandt print that reminded Alan of rainy Monday mornings. He was leaning against the table, its finish dull and spotted, and he knew if he reached up under it he would feel the petrified wads of gum right where he had stuck them decades ago. When his father left, his mother gave up on cooking, gave up the pretense of Sunday meals in the dining room, and the two of them just never went in there anymore; it was a part of their lives that was over.

Except here it was once again, and Stone was in it. He was seated in Alan's father's chair, still wearing the corduroy jacket but now with his own face, his own smile. Julia was leaning against the doorjamb, her eyes closed. "Isn't this fun, Alan?" Stone asked. "Just flexing my muscles, you might say. You want to see any more?"

"No."

Stone's smile widened, and the dining room dissolved into Alan's room at Harvard, records stacked in milk crates, empty beer cans in a pyramid against one wall. Alan saw himself again, this time an acne-scarred teenager trying to make it with an attractive Cliffie. She had heard he was bizarre but was in the process of finding out he was only dull.

"Would you like to listen to one of my Jussi Björling records? He was a terrific tenor."

"No, no, I really don't think so. I must be going."

And which of him wanted to cry at his ineptitude?

Then he was in Marlborough Street (oh, Marlborough Street!) with Agnes Foley, who was explaining why she was dumping him. "You've got no *future*, Alan. You're smart but you've got no get-up-and-go. You *drink* too much, Alan, your apartment is a *mess* . . ." Dusty had never liked Agnes.

And then—oh Lord!—he was in the hotel with Julia. Was it only last night? The two of them lying next to each other in the darkness:

"Would you die for me?"

"I've done my best."

Julia gasped from the doorway, watching the phantoms groan and strain as they made love. And even as he saw how silly he looked he was aroused. Oh, Julia . . .

"What is this, a fucking *Christmas Carol?*" Alan asked.

Stone laughed. "I'm no ghost, Alan, and you won't have a chance to reform by the time I'm finished with you." The grappling bodies faded, and the dining room reappeared.

"What did you have in mind?"

Stone stretched out his long legs. "You think I'm going to kill you—but the killing is past. I don't need to slit any more throats, even yours. Instead, I'm going to make you my first convert. Your life is trivial, Alan, but your mind—your mind may be worth having."

Alan got up off the floor and leaned back against the sideboard. "You'll have to fight for it," he said.

"Oh, I intend to. The better the fight, the more satisfying the victory." And the dining room turned white, transformed itself into Stone's room in the California mountains. Stone was sitting on the bed, and Alan was standing awkwardly in front of the mirror. "Home-field advantage," Stone said with a grin.

"But I have bench strength," Alan responded, gesturing at Julia.

Stone looked over at her, still motionless in the doorway. "Do you think so?" he asked Alan softly.

"I think so."

"What does Julia say?"

"Leave him alone, Seth," she whispered. "You don't need him."

Stone turned back to Alan. "I don't think she'll be a factor in the contest." He got up and moved closer to Alan. "Have you been practicing your Indian wrestling?"

Alan gazed at Julia; her eyes were closed, her arms were folded tight. She looked as if she were trying to disappear inside herself, to do anything that would make this scene, this reality, go away. So much for teamwork. "I guess we've both been getting some exercise."

Stone reached out a hand. "Then let's see who prepared better."

Alan took his hand and moved his right foot next to Stone's. Stone smiled. "Anytime you're—"

And Alan let him have it. He wasn't exactly sure what it was that he was letting him have, but it was powerful. It was what he had given, unwillingly, to Kelliher, only magnified now by the intensity of the danger and of his own emotions. He had just wanted Kelliher to go away; he wanted Stone to die.

The power was not enough to end the match, but it gave Alan the initial advantage—the first he had ever had over the fellow. He could feel Stone hesitate, puzzled, then gasp with pain at the force of the attack. Good—but not nearly enough. He needed more ammunition, but he had none; he would have to get it from Stone himself.

He descended, like a diver searching for skeletons in a sunken ship—searching for Stone, and for a way to destroy him. *Look*.

Stone's father—a grizzled, bent-over man with a Pall Mall drooping from his lip at an impossible angle, leaving ashes behind him like a trail of bread crumbs, showing his young son how to reglaze a window. Seth does not want to learn; he concentrates, and the window suddenly explodes. A lifetime of puzzlement and frustration over the strange creature he has produced finally erupts, and his father shoves the boy. "You idiot! You fucking idiot kid!" And Seth trips and his face ends up in the broken glass, leaving scars that will never entirely disappear.

Look, Stone, a hidden motivation. It's tough to be an enigma when someone is rummaging in your mind.

Stone in high school, drooling over a photo of Ursula Andress in *Dr. No*, masturbating hopelessly to the rhythm of a song by the Dave Clark Five.

Any better than being turned down by a Cliffie? You can't escape your memories; they may not prove you're normal, but they certainly prove you're human.

Stone pacing impatiently through the messy Berkeley commune, fingering the mimeo machine, the ancient typewriter, the stacks of revolutionary leaflets. There is something he wants, but this isn't it, because the people churning out the pamphlets are no better than the fascist pigs they are fighting against. They are all trivial. What really matters is . . . somewhere else. And he is going to find it. So he takes the $147 out of the communal cookie jar and bids farewell to the revolutionary life. But before he does he stands outside the building and narrows his eyes, and soon there is smoke billowing from an open window. He doesn't stay to see the leaflets burn.

How drearily predictable, Stone. You're not really a very interesting person, are you?

Stone sits on a bulkhead concealing two tons of marijuana. He looks out at the serene waters of the Caribbean and thinks: *This is not bad.* But he knows it is not what he needs. When the danger is past there is only the money, piling up in a dozen bank accounts. The powers, unused, fester. The discontent roils beneath the surface of his mind, and the waiting grows intolerable . . .

"Do you like blood?" he asks the woman.

She giggles, afraid, fascinated. She is naked. "What do you mean?"

"Drinking it."

"Not my own," she says with a nervous smile.

"When you drink blood before sex, the gods enter you, make love through you. You breed giants."

"Have—have you ever done it?"

He smiles and descends to her, sinking his teeth into her neck. She screams with pain and desire.

He has never done it . . .

He holds the gun to the man's temple. The man is a peasant; he has betrayed Stone. Stone can smell the man's urine as his bladder yields to his terror, can count the beads of sweat dribbling down from his greasy hair. He listens to the man beg, but then suddenly he is listening no more, he is *inside*, feeling the wetness in his pants, the cold circle of the gun barrel pressed against his head. He thinks of his wife doing her chores at the farm, remembers the long unused prayers of his boyhood, wonders why he ever thought he could cheat this man—and for the first time in his life Stone is happy. He smiles and pulls the trigger. He watches—*feels*—the life explode from the man, and knows that he has found what he needs; each time this happens he will learn a little more, advance a little further, and there is no limit to where he can go because he will not let a limit exist . . .

No. You have reached the limit, Stone. Let the experience of your own death end your search.

Alan could feel Stone's mind cloud over, his legs wobble. But it wasn't enough. Alan had to find another power.

. . . Stone in the dingy West Side apartment. The boy sits in a chair, gagged and bound. The beautiful girl, her eyes glazed with devotion, brings the knife to Stone, happy to be a votary at this ritual. Alan has held that knife. The toilet is running. Stone advances to the boy, who is crying now: his chest heaves, his face is wet, mottled. Stone smiles and holds the knife in front of the boy's neck . . . and Alan forces it back, twists the blade around so that it is aimed at Stone, inch by inch overcoming the weight of reality and Stone's opposition, bringing it closer and closer to the fiend's heart. *I cannot change the past but I can change the memory. And if the memory kills you then you will die, because you, like me, are nothing more than your memories. They make you what you are.*

The knife touches flesh. The walls of the apartment shimmer, revealing the white of the California room, the faded gray of the dining room, the flickering darkness of the burned-out building. And beyond them all is sunshine, sparrows chirping in magnolia trees, a cat lazing on the stoop. Alan needed them, longed for them . . . but the knife would go no farther. The layers of illusion hung suspended in the psychic whatsis—and Alan lifted his gaze from the knife to look into Stone's eyes.

That's as far as you can go, the cold eyes said. *Because you are wrong. There is more to me than my memories. And what is beyond them you cannot hope to conquer.*

And Alan, gazing into those eyes, knew that Stone was right. It was there in the eyes, dark and rock-hard and unassailable. Evil. He could not penetrate the flesh of that evil because it was still somewhere beyond the limits of his understanding—perhaps of anyone's understanding. It simply existed and bided its time, and when it saw a chance, it pushed back.

. . . back from Stone's chest, twisting the knife around till it was pointed at Alan, till it was pressed against *his* heart. Alan could no more stop that knife than he could make the Red Sox win the World Series.

But Stone didn't want to kill him, and the knife remained poised there, a reminder of who was dominant now. And Stone went to work on Alan's mind. *I will take your powers and your memories and your personality, and leave you with only one thing: the need to believe in me. Kneel. Kneel.*

Alan felt his mind disappearing, his legs giving way, like a beaten fighter wobbling through the fifteenth round.

Stay up, stay up, it's for the championship.

But what's the point, I've already lost the decision, the judges are in the bag.

Out of the corner of his eye he saw someone—his trainer?—coming through the ropes, and then he genuflected before those eyes, that evil.

Stone smiled, and then his eyes grew wide—too wide. He seemed to fade away, and then his face was inches from Alan's, twisted hideously. There was a flash of movement behind Stone, and again, and again, and everything turned red—the ring, the apartment, Stone's bedroom, Alan's dining room—all bathed in red, and then they disappeared, and there was only the face, staring, furious, evil. Then that too disappeared—or rather it changed, and changed, and changed. It became everyone Alan had ever known, every human being alive, every human being who had ever lived. For an awful moment it was Alan himself, not a loser now but corrupt, vicious, despicable. Then it jerked away from Alan, and there was a scream, and then nothing.

* * *

Alan found the flashlight in his pocket. It clicked on, and he saw an overturned candle, a box of Nabisco saltines, a gallon of spring water. He saw Stone, still twitching as the blood oozed from his back. He saw Julia crouching by a blackened mattress. One hand still held the knife, red to the hilt; the other covered her face. She was sobbing uncontrollably. He crawled over and put his arms around her. She leaned against him, and the knife clattered to the floor.

"It was my mother," she said, gasping for breath as the tears coursed down her cheeks. "Why did it have to be my mother?"

Chapter 26

The office was on fashionable Newbury Street, next door to a preppie maternity store, one flight up from a place that sold sheepskin rugs and abstract wood sculptures that all looked like gnarled hands. The frosted-glass door was open, so Alan walked into the small waiting room with white walls and gray carpeting. Beyond it was another door, this one closed. From behind it he heard a low murmur of conversation. He sat down in a Breuer chair and considered: an optometrist's office? a C.P.A.? a psychiatrist? Getting warm. Only the magazines on the glass-topped coffee table gave it away: *Fate*, *Psychic Journeys*, *True Stories from Beyond*. He picked one up and thumbed through it: "I Had a Phone Call from the Dead!" "Russian Photographs Prove the Soul Exists!" "Twelve Ways to Test Your Psychic Powers!" Alan was up to way number seven when the inner door opened and a silver-haired fellow in a pinstripe suit came out.

The man looked momentarily abashed when he saw Alan, then nodded politely and strode out the door. Alan smiled and put down the magazine. "Come in, child," his mother said from her office. He went in.

In contrast to the waiting room, the office looked as if it had never left the nineteenth century: flocked wallpaper, Oriental rug, chintz curtains, a couple of over-stuffed armchairs, and a brass floor lamp with a brocade shade. Everything in the best of taste, however, and impeccably neat. "Kiss me, my darling."

His mother was wearing some sort of flowing garment that looked not unlike the lampshade. He made a pass at her cheek and settled into an armchair. "Looks like you're doing quite well," he remarked.

"I even take American Express," she said proudly. She lit up a cigarette. "It's all thanks to you, of course. What was it you said to that reporter: 'My mother is the Boston Celtics of the psychic world; I'm the Los Angeles Clippers'?"

"Yeah. Some people from Los Angeles didn't much like that."

"Oh, I'm sure you told them where to get off. Anyway, my landlords at Charles River Park got very snippy about my seeing clients in the apartment, so I set up shop here. My accountant says it's a lot easier to write off the expenses than if I operated out of my home. And I'm turning people away."

"Sound ideal."

She exhaled a stream of smoke contentedly. "Yes, things have worked out well." Then she leaned forward and grasped his hands. "But you've been through so much, Alan. I've agonized over you—ever since—"

"I remember."

"I tried to help. I hope you're not too angry with me. I was desperate; I had to call up your friend Kelliher. I kept getting these feelings—of evil so strong it almost—"

"I'm not angry, Ma. Kelliher's okay, I'm okay. Everything turned out fine, so what's to be angry about?"

She squeezed his hands and let go. "You're through with all that business, then?"

"God, I hope so. The police were extremely nasty, but that was mostly because I found him and they didn't. I became something of a hero, so they couldn't really charge me with anything. They told me they never wanted to see me again, and I said I'd be happy to oblige."

"And what will you do now? Will you go back to your apartment?"

Alan shook his head. "You've got to move on in life. Can't stay the same. I thought I'd go to Seattle, maybe, take up salmon fishing."

"And root for the—the Whalers?"

"The Mariners. Sure, why not?"

She gave him a try-again look.

"Well, maybe Cambridge. Or even Somerville. No sense getting carried away."

She gestured with her cigarette at her office. "I have moved on too. Perhaps things are looking up for both of us."

Alan grinned and leaned back in his chair. He looked out the window at the busy street and basked in contentment, warm as the autumn sunshine.

"It's gone, isn't it, Alan?" his mother said after a while.

He looked at her and shrugged.

"You lost it down there in New York, fighting your battle. You pushed it too far, and now it's gone forever."

He shifted uncomfortably. "I don't know about 'forever.' Maybe just a . . . leave of absence."

"Bullshit," she said, not unkindly.

"You've been wrong before. Remember that day in my apartment—you said if I ever left Boston, I wouldn't come back. Here I am."

"But this *you* is not the same person as the *you* who left."

"Bullshit," he murmured, and then, after a while, he smiled. "Could be worse."

She nodded, and they both fell silent, communicating, not telepathically, but with the unspoken understanding of people who have known each other too long for words to be necessary. Finally he sighed, and she sighed too. "Mrs. Bradford is looking at the wood sculptures downstairs and thinking about canceling her appointment," she said. "She's afraid I'm going to say her husband is cheating on her with her best friend."

"Is he?"

"Afraid so."

"Will she cancel?"

His mother shook her head. "She can't help wanting to know. Curiosity, Alan. The lust for understanding. Awful things."

Alan gestured at her office. "Where would you be without them?"

She sighed again, and Alan thought of the books infesting her apartment. And then he thought of their dining room in Jamaica Plain, of gray wallpaper and gray pot roast. Was she thinking of the same things? He would never know for sure. He stood up. "We'll have you over for dinner in our new place—wherever it is."

"Yes, I'm dying to meet your—whatever she is. I feel like I know her intimately already."

"I'm sure you do."

She stubbed out her cigarette and extended her hands. "Give me another kiss."

Alan complied. On his way downstairs he passed an elegantly dressed woman in her early forties. She nervously avoided his gaze and hurried up the stairs. There were better jobs in this world than the one his mother had.

He strolled down Newbury Street in the sunlight. A policeman on horseback clopped along, searching in vain for an illegally parked car. A woman in a lime-green skirt and yellow blazer dropped her packages coming out of the Laura Ashley store, and two black teenagers helped her pick them up. "Spare a quarter, pal?" a friendly bum asked. Alan gave him a dollar. Then he cut across Commonwealth Avenue to Marlborough Street.

The street hadn't changed since he left it, only nature had changed. The maple trees were orange and yellow and red; chrysanthemums bloomed in the tidy gardens instead of crocuses; birds twittered nervously on rooftops and fences. It was World Series time; winter was on it way.

In his apartment, Julia had filled five Hefty double-strength trash bags with junk and was working on a sixth. "You said you cleaned this place out *before* you left?" she asked as he came in.

He gave her a hug. "Well, you know, after a fashion."

"How's your mother?"

"Couldn't be better. She's thinking of opening franchises. 'Madame Zelda's Original Psychic Consulting Service. Tell us your problem. We already know the solution.' You find anything worth saving?"

"How about your old Red Sox score cards?"

"Trash."

"This scrapbook of cases you've been involved in?"

"Trash."

"Your opera albums?"

"Hey, let's not go overboard here. Save those."

Julia grinned. "I told the real estate person in Arlington we'd be there around two. Okay?"

"Fine." Alan went into the kitchen and got himself a beer. Halfway through, the memories started crowding in, and he figured it was time to get busy.

Julia was carefully packing his records in Budweiser cartons.

"I'll put out the trash," he said.

"I'll help."

They each lugged two trash bags out into the alley and then just stood there, smelling the fallen leaves and the rotting garbage. "You know, the toilet hasn't run since we got back," Alan remarked.

"Is that a good sign?"

"Who knows? It'll probably run in our new place."

Julia put her arms around him and leaned her head against his chest. "We've got to protect each other from running toilets and flat tires and things that go bump in the night," she said. "I'll study plumbing."

"And I'll learn how to do a tune-up. You can save hundreds of dollars doing your own routine maintenance."

"And with the money you save maybe someday we'll be able to buy a car."

"And twice a year we can drive out to California to visit your mother."

"And we can pick up your mother and bring her over for dinner every Saturday night."

"Together we'll be unstoppable."

She smiled. "We already are."

Alan kissed her. "Let's get out of here."

He drove their rented car along Massachusetts Avenue, headed for Arlington. "Boston drivers," he muttered as a Volvo cut him off.

"We could take the bus," Julia suggested.

"Nonsense. I'll just cut someone off myself, and then I'll feel better."

"Swell."

He inched his way through the congestion around Harvard Square. Julia had never been there before, and her head swiveled back and forth, trying to take everything in. "Is that Harvard over there on the right?"

"A slice of it."

"Everybody looks so strange."

"You must've led a sheltered life, my dear. Come on, buddy, move it or lose it!"

"Look at the guy over there by the Co-op."

"That's the Coop, as in chicken."

"The one with the beret and the dark glasses and the sandwich boards. *Look.*"

Alan obeyed, reluctantly. Guys with berets and dark glasses and sandwich boards were a dime a dozen in Harvard Square. He was coming toward them, his goatee sticking out over the front of the board. Something familiar . . . "Holy shit," Alan whispered. He read the board.

Their is no Meaning

it said in large block letters. Alan stayed where he was, oblivious of the blaring horns and screamed obscenities, until the rear board came into view.

Their is only Life

At the corner the man turned around and marched slowly back the way he had come. No one paid any attention to him.

"You son of a gun," Alan murmured and stepped on the gas pedal.

"Who is it?" Julia asked.

"My ex-employer, with the final chapter of his book. The distillation of a lifetime of study."

"What's he doing here?"

"What does it look like? He's living."

"But I thought he didn't go outside; he has an allergy or something."

"Yes, well, here *I* am driving a car. Next thing you know he'll learn how to spell."

Julia laughed and settled back in her seat. "Do you believe in his philosophy?" she asked after a while, as they waited at a red light.

"Not much there to believe."

"Still."

"Still. It got him out in the moderately fresh air, walking around. Carrying the sign probably improves his muscle tone. Meets a lot of people . . . There could be worse philosophies."

"Well, what is your philosophy, Alan Simpson?"

Alan considered. "Ask me in thirty years."

"I intend to."

The light turned green, and they pushed on toward the real estate agent.